CHASE LIFTED HER CHIN
AND KISSED HER SOFTLY

His infinite tenderness flooded Jessica with emotion. Their lips parted, and she looked at him through misty eyes, helpless to do anything but accept his affection. She wanted it too fiercely.

Chase ran his fingers along the side of her neck and up into her hair, sending tremors through her body. Then he traced the skin at the edge of her neckline, his hands slipping under the fabric to stroke her.

She pressed against him, wanting to feel him more intimately.

"Jessica," he whispered into her hair, "I want you. Now."

Her eyes sought his questioningly. "Chase, I don't think we should." But there was no conviction in her voice, and she could tell Chase knew it too.

ABOUT THE AUTHOR

In 1985 Janice Kaiser took down her lawyer's
shingle to become a full-time writer, and her pen
has barely left paper since. This California author
has four Superromances and one Intrigue under
her belt, and another Superromance coming out
this spring. Though Janice is never at a loss for
story ideas, she does put her writing aside
occasionally to immerse herself in other loves:
opera, theater and gourmet cooking.

Books by Janice Kaiser

HARLEQUIN SUPERROMANCE
187–HARMONY
209–LOTUS MOON
224–MEANT TO BE

HARLEQUIN INTRIGUE
56–THE BLACK PEARL

Janice Kaiser

LOVE CHILD

Harlequin Books

TORONTO • NEW YORK • LONDON
AMSTERDAM • PARIS • SYDNEY • HAMBURG
STOCKHOLM • ATHENS • TOKYO • MILAN

Published January 1987

First printing November 1986

ISBN 0-373-70242-6

Printed in Canada

For Matthew and Sybil Kaiser,
with love.

CHAPTER ONE

HARRIET THOMAS LOOKED UP into his cool blue eyes, certain he would reject every woman she had to offer. His requirements were extremely demanding, and she wasn't at all confident they could be met. "The task you've given me, Mr. Hamilton, has not been an easy one," she said, trying her best to sound self-assured.

"If it were, the money wouldn't be as good, Miss Thomas, would it?" Chase Hamilton let her know by the smirk on his wide handsome mouth that he was in no mood for idle politeness. "What have you got for me?" His voice was deep.

She started to say something to prepare him for her meager offerings, but decided against it. Tentatively she slid the three file folders across the desk. Harriet decided to let her women do the talking for her and hoped to God he wouldn't be too upset.

Without a word Hamilton took the files and, casually leaning back, began perusing the contents as one might examine a fine art book, or a historical manuscript. Harriet felt her heart thumping as she studied his face.

After what seemed like an eternity, he placed the first file on the desk and picked up the second. He hadn't looked at her yet, and there was no hint of what he was thinking. She swallowed hard, hating the man for making her feel so inadequate.

Hamilton looked through the second as he had the first, with excruciating patience, but still refused to betray a reaction. By the time he got to the third folder Harriet was certain she couldn't bear the suspense. She fidgeted nervously just before he looked up, his blue eyes settling on her with vacant impersonality. He sighed, pressing his lips together thoughtfully.

Harriet knew she should keep her mouth shut and wait, but the pressure was too great. "There are not many women who meet your specifications and who would be willing to do what you want, Mr. Hamilton."

"Is it the money?" he asked after a moment. "Do they need more money?"

"No, it's not just money. All three of these women—"

He cut her off with a wave of his hand. "Forgive me for being uncharitable, Miss Thomas, but these... these... *women* hardly approach the standard I'm seeking." He picked up the folders brusquely. "This first one...she looks like a...forgive me...a cow!" He glanced up at her. "I want a sleek filly, not a *cow*. And this one," he said, opening the second file folder again. "What can I say? A bored housewife looking to supplement the family income?" He picked up the third. "And this one!" He opened his mouth to say something, then thought better of it and tossed the folder back on the desk.

"I'm sorry, Mr. Hamilton."

He was thinking, not showing any sign of concern over Harriet's anxiety. "Look," he said finally, "would a hundred thousand dollars get me the woman I want?"

"A hundred thousand?" Harriet's lips trembled as she pronounced the words.

"But I won't compromise on standards," he warned. "If anything, I'd be even more demanding."

Harriet Thomas was speechless.

"Of course, the problem may not be the money," he added. "It may be your agency. Let's be frank, Miss Thomas. *Are* you the right one for the job?"

Harriet felt her neck and cheeks turn red. "Certainly we are the ones," she stammered. "If anyone can find the right woman for your needs, we can."

Hamilton laughed softly. "Would it be too trite to say actions speak louder than words?"

Harriet knew it was her last chance. "Give me a week."

Chase Hamilton looked at his watch as though he had just set the countdown in motion. Then he looked up at her and almost smiled. "All right, a week." Without another word he got up and walked out of the office.

JESSICA BRANDON FOUND HERSELF staring at the diamond ring on Helmut Geisel's little finger. It spoke volumes about the man. It was the neon sign proclaiming his success, his wealth, his need to look down on lesser rings, or—God help him or her—those without rings at all.

Geisel smiled at her with his fat little mouth despite Jessica's bare fingers. "You have tremendous talent, Jessica—a little primitive and naive for some of the salons I cater to perhaps, but talent nonetheless."

"So what does that mean, Mr. Geisel? Can you sell enough of my paintings so that I can feed my child? That's what I need to know."

The gallery owner and art dealer leaned back, smiling benevolently, eyeing the strikingly beautiful woman seated across his desk. Jessica Brandon's frothy beige eyes were full of the innocence of a child, though she was already thirty. Still, she waited with the cunning patience of a woman, enduring the man's lascivious thoughts.

She was dressed simply: a silk blouse and pants that flattered her trim model's figure, and pearl stud earrings, no other jewelry. Her blond hair was short and swept back from her face in soft waves. Her makeup was understated, permitting the natural purity of her skin to show. Only the glossy peach of her lips suggested a sexuality beyond the allure of her basic wholesomeness.

"That is not an easy question to answer," Geisel said, his eyes sliding down her as though she were a nude sculpture. "I have no idea of the way you live, or of your expectations."

"I live very simply and, to be blunt, my immediate expectation is subsistence."

"I believe I understand your predicament." His smile was patronizing and his diamond flashed as he gestured. "Let me be as direct as I can, then, Jessica. You have talent, as I said. Your immediate problem is not so much quality as it is quantity. I have two of your pieces on my walls. They have not sold, but there has been interest in them. That is encouraging. But the problem quite simply is that the marketplace has not seen enough of you."

"Will you display more if I bring more?" Jessica asked anxiously.

"You mean after you have painted them, of course. But you see, that is what I allude to. To earn money, to be commercially successful in this kind of market, an artist must have inventory. You are fairly new at this, I know, and only your most recent work has been of a quality that I would even consider handling. The two canvases I have now could mean anywhere from two to perhaps three thousand dollars to you when they are sold, but that could be six months from now.''

"I can't wait that long.''

"Look, Jessica, if you want to do this for a living you need a one-woman show, and that means twenty-five or thirty canvases—preferably more so I can pick and choose. That's the sort of thing that launches a career. Otherwise you're talking nickel-and-dime, hand-to-mouth.''

"That's a year's work,'' she lamented.

"It's called paying one's dues.''

Jessica ran her fingers through her tawny hair. "My son can't wait a year to eat.''

Geisel shrugged. "What can I say? Find yourself a patron, or a husband.... Paint at night. All I can do is try to sell what you bring me.''

Jessica stood up and the dealer hurried around the desk to say his goodbyes. Geisel, at about five-six, was an inch shorter than she, and judging by his expression, he rather liked her height. He clasped her hands with undue familiarity.

"I'll do my best to sell your pieces. And that's not charity. I like them...and I like you." He reached up and pinched her chin almost as one might a child, his fat lips twisted into a smile.

Jessica smiled, too, but it was an effort to do so. She felt devastated by Geisel's equivocal report, and she had no use for him personally. She had prayed all the way in on the train from Peekskill that morning that there might be a check waiting for her when she arrived, but instead there were only compliments and encouragement. Neither would pay the rent.

"I'll phone if anything happens," he called after her, but Jessica was in a hurry to leave before the tears she felt welling began running down her cheeks. She stepped out into the streets of Manhattan feeling hopeless and desperate.

Jessica walked vaguely in the direction of Park Avenue, trying not to let her depression overwhelm her. It was a warm day in May, a nice day for walking. She had half an hour before she would be meeting Harriet Thomas for lunch, so there was no rush. She could kill time wandering and thinking, and possibly get herself into a better frame of mind before seeing her friend.

Jessica looked at the faces of people passing on the streets—something she normally didn't do in New York—perhaps in an attempt to bring perspective to her tangled life. She felt desperately alone, cut off from people, in need of a little human compassion. But there was nothing to encourage her in the faces she saw, not that she really expected there would be.

It would be good to see Harriet, though. Most of Jessica's friends in the city had forgotten her, or found the circumstances of her life too depressing to deal with. But Harriet at least called occasionally, and they got together for lunch whenever Jessica came into town.

As she walked, the first waves of the noontime crowd began spilling into the streets. People were rushing to keep up with the hurried pace of life in New York: hurry to work, hurry to lunch, hurry home, then hurry to work again the next morning. In a way Jessica envied them, because somewhere in all that rush and hurry there was a form of security—financial security. She, on the other hand, had no place to hurry to, no pressing obligations, no paycheck waiting at the end of the week.

Jessica felt as though her life the past two years had been a struggle just to keep her head above water. The insurance settlement covered most of Jamie's medical expenses, and the welfare payments from the state had kept them from starving, but what few resources she'd had at the time of Alex's death were now gone. He had been convinced he'd live forever and wouldn't consider life insurance, even after their son had been born. Now she and Jamie were paying for that error in judgment.

Their marriage had not been perfect by any means, but she had loved Alex, and in his way he had loved her. All he had left her were dozens of incomplete manuscripts that lost what potential value they had with his death. In one fiery crash she had lost her husband and what little financial security they had, and was left with an injured child totally dependent upon her.

After a while Jessica found herself in front of the salad bar where she and Harriet normally met. She looked in the window but didn't see her friend, so she decided to wait outside, rather than stand in the crowded entry. Mentally she calculated how much of the fourteen dollars in her purse she could spend on lunch and how much she would have to save for the return ticket back to Peekskill.

Looking up and down the sidewalk for the familiar face of her friend, she remembered the conversation they had had the last time they'd met for lunch. "Why don't you go back into modeling?" Harriet had asked.

"I would, but I'm too old. Women in the business my age are peaking, not beginning."

"But you're not a beginner," Harriet had insisted. "You were on the verge of a wonderful career when you quit to marry Alex."

"There's a big difference between being established and being 'on the verge,' Harriet. Besides, a model is like a perishable fruit, too much time out in the sun and nobody wants her."

"But you're as gorgeous as you ever were. Even more elegant than when you were a kid. Surely someone would recognize that."

"Sure," Jessica had told her, "I could pick up jobs here and there, enough to pay for the portfolio, the clothes, the haircuts and all the other things I'd need. But who'd take care of Jamie? No, the only way to be a model is to be really big. I'm too old, Harriet. It's too late for me. Besides, my marriage was only an excuse for quitting. It's a tough business. I'm not quite tall enough and I never felt really comfortable being on display. I suppose I'm more of a private person than that."

The lunchtime crowds on the sidewalk had swelled and Jessica found herself being bumped and jostled. She decided to step inside the restaurant when she heard Harriet's voice over the hubbub.

"Jessica! Sorry I'm late." The thin brunette in her early thirties slipped through the flow of bodies to embrace her friend.

"Hi, Harriet," Jessica said smiling.

"You're looking fabulous. How's Jamie?"

"Fine. He's fine."

Harriet looked into Jessica's eyes hesitantly. "How'd it go with Geisel?"

Jessica tried to be brave. "He says there's been interest in my paintings, but neither of them have sold."

Harriet touched her friend's arm. "Don't worry, they'll sell and you'll soon be New York's most famous young artist." She turned with annoyance at being bumped by a passerby.

"Come on, let's go inside."

They were fortunate in that the line was short. They quickly went along the cafeteria-style salad bar, making their selections. Jessica took a green dinner salad and a French roll, Harriet a seafood salad and iced tea.

"So, will he take more of your work?" Harriet asked when they were seated at one of the cramped little tables.

"Yes, but that's my problem. He doesn't feel I'm ever going to get anywhere on a piecemeal basis. He said I need a one-woman show."

Harriet's face lit up. "And he's willing to give you one?"

"Yes, but that's just it. He wants twenty-five or thirty canvases, and I don't have them. That's the better part of a year's work. There's no way I can survive that long."

Harriet bit her lip anxiously. "God, that's almost worse than rejection, isn't it?"

"Yes."

"Well, maybe something will come up."

For a while they ate in silence. Jessica glanced at her friend, sorry that she was always such a burden. It was no wonder people didn't want to spend time with her anymore. "So how's business, Harriet?" she asked, trying to sound chipper.

"Oh, God, don't ask."

"What's the matter?"

"I've got a client I just can't make happy."

"You can't please everyone."

Harriet laughed. "But this, my dear, is one I want to please, desperately. It could mean twenty-five thousand dollars for the agency.

Jessica's eyes rounded. "Twenty-five? What do you have to do for that kind of money?"

"I've got to find a woman willing to give a man a child for a hundred thousand dollars."

Jessica blanched. "I thought you were in the surrogate mother business."

"I am."

"What do you mean, a man wants to buy a child?"

"He wants me to find a woman to have *his* baby."

"And he's not married?"

"No. He wants a child, not a wife."

"But Harriet, doesn't your agency find surrogate mothers for childless *couples*?"

"That is what we do normally, but this is an unusual case. That's why all the money."

"He's willing to spend a hundred and twenty-five thousand dollars?"

"Yes, that's how determined he is. The man's eccentric, there's no question about it. Eccentric, determined, stubborn, particular. He's made my life miserable the past month."

"Is he a weirdo, or what's his problem?"

"Oh, he's no weirdo. He's filthy rich and he wants an heir."

"Then why doesn't he just get married?"

"He's not interested in marriage, Jessica. He's made that plain. He does seem to be very interested in parenting, however. His motives are good, and a child is very important to him. Heaven knows he's got the money for the help and care that will be required."

"So what's the problem? Don't any of your mothers want to bear a child for a single man?"

Harriet rolled her eyes. "Don't I wish. No, the problem is the bastard is so particular that he's turned down everyone I've presented to him."

"Why?"

Harriet scoffed. "He wants somebody who looks like Grace Kelly—somebody with brains, class and, of course, the usual qualifications that we require."

"You mean a woman who already has a child of her own?"

"Yes, that and good health, the proper psychological profile, a humanitarian spirit...et cetera, et cetera. In other words, he wants someone who doesn't exist." Harriet took a bite of her salad, then glanced up to see a faraway look on Jessica's face. She watched her friend for a moment before she realized what was going on in her head.

Jessica returned from her contemplation and looked squarely at Harriet. Her eyes brightened. A slight smile was on her lips.

Harriet shook her head. "No, Jessica. Erase that thought from your brain this instant."

Jessica smiled more broadly now. She slapped her hand on the table. "Harriet, I'm going to do it."

"You aren't going to do any such thing. Forget it."

"But why? It'll solve all my problems."

"I said forget it and I mean it." She pointed an authoritative finger at her friend. "You're not the type for this business and financial desperation doesn't qualify you."

Jessica ignored the admonition. "It's all done by artificial insemination, isn't it?"

"Yes, but that has nothing to do with it."

"I don't even have to meet him, do I?"

"Well, yes, there are meetings required at the beginning. That's all part of the psychological preparation. But it doesn't matter. I wouldn't let you do it."

"Is the money paid in advance?"

"Jessica!"

"Is it?"

"Half at the time the pregnancy is confirmed, half at the birth of the child."

Jessica Brandon beamed.

"Wipe that silly smile off your face. This is not your thing."

"Give me one good reason why not."

"Because you have to be willing to carry a baby, give birth to it, then give it away to a stranger. Your own flesh and blood, Jessica. Your child!"

"Harriet, I already have my child. Jamie is all I'll ever want or need—he's mine and Alex's. And now that Alex is gone, there'll never be another baby...not that's *mine*. If I can make a hundred thousand dollars and spend nine months painting, think what that'll mean to Jamie's future!"

Harriet turned and looked out the window at the crowds in the streets. "No," she said emphatically, engaging Jessica's eyes again. "I know this business. I know the kind of person it takes. I know it's not for you. No, Jessica, no."

"What do you want me to do? Rot on welfare? Or leave my child and sit on my rear end in a bank all day long so I can pay someone else to play the role of mother? What about your other mothers, Harriet? Are they more insensitive than I, or more saintly? Can't I be capable of sacrifice like anyone else? Am I too good for what you do? Or too selfish? Or too much in need?"

Harriet seemed to wilt under Jessica's onslaught. She shook her head. "I'm just trying to protect you."

Jessica looked at her for a minute, then reached over and took her hands. "Harriet, I know you want to protect me, and I appreciate that. I really do. But I don't need any protection right now. I need an opportunity.

Look, I meet all the requirements and you know it. I had a very easy time with Jamie—and he was my first. I am a generous, caring person capable of sacrificing for other people's happiness. Most important, I already have my child. Jamie's my life, Harriet.''

"You're really serious, aren't you?''

"Think what it would mean—financial security. I could paint for nine months, stay with Jamie and still afford the care for him that's needed.''

Harriet started to speak, but Jessica cut in. "I know, there's the discomfort of pregnancy and the birth, but what's a little pain after what I've been through?''

"The baby, Jessica! What about the baby?''

She sighed with exasperation. "Do you do this with all the mothers? Or are you singling me out for harsh treatment?''

Harriet frowned, silent for a moment. "Okay, I'll tell you what. You go home and think about it. I want you to get out all of Jamie's pictures when he was a baby, the earliest ones. I want you to imagine another little face in them, half *yours*. And I want you to think in terms of never seeing it again after the delivery.''

"You're trying to brainwash me, Harriet.''

"You just do what I say. Then if and when you want to discuss it some more, give me a call, but not unless. I'm going to dismiss this conversation as rash fantasy and expect that we laugh about it every time we have lunch.''

"All right,'' Jessica said. "I'll do it your way, but I want my interview with this guy as soon as possible. I want to get started.'' She smiled broadly. "I have a feeling that Jamie and I have a whole new life ahead of us.''

JESSICA PEERED through the venetian blinds at the traffic on Park Avenue. Harriet's building was old and her suite of offices was located unprestigiously on the second floor. The address was the one concession the agency had made to image. Jessica turned around as Harriet entered the reception area from her private office.

"Wow," Harriet exclaimed, "you look terrific."

Jessica smiled tentatively. For the interview she had decided on her navy linen suit and white silk blouse with a soft bow. The suit was three years old, but still in good condition, and the cut was flattering. She reasoned that he wouldn't notice or care if she didn't wear the latest fashion, as long as she looked good.

"You look just fine," Harriet replied. "I know I told you that appearance is important to Mr. Hamilton, but this isn't a beauty contest. If *you* aren't pretty enough for him, no one is."

Jessica sighed. "I haven't been this nervous about an interview since my first modeling job eight years ago."

"Listen, why don't you wait in the conference room. I'll probably talk to Mr. Hamilton in my office for a while before I introduce you. There were some things we didn't cover on the phone." Harriet looked at her watch as she opened the door. "He's always been prompt, so I expect him anytime. Come on, you'll be more comfortable in here."

Jessica sat first on the couch, then switched to one of the easy chairs, where she felt a little more secure. She could hear the traffic outside, a low hum that seemed everywhere in New York. It was the sort of detail she'd never paid attention to when she'd lived in the city, but her year and a half in Peekskill had changed that.

Her heart was pounding noticeably in her chest and her palms were wet, though the room was air-conditioned. For the first time since she had decided to be the surrogate mother to Chase Hamilton's child she had doubts.

In the four days since her lunch with Harriet, Jessica had done everything that her friend had asked. She'd looked at Jamie's baby pictures, but that had only served to amplify her desire to improve his life. She'd lain in bed trying to remember every detail of her pregnancy: the discomfort, the pain, the endless wait. She'd conjured up the birth. Time had blurred much of the unpleasantness, according to nature's design, but she also knew it was something she could do again.

There had been no one to talk to, so the decision had to be made alone. Jessica's mother had died when she was a toddler and her father when she was in high school, so being on her own was nothing new. The only family she had apart from cousins were an aunt and uncle who lived on a small ranch in eastern Oregon. It had been years since she had seen them, and they would hardly be the sort of people to discuss surrogate motherhood with.

And she had never even met her in-laws. Alex's father had deserted his wife and child when Alex was a boy. His mother was a troubled woman who remarried and cut all ties with her son.

Jamie was the only one in her life who would be affected. She decided he was young enough to accept without trauma what she planned to do. She would have to be careful how she presented it to him, but she knew for a child of that age pregnancy was not the problem—the disruption of a brother or sister was. And he would never know the baby.

The idea of carrying a strange man's child was the part that had concerned her the most. She had asked Harriet about Chase Hamilton and was pleased to hear that he was most attractive, though his appearance really didn't matter.

Jessica knew that the entire procedure required only an encounter of their reproductive cells. Artificial insemination made the whole thing rather clinical and impersonal—not unlike a routine visit to the gynecologist. Nevertheless, she was relieved that the man was decent, the sort of person she might choose to father her child if their roles were reversed. That made the idea palatable.

Now all she had to do was meet him, the human being who was to father the child—*if* he decided to select her, that is. To be rejected after mentally committing her body to this man would be a difficult blow, indeed.

Jessica heard voices out in the reception area—a man's and Harriet's. She felt her stomach clinch. Chase Hamilton had arrived.

Minutes later, when the door finally opened, Jessica saw him. At first she was only aware of his maleness and the threat to her that he represented. She looked at his face without seeing his eyes, feeling the shyness and trepidation of the bride of an arranged marriage upon seeing her betrothed for the first time.

She stood, aware by now that he was tall and dark. Harriet's voice came vaguely from the background.

"Jessica, I'd like for you to meet Chase Hamilton."

He didn't move for a moment, but in the blur of him there was the impression of a brief smile.

"How do you do, Mrs. Brandon." The voice was deep, gravelly.

Jessica looked at his eyes for the first time. He was handsomely mature, perhaps forty, with lines at the corners of his eyes that smiled even when his mouth didn't. He stepped toward her and his face blurred again.

She was aware of his European-cut suit in a navy almost identical to the shade she wore. His hand extended toward her. It was large but narrow, the hand of an artist. It took hers firmly, warmly. It was a dark hand, unlike Alex's, which had been ruddy. Jessica looked into the eyes again. The man was very handsome.

"How do you do, Mr. Hamilton."

His wide mouth was drawn into a thin line, his eyes narrowed as he examined her face. Bone structure, complexion, coloring—he seemed to be taking it all in.

Again Harriet's voice came to her from the background. "Shall we sit down?"

Chase Hamilton didn't move. He seemed to be thinking while he observed her. The corners of his mouth curled ever so slightly, as though something had amused him, but it wasn't clear what.

Jessica blinked self-consciously under his gaze, but she managed to look back into his eyes.

"No, Miss Thomas," he said without turning from Jessica, "I think Mrs. Brandon and I will speak for a while, alone."

Jessica's heart lurched and she felt more vulnerable than she ever had in her life. Chase Hamilton was still looking deeply into her eyes when she heard the door quietly close. They were alone.

CHAPTER TWO

"PLEASE SIT DOWN, Mrs. Brandon." He gestured toward the couch.

Jessica complied, her stomach in knots, her hands trembling almost imperceptibly. She watched Chase Hamilton take the chair she had been seated in, noticing for the first time the file folder in his hand.

He studied her for a moment before speaking. "Thank you for coming, Mrs. Brandon." There was a half smile on his face. "I won't promise you this will be a pleasant session. My intent is not to charm. I'm going to be asking some very hard questions."

"I understand, Mr. Hamilton."

"Good. Let me say first of all that I'm dead serious about having a child, and the woman I select to be the mother has to be perfect—absolutely perfect—for my purposes. That's one reason the fee is so high. The other reason is that I expect more than is usual."

"What do you mean?"

"We can discuss the specifics later, but let me sum up what I mean this way. I consider this to be much more than just an employment situation." His eyes were vacant, his expression matter-of-fact. "To be blunt, if you are selected, I will, in effect, be purchasing the use of your body for a period of nine or ten months."

His words settled over Jessica like a pall, and for the first time since her lunch with Harriet she had serious doubts about becoming a surrogate mother. *Purchasing the use of my body!*

"I see by your expression that that notion doesn't sit well. But let me assure you that if we don't see eye to eye on what is expected, there's no chance whatsoever that either of us will be satisfied."

"What exactly do you have in mind?"

"Let me answer that with a few questions of my own, if I may." He opened the file.

"All right." Jessica studied the handsome visage of the man, half deciding that she didn't like him. It was an inauspicious beginning.

"I understand that you're a widow, Mrs. Brandon."

"Yes, my husband was killed in an automobile accident two years ago."

"Were you involved?"

"No, Alex was with our son. He apparently lost control of the car and hit an abutment. No one knows for sure what happened. Alex wasn't the most cautious driver, but he wasn't reckless."

"I'm sorry."

"I'm just thankful my son survived."

Hamilton glanced down at his file, ruminating. Jessica waited.

"Mrs. Brandon, do you presently have an active sex life?"

Jessica couldn't help her mouth dropping open.

"Please don't take offense, but the question is completely relevant, I assure you. Obviously I would be concerned that the child conceived would actually be mine. Second, the doctors tell me that a...shall we say... unwholesome sex life can cause problems for the baby. Third—"

"Let me spare you the litany, Mr. Hamilton. I haven't had intercourse since my husband died."

"I see."

Jessica saw a flicker of embarrassment cross Chase Hamilton's face and she thought he might be human, after all.

He lowered his eyes. "I realize I'm sounding rather clinical and insensitive, and I apologize for that, but my experience has been that the best way to avoid surprises is to be up-front about things. There'd be no point in acting indifferent at first, only to drop exacting requirements on you at the eleventh hour."

"Please don't apologize. I understand perfectly. And now that I do, let's dispense with the niceties and be direct. What else do you want to know about me?"

"I've had my attorney amend the agency's standard contract considerably. You'll be asked to agree, for example, not to have intercourse during the insemination stage or during the pregnancy. And as for your representations, you'll be asked to agree to a background investigation. I intend to verify everything you tell me."

"If that's designed to make me tell the truth, it's not necessary, Mr. Hamilton. I'm an honest person." Jessica drew a deep breath, beginning to understand what she was getting into.

He was looking at the file, seeming to have disregarded her rejoinder. "Do you drink?" he asked in a level tone.

Jessica could see he had every intention of doing this his way. "Yes. Socially."

"Would you be willing to forgo drinking during the pregnancy?"

"When I was carrying Jamie my doctor said an occasional drink was all right."

"Would you be willing to comply with the prescriptions of *my* doctor on the subject?"

Jessica decided Chase Hamilton's problem was that he needed to hire a surrogate because no woman would have him. "Yes."

"What drugs do you use?"

"Aspirin," she replied dryly, and was surprised to see him smile.

"We'll discuss that one with the doctor, shall we?" His tongue actually poked at his cheek.

Jessica smiled, too.

"Your medical history appears satisfactory," he continued, "but of course, I'm no expert. My doctor is reviewing your file before you see him for a physical. I require that *my* physician have a look, you know."

"Certainly. I would have been surprised if you didn't." Jessica's tone was less than complimentary, and Chase Hamilton looked up sharply.

"Was that sarcasm I heard?"

"Yes."

He smiled again. "You were right, Mrs. Brandon. You are honest."

"It hasn't always served me well," she admitted.

"In this case it doesn't matter. I'll tolerate the sarcasm to get the honesty."

It was the first thing he said that she liked. Maybe he wasn't so bad, after all. "I'll do what I can to accommodate you," she said with a smile.

His expression was actually warm; his pale blue eyes seemed to dance. "Good. We just might get along well."

Jessica felt the interview was beginning to shift in her favor. Back in her modeling days she used to be able to tell when a photographer had decided to hire her. There

was always an unspoken familiarity that came over them.
She saw some of the same signs in Chase Hamilton.

"Tell me," he said, looking up from his file, "what is
your worst character trait?"

"Character trait?"

"Yes."

She waited for further explanation, but saw that none
was forthcoming. She shrugged. "I don't know. Maybe
my sarcasm."

He grinned. "I've already witnessed that firsthand.
Give me another."

Jessica frowned, running her fingers through her styl-
ishly curled hair. "What's that got to do with being a
surrogate mother?"

"Mrs. Brandon, I believe that many character and
personality traits are inherited, not nurtured. In other
words, my child—our child—would have as many of
your traits as mine. The physical is important, of
course," he said, letting his eyes slowly drift down her
body, "but the psychological is just as important."

"So now you have to worry about having a sarcastic
kid?"

Chase Hamilton smiled broadly. "You might say so,
yes."

"What are you, anyway? A geneticist?"

"No, I'm a horse breeder."

"A horse breeder?" Jessica's tone was incredulous.
"My God, no wonder."

"No wonder what?"

"You're a breeder," she exclaimed, as though the point
were obvious. "You breed horses and now you want to
breed a baby. You've got the stud. All you need is the
mare!" She laughed, starting to enjoy herself, but Chase
Hamilton was not amused.

"You're funny as well as sarcastic," he said dryly, "but my experience is not irrelevant."

"Sorry, I thought for a minute you were interested in something other than just a normal healthy child. It all seemed to fit."

"Well, I'm pleased that you've got me figured out, but all I've been able to learn about you is that you're sarcastic and you have a sense of humor."

Jessica heard the irritation in his voice. "I'm sorry."

"Getting back to my point about your character and personality, I am very interested in learning what you are like under this interview facade."

She bit her tongue.

"You see, I can look at a good piece of horseflesh—an animal with all the physical traits, perhaps even the pedigree—but if the spirit's not right, if it doesn't have heart, it'll never be a winner. The same is true of people. Just because you're pretty and quick doesn't mean you're a shoo-in for the job."

Jessica felt things slipping away and secretly kicked herself. She had gotten so wrapped up in the conversation that she was losing sight of her objective. "I apologize, Mr. Hamilton. I meant no offense."

"Good. You know when to back down. Let's add common sense to the plus column of your list of traits. In light of the other things I've seen, that one must come in handy."

Jessica felt duly chastened but had an overwhelming urge to stick out her tongue at him. The pompous bastard. If it wasn't for his lousy hundred thousand dollars, she'd tell him to go to hell in a flash.

"Let's talk about your temper. What sort of thing makes you angry?"

She chuckled. "You're doing a pretty good job right now."

He glanced up at her but did not smile. "Do you feel hate easily?"

Jessica thought for a moment. "I don't think so, no."

"Do you enjoy your poverty?"

Her eyes flashed. "What do you mean by that?"

"It says here in your file you're living on welfare. Why don't you get a job?"

He was looking at her with flat, cold eyes. Jessica could almost smell his smugness. "What are you trying to do—test the limits of my temper?"

Chase Hamilton's mouth widened into a grin. "As a matter of fact, yes."

"You're doing an excellent job."

"Answer my question, please. Why do you sit around when you could be working?"

Jessica struggled to control her anger. "Because of my son, Mr. Hamilton. I don't want to leave him. Most jobs I could get would barely pay me enough for rent, groceries and a baby-sitter. What's the point in that?"

"What about your self-respect?"

"What about my self-respect? It happens to be just fine, thank you."

"Shall I put complacency in the negative column? Or do you think it goes on the positive side?"

Jessica glared with such hostility that even he looked surprised. *The money! The money!* she screamed to herself. *Hold your tongue!* "May I ask just how much of this I have to put up with?"

"To get the money, you mean?"

She was so livid she could have strangled him, but she said nothing.

"That brings me to the principal point of all of this, Mrs. Brandon. Why do you want to have my child? Is it the money?"

"It certainly isn't your charm." She had to laugh at her own sarcasm. In spite of himself, Chase Hamilton did, too.

"Seriously, though, what are you going to do with the money—if you get the job, that is?"

"I'm going to paint as many first-class canvases as I can in ten months, have a successful exhibit at the Geisel Gallery and give my son an education and financial security."

"Then you're doing it strictly for the money, no humanitarian sentiment whatsoever?"

"I'm sorry if that's not what you want to hear. But the truth is I am doing it for the money. To be honest, I don't have a great deal of sympathy for you or your purposes."

"That's very interesting, considering you know nothing about me or my purposes."

"You mentioned your breeding theories."

"Yes, but those are my theories, not my reasons for wanting a child."

"What *are* your reasons, then?"

"Believe it or not, I want a child for the same reasons most people do. I want someone to love, someone who's a part of me—my flesh and blood—someone to leave behind and carry on when I'm gone."

"It sounds rather noble. Why don't you just get married and have a baby the normal way?"

"Heartless as you may think I am, Mrs. Brandon, I wouldn't marry just to have a child. The thought of creating my own flesh and blood thrills me. The thought of marrying—in the abstract, I mean—does nothing for me. A special woman, the right woman, could make me think in those terms, but marrying just to be married or just because I want a baby is abhorrent.''

"Maybe you're too impatient. Isn't using a surrogate a rather drastic step? What if you marry later? How will a wife feel about the child?''

"No differently than if the child were the result of a previous marriage, I would hope. In any case, this hasn't been an impulsive decision on my part. I've considered the alternatives . . . I really have.''

There was a warmth about him now. Jessica even felt a little charitable toward him.

"I'll tell you the truth,'' he said, his eyes crinkling in a friendly sort of way. "The fact that you're in this for the money doesn't concern me in the least. I prefer it that way.''

"Why?''

"Most women who have a child and are willing to give it up do so as an act of kindness and generosity—as well as for money, perhaps. Compassion for the childless couple, a desire to share the joys of motherhood, and so forth. You know the story, I'm sure.''

Jessica felt a twinge of guilt, though she was sure he hadn't intended it.

"That's all well and good, but I don't trust a woman's willingness to sacrifice for my benefit, for a stranger's benefit. But to do it for pay, that's another matter.''

Her eyes dropped. For some reason his words were turning her sacrifice for her son into a cynical, mercenary act.

"Is that remorse I detect on your face, Mrs. Brandon?''

"Not remorse, no.''

"What then?" The glimmer of friendliness was gone. The biting, aggressive attitude was back.

"To be frank, I feel like you just called me a prostitute."

"With all due respect, it's not a lot different, is it?"

Again Jessica's eyes flashed, but this time it was his logic that stung her, not his tone or attitude. "If it wasn't done by artificial insemination, I wouldn't do it."

He tried to suppress a smile. "Granted there's a difference, but how much of one, really?"

"Enough for me," she snapped.

"Don't get me wrong, the arrangement is satisfactory. I'm just curious about your ethical position. What is the difference, *really*? Would, say, two hundred thousand dollars make the other arrangement acceptable?"

"No." Jessica felt her temper rising.

"Why?"

"I thought we've already had the anger test."

"Forgive me, but that's not my intent at all. I have a legitimate concern."

"What concern?"

"Well, if money makes you do it, where's the cutoff point? I mean, if a hundred thousand dollars is enough for you to agree now, will it be enough, say, in month eight? If your rich uncle died and left you a million dollars would you change your mind? When you see the baby will a hundred thousand dollars still seem like enough?"

"I'm sure your lawyers have all that covered for you."

"Indeed they have. However, problems are never pleasant. I want to know exactly where you're coming from."

"Look, Mr. Hamilton, this game playing might be amusing to you, but it's not to me. I'm willing to have your child for the price you've offered. If you want a financial statement from me, and if you want to see my bank account and budget, that's fine, too. No, I wouldn't have your child as a favor, and no, I wouldn't do it for less than what I need for the purposes I've mentioned." Jessica looked him square in the eye. "And no, I wouldn't go to bed with you for a million dollars."

She stood and walked across the room, unable to sit calmly and talk to the man. She was at the window, looking down at the traffic in the street. Behind her, he was silent. A sinking feeling came over her. Jessica knew she couldn't take any more. She spun around. "Look, if I'm not what you want, I wish you'd tell me right now so I could leave."

His voice was gentle. "I haven't decided yet. But please don't be upset. Come and sit down. Please." He stood up and extended his hand, almost as though he were beseeching her. Just then Chase Hamilton seemed terribly human and terribly attractive.

She walked toward the extended hand, putting hers in it when she reached him. He felt warm and strong and she forgot immediately how angry she was. Standing close to him, she could smell his cologne and sense his powerful masculinity, which struck her completely without warning.

Treating her more as a shy child than a woman, he helped her to the couch. Sitting, he smiled at her benevolently. "I warned you this wouldn't be easy."

"I'm sorry if I got upset."

"Don't worry about it. I honestly wish this weren't necessary."

"Is it, really?"

"I'm afraid so."

Jessica shrugged. "It's your money. You're the boss."

"I have only a few more questions."

"Okay. Shoot."

Chase Hamilton glanced at the file for a moment, then looked up with uncharacteristic constraint. He hesitated. Jessica was surprised.

"I'm told the hospital will require you to carry the baby out. You won't be able to turn it over to me until after we've left the premises. You'll have to hold it until I take it from you, even if you choose not to see the baby after the birth."

Consternation filled Jessica's face. "I wasn't aware it was done that way."

"Unfortunately it is—apparently for legal reasons. Third parties are reluctant to be involved in the transfer from the mother."

"I see."

"Since you won't be able to close your eyes and pretend the baby isn't in your arms, you won't be able to ignore it, Mrs. Brandon. I need to know now...will you be able to give me that baby—one you've given birth to— and let me leave with it, never to see it again?"

"You're saying you can't believe I could give up a baby I carried and delivered."

"I'm asking, in effect, if you can."

"I suppose that's the heart of the matter, isn't it?"

"I think so, yes."

"Let me tell you something you might not understand, or maybe even believe, Mr. Hamilton. I have my child already. Jamie is the product of the love of my husband and myself. We didn't breed him. He was brought into the world as a result of the love we shared. He's not a fine young colt who'll grow up to be a wonderful racehorse some day. The same accident that killed Alex broke Jamie's little body. He's a cripple, but I love him just as much as if his body were perfect. I love that little boy more than I could love anything or anyone. I'd give my life for him. I'd sell my body for him. In effect, that's what you're proposing I do. And I will.''

Chase Hamilton had looked down, away from Jessica's face. He had seen the tears welling, and he could no longer look into her eyes.

"I don't pretend that I'll be indifferent to your child. I know that it will be mine, too, biologically. But since I'll never know it, since I won't be giving it to you out of love, it won't be mine—not in the way Jamie is.''

"That's all I needed to hear, Mrs. Brandon." He stood and Jessica did, as well.

She wiped a tear from the corner of her eye and saw that his eyes, too, were misty. He was a totally different man from the one she had seen at first.

Chase Hamilton extended his hand again and, taking hers, gathered her closer. He looked down into her eyes, fighting emotion as he wrapped both of his hands around hers. "I'm sorry I was so rough on you, but I found out more than all the kindness in the world could possibly have produced. It was very important to me." He smiled sympathetically. "You're a fine filly, Mrs. Brandon, a very fine woman. I'm impressed with you and, I must say, favorably disposed at the moment.''

Jessica bowed her head, looking at the large strong hands that enveloped hers. "Thank you," she whispered.

"I'm going to think about our conversation and hopefully be making a decision soon. I'm sure Miss Thomas will be advising you what I decide to do.''

Jessica looked at the door, realizing how anxious she was to leave, to distance herself from the strong feelings that the conversation and the man had produced. She smiled at him as best she could. Then, when he released her hands, she quietly made her way to the door.

HARRIET COULD HARDLY CONTAIN her excitement when she called Jessica the next afternoon. "He wants you to talk to the psychiatrist, Jessica!"

"Does that mean I've got it?"

"Not quite, but almost. It's the second step. We can't proceed in any case unless you pass the psychiatric evaluation."

"To verify I've got all my marbles?"

"To verify that you're emotionally stable and able to bear the pressures of surrogate motherhood."

"Oh, Harriet," she enthused, beside herself with excitement. "Imagine! My problems will be over."

"You'll be trading one set for another, but a hundred thousand will go a long way toward making the new set palatable, I must admit."

Jessica laughed. "Then you've finally come around, Harriet? You agree now that I'm doing the right thing?"

"You've gotten this far and you're still enthusiastic. I may have been wrong about you, after all."

"I know it's right. I can feel it deep down. And Chase Hamilton didn't make it easy for me. It was like the Grand Inquisition yesterday."

"You don't have to tell me what you're up against in him, believe me. I've been that man's whipping boy for weeks now. But I'll say one thing, Jessica, he sure was impressed with you. He was so surprised that I don't think he believed you were real."

"What'd he say?"

"After you left he just babbled away about racehorses and fillies.... That's all he thinks about as far as I can tell."

"He is a strange one, isn't he?"

"He's got his eccentricities, true, but he's quite a man. God, you ought to be wishing he was looking for a wife, not a kid."

"Harriet, what a strange thing to say. The thought never occurred to me."

"You're kidding! God, the minute he walked in my door I began drooling."

"Then why don't *you* marry him?"

"Chase Hamilton's not interested in me, Jessica. You're much more his type. Hell, he wants you to be the mother of his kid."

"That doesn't mean anything and you know it. You're in the surrogate mother business, you ought to know better."

"Well, we don't normally deal with single men, and besides, the basic idea is not as dumb as you think. Of course, the surrogate mother is usually selected by the couple, not just the husband, but what sort of woman do you think anybody would choose? If it's a couple, as much like the wife as possible. If it's a man, as much like the woman he'd want for himself."

"I don't care what you say, Chase Hamilton is interested in horses, not women. He told me so himself. Besides, I don't have the remotest interest in him—just his money."

Harriet laughed. "Fifty percent of his millions is a lot better than a hundred thousand dollars, love."

"Yes, but for a hundred thousand dollars I only have to put up with him for ten months, and even then only at a distance. The other way it'd be a lifetime. I don't think there's enough money on earth—"

"Well, think what you will, our first order of business is to get you certified. Incidentally, the next ten months may not be at quite the distance you might think."

"What do you mean?"

"Chase Hamilton wants a lot more involvement in this pregnancy than just donating the sperm."

"Like what? He didn't say anything to me."

"Well, he did to me. He intends to watch you like a prize mare in foal. If that's a problem, you'd better get it worked out now."

"What do you mean 'watch,' Harriet?"

"I think a lot of checking up, supervising, joint visits to the doctor, that sort of thing. But talk to him about it."

"Yes, I intend to."

"Well, let's get down to brass tacks. I've got to schedule all sorts of appointments for you and draw up a time chart. When's your period due, Jessica?"

The question was innocent enough, and coming from Harriet, Jessica didn't mind. However, it did serve to remind her how public, rather than private, the whole process would be. What's worse, she had no doubt that Chase Hamilton would be involved in every intimate detail. Come to think of it, he already knew about her sex life. That had been one of his first questions.

What was the old saying? Nothing in life was free? Jessica could see that her road to riches wasn't going to be the smoothest she had ever traveled. Chase Hamilton was going to get his money's worth. There was absolutely no doubt about that.

CHAPTER THREE

THE SUBSEQUENT DAYS were busy ones. Jessica went to see the psychiatrist and Chase Hamilton's doctor. Harriet called with the news that both physicians had given their blessing and now they were all waiting for the father-to-be's final decision. He had promised it would be forthcoming.

Jessica was getting impatient. If he thought this a business proposition, as he claimed, then he wasn't acting like it. He was behaving more like a nervous bridegroom before the wedding. "What's wrong with him?" she had asked Harriet on Friday.

"Nothing, Jessica. The man's cautious. He just doesn't want to make a mistake."

"Well, if he keeps me on tenterhooks too long," she had joked, "I might just leave him waiting at the clinic."

The next day Jessica wanted to get some painting done, but Jamie was not feeling well and she spent almost all of her time with him. He was in pain and was consequently very cranky. After she put him to bed and did the dishes she primed a new canvas, but was too tired to do any creative work. She ended up watching an old movie on television and going to bed early.

Sunday morning was a lovely one. Jessica and Jamie sat for several hours on the front porch in the sunshine, watching the bees humming around the flowers she had planted early that spring. When Jamie had decided he wanted to play with his trucks, Jessica took her sketch pad and sat drawing the trees that graced the lawns across the street. Their place was modest, just a small old house several blocks from the shopping district of Peekskill.

After lunch Jessica put Jamie down for his nap and sank into the big overstuffed easy chair that had been Alex's favorite. It didn't go with the old house at all, but she wasn't going to give up her furniture, at least that which she still had. The extra pieces that had been put in storage were confiscated for lack of payment, and she was determined to hang on to what was left.

She had just picked up the *Sunday Times* when she heard footsteps on the wooden porch. Jessica turned and saw the figure of a man through the screen. Approaching the door, she was amazed to see Chase Hamilton standing there, wearing a linen sport coat and a tie. There was a friendly smile on his face.

Jessica looked down at herself, horrified at being caught in an old pair of jeans and the paint-spattered shirt she wore when working. Fortunately she had showered and cleaned up first thing that morning. Her hair, though, was a mess. She had shampooed, but hadn't really done anything with it.

She looked at him through the dark screen, noticing for the first time that he held some packages in his hands. "Thanks for the warning, Mr. Hamilton. I look almost as good as my house." Jessica pushed the screen door open.

"I'm sorry, but I confess that it was entirely intentional. I wanted to see you without the interview facade," he said, stepping inside.

She looked down at herself. "You succeeded beautifully."

He quickly glanced around the room and Jessica looked at the objects in his hands. His eyes engaged hers and he smiled again. "Here," he said, offering her the packages, "A basket of fruit for you and a little gift for your son."

"Thank you. That's very thoughtful," she said, putting them on a side table.

He was looking at the toys on the floor. "Where is he?"

"Taking his nap. But he'll be up soon enough if you'd like to meet him."

"I hoped I might."

She turned toward the couch and chairs. "Please sit down."

Chase followed her and waited as she picked up the newspaper scattered over the couch.

"As a housekeeper I err on the side of messy."

He laughed and sat in Alex's chair as if it were obvious she was clearing the couch for herself.

Jessica looked at him, noticing the incongruity of seeing another man in her husband's chair. "I guess, though," she said, "messiness is not among the criteria for selection, is it?" She sat opposite him.

"Not unless it's an inheritable trait," he replied. "But don't worry, I tend to be a little messy myself, so we would never be able to prove who donated the defective gene."

Jessica smiled politely, then studied him for a moment. "I take it I'm still in the running?"

"Oh, yes, very much so." He let his eyes drift down her body and his expression slowly changed from sunny to thoughtful. "I'm sorry to hold you up like this. I imagine you're feeling a bit in limbo, but I promise you'll get a decision tomorrow."

"Am I right to assume that this is the final exam?"

Chase Hamilton looked squarely at her. "In a sense, Mrs. Brandon, this house will be my baby's home, at first. I thought I ought to have a look."

Jessica's smile was rueful. "Well, since you happen to be here, feel free to look around."

"This isn't easy for you, is it?"

"No. To be honest, it's pretty tough."

"I don't mean to sound callous, but it ought to be tough. First, you're being well paid, and second, if you can't hack it, you're not the one for me."

"You certainly have a way of putting things on the line, don't you?"

"That's my style, yes."

"Well, it's fine with me. The less personal and more businesslike we keep this the better."

"It is business, that's true, but it concerns me that we seem to have gotten ourselves into an antagonistic state."

"Oh? Why?"

Chase Hamilton looked a little uncomfortable. "Well, you aren't exactly a concubine captured in battle. I don't intend that you resent me."

Jessica smiled wryly. "Well, you have come on like gangbusters."

"I've been that bad, have I?"

Jessica searched the handsome face that seemed far less ominous than the first time they had met. His eyes and mouth were somehow softer, less critical, but his devil-may-care attitude persisted. He was just being a little more subtle than he had been at the agency.

"Obviously I prefer being friends to enemies, Mr. Hamilton. But if you're suggesting something else, I'm not sure I'd be interested."

"Let me ask you what sort of relationship you expect during the pregnancy."

Jessica hesitated, knowing she still didn't have the job and shouldn't do anything to jeopardize what she had come to want so desperately. "I'm not saying this is all I'd agree to, but if I had my druthers I wouldn't see you again until I gave you the baby—and only then if it's absolutely necessary."

"That isn't quite how I pictured it."

"Harriet said you had strong feelings about being involved, but she didn't elaborate and you didn't say anything when we met. May I ask how *you* see this thing going?"

"To be blunt, I don't plan on missing any of the experience of fatherhood, before or after the birth."

"Mr. Hamilton, I don't—"

"Look...this Mr. Hamilton and Mrs. Brandon business is more suitable for lawsuits or back-to-school nights. Let's switch to Chase and Jessica. Do you mind?"

"Okay, if you wish."

He contemplated her, his face a curious mixture of handsome and smug. "I believe I interrupted you. You were about to comment on my view of the way this thing would go—if you are selected."

"Yes...." Jessica had been noticing again the incongruity of seeing him in Alex's chair. It not only looked strange to her, Chase Hamilton did, as well—not so much *him* as the way she saw him. She realized immediately what the problem was. She was reacting to his attractiveness, his manly appeal. It was not a feeling she was accustomed to. "Yes...Chase..." He had distracted her to the point where she didn't know what it was that she had intended to say.

"Does it bother you that I would be interested in the baby before it's born, Jessica?"

His question reminded her of her feelings. Of course! She did mind. Very definitely. "Well, yes," she said, as though it ought to be obvious. "That's a very personal sort of thing between the mother and the child."

"What about the father?"

"If the father is the husband, then yes, of course, but—"

"I don't see what difference it makes."

Jessica had the sudden realization that Chase Hamilton was expecting much more of her than she was willing to give him. "Exactly *how* involved in the pregnancy do you want to be?"

"Like I said, I don't intend to miss a thing."

Jessica gave a little laugh. "You mean you intend to sit and watch my stomach grow?"

"Well, I do have other things to do, of course, but that's the gist of it, yes."

She stared at him, wondering what she had gotten herself into. It obviously was not the routine surrogate arrangement. Jessica sighed.

"Having problems with the idea?"

"God," she lamented, "why can't anything ever be simple?"

Just then Jamie made a sound in the bedroom. She glanced at Chase.

His expression brightened. "Well, looks like I'm going to meet Master Brandon."

"You'll learn that one of the joys of being a parent is that things are done on *their* schedule, not yours." She smiled and stood up. "Please excuse me, Chase."

He watched her leave the room, admiring the shapely curve of her hips and legs under her jeans. She was a damn good-looking woman and that was nice, especially if the child were to be a girl. The women in his own family were attractive, perhaps more handsome than delicately beautiful like Jessica Brandon, so the combination might work out very nicely.

On the other hand, if the child were a boy he'd be concerned about durability, mental toughness and strength. His gene pool couldn't carry the burden alone. He'd have to look for evidence of familial traits. The boy, Jamie, might give him some clues in that regard.

But the woman did please him. Her femininity spoke to the masculinity in him, and that he considered a bonus. After all, people weren't horses, and Chase had always appreciated a nicely turned ankle and a well-shaped derriere. But best of all she had spunk. She was unique, and that pleased him.

Chase heard her in the next room with the boy, heard the patter of mother and child, and had a curious feeling. Jessica Brandon's qualities as mother were not really relevant to his plans for her because she would never know the baby. But they were a part of who she was, and that was interesting because of what it revealed, if nothing else.

A moment later, Jessica appeared at the bedroom door with a small boy in her arms, blond like her, with the same frothy beige eyes. The child was rather endearing with the metal braces on his legs, but more than anything, Chase was aware of the woman, her manner with the boy. Her face was filled with pride as she looked at her child, speaking to him in a soft, reassuring, maternal way.

"Come and meet Mr. Hamilton," she was saying.

Chase stood as they approached. "Well, who's this?"

Jamie looked at him with wide eyes and shrank a bit at the proximity of a stranger. Chase took his hand. "I'll bet you're Jamie Brandon."

The boy nodded.

Jessica smiled proudly. "Jamie's not accustomed to strange men, I'm afraid." She sat down on the couch with the boy on her lap.

Chase sat beside them. He smiled at the child. "How old are you, Jamie?"

The boy held up three fingers.

"Three! Hey, that's pretty big. When are you going to be four? When's your birthday?"

Jamie shrugged.

"He was just three in March," Jessica said, "so he has a long way to go."

"What'd you get for your birthday, Jamie?" Chase asked.

The boy shrugged again.

"Oh, you remember," Jessica prompted. "You were playing with it on the porch this morning."

"A truck," he said to Chase shyly.

"A truck! That's terrific. What color is it? I'll bet it's red."

Jamie nodded, slipping his fingers into his mouth. Jessica pulled them out and glanced at Chase.

"Red is always a safe guess," he said to her, noticing the soft beauty of her smile. He turned his attention to the boy. "Guess what? I brought you a birthday present. It's a little late, but better late than never."

"Where?" Jamie asked, showing real interest.

Chase and Jessica laughed.

"It's over there on the table," he said, pointing. "See that big box with the red ribbon?"

Jamie nodded and squirmed on his mother's lap.

"Can he walk over and get it?"

"I'm afraid Jamie has to learn to walk all over again. He had just been walking a few months when he had his accident. We go to physical therapy twice a week to strengthen his legs and back. If we work real hard the braces will become a thing of the past."

"Can he walk with help?"

"Yes, but he has to be held under the arms, not by the hands."

"Is it okay if I walk him over to get the present?"

"Well . . . I guess so."

"Hey, partner, how'd you like to walk over and get that present?"

Jamie nodded eagerly.

"Come on, then." Chase reached over and lifted the boy off Jessica's lap. Putting Jamie on the floor, he held him under the arms. "Can he take his full weight?"

"As long as he doesn't complain. Pain is the only limitation."

Jessica watched in amazement as Chase and her son inched their way toward the table. She was supposed to get him to walk as much as possible, but he was seldom interested. Whenever she encouraged him, he usually cried after a step or two and asked to be picked up.

When they had negotiated the distance to the table without any complaints from Jamie, Chase lifted him up so he could reach the package himself. Then he lowered the boy and the package to the floor, letting him sit at his feet to unwrap it.

"Chase, that's amazing. He won't walk like that for me!"

"Maybe I just understand the male psychology a little better than you, Jessica. With animals motivation is the key to performance, and people are no different. We're animals, too, just a little more complicated than the other species.''

Jamie was tearing the paper and jerking at the ribbon with frustration. He looked at Jessica with a distraught expression. She started to get up, but Chase raised his hand, indicating that she shouldn't come. He squatted beside the boy.

"See this end, partner? Try giving it a pull."

Jamie gave it a halfhearted tug.

"That'll never get you what you want in life, Jamie. Pull harder."

The boy gave the ribbon a ferocious tug and it dropped from the box. He looked at his mother and giggled gleefully.

"You see," Chase said, winking at Jessica, "his sugar cubes are in the box."

"Have you been a father before?" she asked, giving him a skeptical look.

"Yes, to hundreds of little colts, but not of this variety." He grinned, and Jessica felt an odd twinge go through her.

For the next few minutes she watched Chase Hamilton and her son opening the present, the man only intervening when the obstacles became insurmountable. Finally Jamie pulled a lifelike miniature of a racehorse from the box.

His eyes lit up. "Horsey, Mommy." He held it up for her to see, then began bouncing it along the floor. Chase was grinning with satisfaction.

"I'm impressed," Jessica said approvingly. "I couldn't have done that."

"Well, mothers have other functions. Women seem to have natural talents in the emotional realm. You look like you do a pretty good job in that regard."

Their eyes met and Jessica felt a strong current of emotion pass between them. There was a closeness that she wouldn't have thought possible on the day they had met. The difference, obviously, was her son. She wondered whether it was a good sign or a bad one.

After Jamie had played for a few minutes with the horse, Chase picked them both up and went to Alex's chair. He sat down with the boy and the horse on his lap. "How do you like that horse, Jamie?"

"He's nice," the boy replied, beaming at his mother.

"You ever been on a real horse?" Chase asked.

He nodded.

"When were you on a horse?" Jessica asked incredulously.

"At the store," he replied, making the horse bounce along the arm of the chair. He looked over his shoulder at Chase shyly.

"What store is this?" Chase asked.

"I think he means the supermarket horse," Jessica explained.

"Well, that's a pretty sorry excuse for a horse. How'd you like to see a real one, Jamie?"

The boy's eyes grew round and he nodded emphatically.

"I'll tell you what. I've got some nice horses at my house that'd probably like to see you as much as you'd like to see them. Since it's such a nice day, why don't you ask your mom if she'd like to drive over and have a look?"

Jamie's eyes lit up and he looked at his mother.

Jessica was surprised. "Do you live around here?"

"I've got a small farm outside of Cross River."

"Where's that?"

"Due east of here about fifteen miles, near the Connecticut border."

"Goodness, we're practically neighbors. I had no idea. I thought horse breeders lived in Kentucky and Virginia, places like that."

"Actually, my main operation is in Kentucky, but I live in New York most of the time. I keep a dozen horses here, mainly so I don't forget the feel and smell of horseflesh." His eyes settled on her in a way that made Jessica feel strangely uncomfortable. "I was serious, by the way, about letting Jamie see the horses. Let's drive over to my place."

Though Jamie hadn't comprehended everything that was said, Jessica could see that he understood that the horse adventure was clearly in her hands. His look was beseeching.

"You seem to have put me in an awkward position, Chase."

He grinned. "Not unintentionally, I must admit."

"You do have a knack for that, don't you?" The corners of her mouth twisted wryly. She was secretly pleased.

"I would have said put on your sneakers and let's go, but on second thought, I've decided to take the two of you to the country club for dinner. So why don't you slip on something suitable before we go?"

"We've had the bathing suit competition, now it's time for the evening-gown part of the contest. Is that it?"

"You're one of those rare women who understand the male mind." He nodded, smiling. "I like that."

Jessica was caught completely off guard by his comment.

"Well, you go ahead and get yourself together," he said, standing up with her son in his arms. "Jamie and I will go out on the lawn for a bit."

Jessica started to protest, not only because she wasn't sure she wanted to go with him, but also because he was carrying off her child and that made her feel uneasy. But he was already headed for the door, apparently never doubting the propriety of the liberties he was taking. She looked after them for a minute, thinking about what he had just said about her. She wished she could return the compliment, remarking on his understanding of the feminine mind, but knew it would be a filthy lie.

FIFTEEN MINUTES LATER she stood inside the screen door and watched Chase Hamilton and Jamie on the little strip of lawn next to the porch. The toy horse was at the far edge of the yard and Chase and Jamie were at the near end. The man had removed his jacket and loosened his tie. He was supporting the boy.

"Let's go get the horse again, Jamie," he said. "Let's catch him before he runs away."

She watched her child taking awkward but determined strides toward the toy. Little excited laughs emanated from his mouth every few seconds. Chase was above him, urging him on. "Just a little more, Jamie. You can do it. Hurry, before the horse runs away."

When the boy had finally captured the prize, Jessica stepped onto the porch. Both of them glanced up when they heard the screen door slam.

For a moment the man looked at her, his eyes taking in her taupe linen skirt and coral silk blouse, her legs, her hair, her mouth. Feeling very feminine in the clothes she so seldom had a chance to wear, she slowly walked along the porch toward them. Her strides were languorous. It was a little like the days when she had been a model and walked down the ramp under other admiring eyes.

Chase Hamilton had made her aware of her body, her female sexuality, in a way she hadn't been for years. His admiration felt good.

Seating Jamie on the grass with his new toy, Chase walked over to the edge of the porch and looked up at her. The afternoon sun shone on his face, making her even more aware of his robust masculinity.

"Not bad. All you need is a crown."

She laughed, then leaned against the post, looking down at him, her fingers self-consciously touching the ivory beads at her neck, the ones Alex had given her on their last wedding anniversary. "Easily said. I don't have any competition."

"Don't get smug," he said with a grin. "The race ain't over."

Jessica frowned. "I'm beginning to see that your technique is bait and hook."

"No, carrot and stick."

"Lest you forget, Mr. Hamilton, all that interests me about you is your money."

"That's what I'm counting on." He chuckled. "Amazing what a few pounds of gold does to people."

Jessica's eyes flashed. "Well, I hope your horses appreciate your generosity. Nobody I know would be impressed by your way with your own species."

"Now, now. No offense intended. I think you're the one who's been talking money ever since we met. That *is* what you're in this for, isn't it?"

"Yes, it is. But I'm beginning to have second thoughts about whether a hundred thousand will be enough."

Chase turned and looked at the boy, then at Jessica. "I suppose we could stand here charming each other all evening, but I think your son is ready for a horseback ride. Shall we go?"

Jessica wanted to take another shot at her would-be employer, but she remembered what that meant to her bargaining position. He obviously was having a great deal of fun, wringing all he could out of his advantage over her. "Yes, I just want to take Jamie into the bathroom before we go and put a clean shirt and pants on him."

Chase brought the boy and his horse to Jessica and she disappeared inside. Several minutes later she reappeared, having herself put on a white raw silk jacket. Jamie looked scrubbed and fresh. Chase took the boy from her and they walked up the street to where he had parked.

"My goodness," Jessica said, looking at his car. "What's this, a Rolls?"

"It's a Bentley—virtually the same thing."

"Very pretty." She climbed into the silver-gray car and Chase handed her the boy, who settled quietly on her lap, still clutching his horse.

For twenty minutes they drove along country lanes through the rolling hills and villages of Westchester County, past a hodgepodge of secluded executive homes, farms and country cottages. Chase didn't say much, but Jessica was very aware of him, disliking him in a way, but also finding herself fascinated. She was glad that Jamie had become the focus of attention.

Eventually they came to a small valley of open fields surrounded by wooded hills. A board fence painted white separated the pasture from the road. There were several horses grazing on the luxuriant grasses at the far end of the field.

"This is my place," Chase announced casually.

"What a lovely setting."

"I like it."

They turned off the road and went up the driveway that led to a stately house that looked very much like an

English country estate. It was surrounded by large shade trees, maples and elms, now richly verdant with spring foliage.

The house itself was two stories, and judging by the size, Jessica thought there must be fifteen or twenty rooms at least. She glanced at Chase as they pulled into the graveled area outside the porte cochère, but said nothing. Harriet had said Chase Hamilton was wealthy, but between the car and the house she was beginning to gain an appreciation of just what they meant.

"If you'd like to see the house we can go inside, maybe for a drink before we leave. But I think we'd better put the horseback riding at the top of the agenda, don't you?"

Jessica looked at Jamie's expectant face. "Yes, I think so."

Chase drove on to the stables and they all got out of the car. He had his farmhand bring out a gentle old mare named Velvet and saddle her where the boy could watch. Jamie was beside himself with excitement.

When the mare was ready, Chase tossed his sport jacket in the car and handed Jessica the toy horse. Then, as he carried Jamie to Velvet, Jessica felt a little clutch of fear for her child, not knowing whether she ought to permit so ambitious a venture.

There was a little trepidation on the child's face, too, until Chase swung himself up behind him. He adjusted Jamie's little braced legs so that he was virtually sitting on his lap. Jessica stared up at the broad-shouldered man, his nicely chiseled features at once challenging and admiring. By the grin that finally crossed his face he was aware of the sex appeal he exuded.

Jessica tried to concentrate on her son as Chase gave a command to the farmhand, who opened the gate to the adjoining riding ring. The horse and riders entered the enclosure.

Jessica went to the fence to watch. At first they walked in lazy circles around the ring. She looked on quietly, full of maternal pride and joy for her child, uneasiness toward the man. At one point Chase leaned over and said something to Jamie, then pointed toward Jessica. The boy then waved at this mother. "Hi, Mommy," he called, and she felt tears of gratitude welling in her eyes.

JAMIE SAT on the Oriental carpet at his mother's feet, playing with his horse, which he now called Velvet. Jessica was surveying the finely furnished sitting room that was about three times the size of her entire house. Chase had gone to ask the maid to bring Jamie a glass of milk and to get drinks for the two of them.

When he returned a few minutes later, Jessica smiled up at him appreciatively. She took the vodka tonic she had requested and a cocktail napkin, then waited for him to sit down. "Your house is just lovely, Chase. Did you do it yourself, or did you have a decorator?"

"A friend did most of it, but she was a professional decorator—still is, actually."

"She did a lovely job."

"Yes, Carolyn is very good."

There was something about the way Chase referred to the woman that told Jessica she was more than just a friend. The notion intrigued her, filling her with curiosity about his personal life. She glanced at the painting over the mantel, a hunting scene filled with horses and hounds that looked to be early eighteenth century. "I guess you have a taste for things English."

"Yes, Carolyn was . . . is English."

"Oh, did you have a taste for her, too?"

Chase laughed. "I guess I did walk into that, didn't I? As a matter of fact, Carolyn and I were engaged at one time."

"Why didn't you marry?"

"She didn't like children and horses." He sipped his drink and looked at her. "It proved to be an insurmountable obstacle."

"You wanted children and she didn't?"

"Yes, that pretty well sums it up."

Just then the maid, a big-boned Irish woman, entered the room, carrying a glass of milk on a tray. "Excuse me, ma'am," she said, addressing Jessica, "but I brought the young gentleman a few biscuits on a plate, as well. Would that be suiting you, ma'am?"

"What sort of biscuits?" Jessica asked.

"I believe they be oatmeal, ma'am."

"Oh, that would be fine, thank you. But I'm not sure I want Jamie eating on your carpets or furniture, Chase."

"Don't worry about it," he replied. "They're meant to be used, even by children. I'm only sorry there aren't more nicks and spots around here."

Jamie watched with curious eyes as Maggie spread a cloth beside him on the floor and placed the glass of milk and plate of cookies on it. "There you be, lad," she said, and playfully tousled Jamie's hair. "You can have a proper picnic if you like." The woman nodded to Jessica and left the room.

Jessica's attention immediately returned to Chase. "So what happened to Carolyn? You couldn't agree on the children issue so you broke it off?"

"It was a mutual parting of the ways. We both saw the writing on the wall."

"But you loved her?"

"Yes."

"That must have been hard for you."

"I suppose it was." He was watching Jamie attack the cookies.

"Is that why you don't want to get married? Because of Carolyn, I mean."

"I never said I didn't want to marry. I said I wouldn't marry just to have children. Unfortunately women and I rarely see eye to eye."

"Yes, I can appreciate that."

He shot her a glance, but Jessica managed to keep a straight face.

They both sipped their drinks.

"Do you like Gainsborough?" he asked after a while.

"Yes, why?"

"I've got a minor painting suspected of being one of his. It's in my study, if you'd like to see it."

"I'd love to."

"I've got a modest collection of contemporary art, too, if that interests you."

"Very much."

"Good." He stood up. "Jamie, my friend, would you like to stay here with Velvet while I show your mom some paintings?"

The boy nodded.

"We'll be back in a minute," Jessica said.

Chase took her by the arm. She was very much aware of the feeling of his hand. "We'll have to leave shortly for the club if we don't want to lose our reservation."

Jessica walked with Chase into the adjoining room, deciding that he was a very curious man: wonderful with children on the one hand, but heavy-handed with women, or at least with her, on the other. He would be an excellent father, she concluded, one she could feel good about giving a baby to, if she got the job. Somehow that made up for the bad time he had been giving her.

IT WAS DARK when Chase Hamilton's Bentley pulled up in front of the little house in Peekskill. Jamie was asleep in Jessica's arms, the catsup stain on his shirt belying the angelic pose.

"Sit still for a second," Chase said, touching her hand. "I'll come around and get him."

A moment later they were climbing the steps to the porch. Chase was carrying the sleeping child; Jessica was fishing her keys out of her purse in the dark. She opened the door and led the way back to the bedroom that she shared with the child. Because of his handicap, Jamie slept in a large crib.

Chase gently laid the boy down, then stepped back while Jessica removed the braces and his clothing. When she had finished she glanced self-consciously at her own single bed before leading the way back into the living room.

"Can I offer you a cup of coffee or something to drink?"

"It's late and I know you're tired." His eyes roamed her face, indicating an awareness that both frightened and excited her.

The evening had been delightful, a complete change of pace from her rather Spartan existence with Jamie. During dinner at the club and afterward they hadn't discussed the subject that had brought them together, but they'd talked a lot about Chase's work, about horses, about her painting and about Jamie and his rehabilitation program.

Chase had looked at her in a strange way from time to time—she knew it was the look of a man appreciating a woman—but he neither said nor did anything that would suggest more than awareness.

"It'll only take a minute to put the tea kettle on."

"Thanks, but no."

He looked genuinely uncomfortable just then and it surprised her. "Thank you for a wonderful day, Chase. It was a delightful surprise. Thank you for the gifts, and especially thank you for your kindness with Jamie."

He nodded. "He's a great kid."

"I'm sure he'll never forget that horse ride."

Chase had a contemplative look on his face. "Well . . . I'd better go."

Jessica could tell he wanted to say something, but was hesitant. She knew he was thinking about the surrogate mother thing and was troubled by it. That concerned her. "What happens now?"

"You mean about the job?"

"Yes, the job."

"I promised you a decision tomorrow. Harriet will call to tell you what I've decided." His blue eyes were cold, flat.

It was back to business again. As Jessica watched, Chase went to the door. He stopped and looked back at her. "She'll give you the official word, but I suppose there's no harm in telling you that I've made up my mind."

Jessica felt her blood stop in her veins. She swallowed hard.

"If you'll agree to my terms," he said, letting the words roll slowly off his lips, "I'd like you to be the mother of my child."

Without waiting for the announcement to have its effect, he turned and was gone.

CHAPTER FOUR

JESSICA DIDN'T FALL ASLEEP until three o'clock the next morning. Her mind was crackling with the excitement of Chase Hamilton's announcement. But at the back of her thoughts there was a nagging uncertainty about what he meant by the qualification "if you'll agree to my terms." Given her excitement she didn't want to worry about that just then; the important thing was she'd gotten the job!

For the first time in a long time, everything seemed as if it might end up all right. She and Jamie would be rich. She could paint to her heart's content. Their problems would be over!

Jessica lay in bed, feeling the joy and trepidation of a schoolgirl. She reflected even as she smiled blissfully into the darkness of the room. The thought of being pregnant by a man she didn't love couldn't dampen her spirits, because Chase Hamilton was a decent man, if a little eccentric and heavy-handed. He had been kind to Jamie, and despite his capacity to annoy her, she was glad he would be getting what he wanted, too.

Jessica thought about the pregnancy, the impersonal insemination that would cause dramatic changes in her body and bring another life into the world. But it didn't frighten her. The change would be temporary. The child would belong to Chase; it would brighten his life just as Jamie had brightened hers. In ten or twelve months her life would be just where it was now, except that there would be no poverty, her career as an artist would be under way and she'd feel secure instead of afraid.

The next morning Jessica awoke to Jamie imploring to go to the bathroom. Mercifully he had waited until eight-thirty to awaken her, having played quietly in his crib with Velvet, which Jessica had placed next to him on the dresser the night before.

When they both had cleaned up and dressed, she carried the boy into the kitchen and propped him in his high chair while she started breakfast. She had just handed him his juice, when the phone rang. It was Harriet.

"Congratulations, love! Looks like you've done it, after all."

"Oh, Harriet, I'm so pleased!"

"Are you really? No sleepless night tossing and turning, wondering what you had gotten yourself into?"

"Not at all. I'm on cloud nine. Couldn't be happier."

"Well, I'm pleased for you, Jessica. And I know you've made my client happy. The man certainly was chipper when he called this morning."

"Was he?"

"He wasn't the hard-nosed, intimidating Chase Hamilton I've come to know and love, let me put it that way."

Jessica laughed. "Poor thing, he's probably just been frustrated, that's all."

"Apparently you changed that."

"Then it's done?"

"There still are the formalities ... the contract."

"Yes, I guess that's when his terms get spelled out, isn't it?"

"What do you mean?"

"When he told me last night, he said I had the job if I agreed to his terms. Should I worry, Harriet?"

"He's got his own ideas, that's for sure. But I don't know of anything in particular other than what I've already told you."

"What happens now?"

"I've got to schedule you with the attorney. When are you free?"

"Anytime. The sooner the better."

"We'd better get cracking, then. With luck, you'll be pregnant in no time."

Jessica pondered the curious notion. Then a thought struck her. "God, Harriet, what if it doesn't work? What if I don't get pregnant?"

"The doctor doesn't feel there'll be a problem, so I wouldn't worry about it."

"But if I don't conceive there'd be no deal, no money."

"That's true, but there's no reason to think it won't work. It doesn't always take the first time, of course. I believe the average is something like two or three tries."

"Lord, I could have a nervous breakdown if it went on for months."

"Presumably you didn't say that to the psychiatrist."

Jessica laughed. "No, but we weren't discussing my financial problems at the time."

"Well, let's see what we can do about getting you pregnant right away."

Jessica was still considering Harriet's words.

"Jessica?"

"Sorry. I was just thinking how strange that sounded—getting me pregnant. You'd think I was a heifer."

"Mare, I think would be the correct analogy, given the circumstances."

"Lord, no question he regards this as a breeding exercise, is there?"

"I warned you it wouldn't be easy."

"You know, the involvement he wants is the only thing about the deal that bothers me, Harriet. It'd be so much easier if he just came and picked up the baby when I've delivered."

"That's not the way he wants it. And it's his party."

"Yes, that fact is becoming clearer by the day."

"Well, back to the business at hand. After you finish with the attorney we'll want to schedule the first insemination. Any idea when your next fertile days are?"

"I've been taking my temperature each morning since my visit to the doctor. I'm supposed to see him the end of this week. Since I'm regular, he thinks we'll be able to pinpoint it pretty accurately. He was talking in terms of the week after next."

"Wonderful! With luck you may be with child before June's out."

Jessica smiled, but with less enthusiasm than before.

"Still sound like what you want to do?"

"Yes, Harriet. I'm committed."

"Well, just remember until the contract's signed you can change your mind."

"I won't change it. I'm going to have Chase Hamilton's baby."

WHEN THE INTERCOM BUZZED, Arthur Netley, a large man with thinning gray hair, glanced at Chase Hamilton, sitting across the desk. He picked up the telephone receiver, punching one of the buttons on the console.

"Yes?" He listened. "Fine. Bring her in." He replaced the receiver. "Mrs. Brandon's here, Chase."

Netley got up and walked across his large book-lined office with a view of the Manhattan skyline as the door opened. Jessica, wearing her navy suit, walked past the secretary and into the room. The lawyer greeted her ceremoniously and turned to escort her to where Chase sat waiting.

Jessica's eyes rounded in surprise upon seeing him. Languorously he got to his feet.

"You know Mr. Hamilton, of course," Netley said. "He felt it might be useful to be here in case there were any questions."

"Hi, Jessica." He gestured for her to sit in the vacant chair next to him.

"Well, I hadn't expected to see you, Chase. I hope it's not a bad omen."

"No, I just think it's important that we be on the same wavelength."

The lawyer had returned to his desk. "Obviously the purpose of this meeting, Mrs. Brandon, is to review the agreement. I will be happy to answer any questions you may have, but since I represent Mr. Hamilton, I can't render any legal advice. I recommend that you have your own counsel review the documents for that purpose."

"I don't have a lawyer."

"I'm sure any competent attorney could evaluate the agreement for you. It is important that you have independent counsel."

Jessica glanced at Chase, who sat with his fingers steepled, listening. He didn't look at her. "Unless there's something strange, I'm sure I can evaluate it for myself," she replied, feeling a little uneasy.

"The decision is yours, but I can't stress enough the importance of having an attorney look over the contract for you."

Jessica nodded. "You've made your point, Mr. Netley. Shall we get started?"

The lawyer opened the folder on the desk before him, then slid it toward Jessica. She picked it up and flipped through ten typed pages.

"The reason I'm here," Chase said casually, "is because of the last few paragraphs I had Arthur add. You might want to look at those—the rest of it you're pretty much aware of."

Jessica eyed him warily, then turned to the last pages of the document. She read carefully, working her way through the legalese. After several moments she looked up at Chase, her face registering disbelief.

"It says here that it's a condition of the deal that I live with you."

"That you live at the farm, yes. And Jamie, of course."

"That's impossible!"

Chase stared at her, his face unexpressive. "Impossible?"

"You expect me to live with you?" she asked incredulously. "That's ridiculous!" She glanced at the attorney, then back at Chase. "I'm surprised you have the gall to suggest such a thing."

Chase sat upright. "Wait a minute. I'm not suggesting anything unsavory. My place is large. There are servants, a staff. If you'll read on you'll see that all of your and Jamie's needs are to be taken care of. I'm providing you with a studio and a full-time governess for the boy—"

"That's not the point, Chase. I have no intention of living in your household under any circumstances. I cherish my independence and I'm not about to become anyone's childbearing concubine."

"Isn't that a little strong? There isn't a thing in there that suggests that anything untoward is expected of you.

It simply requires that you reside at my place before the baby is born.''

"But why? Don't you trust me?''

"It's not a matter of trust. I simply prefer it that way.''

"That wasn't part of the deal!'' Jessica shot back.

"We're making the deal now.''

"You may be, Mr. Hamilton, but I'm not.''

Chase shook his head. "I don't know what you're so upset about. This is a better deal than what was originally proposed. On top of your hundred thousand you and your son get free room and board, a studio, child care, even physical therapy for Jamie. That's hardly grounds for being offended.''

Jessica couldn't believe what she was hearing. "You act as though money is all that counts.''

"Isn't that what you're in this for—the money?''

She rose to her feet and glared at him. "If you think you can just take out your checkbook and buy me, you're nuts!''

Chase remained composed, looking up at her. "When you've calmed down and had a chance to look at this logically, you'll be welcome to sign the agreement.'' He slowly got to his feet. "But be advised I'm not going to wait around forever.''

Jessica's eyes narrowed. "The gall...'' she said, her voice husky with restrained rage. Then she turned on her heel and marched toward the door. "Nice to have met you, Mr. Netley,'' she called over her shoulder, and left the room.

Jessica was still seething by the time she got to the bank of elevators. She pushed the Down button and waited impatiently, tapping her foot on the marble floor. Watching the lights indicating the location of the cars, she thought how, in one brief, incredible conversation, her dreams had been shattered. Chase Hamilton had pushed her too far, taken one too many liberties.

Tears came to her eyes as she thought how Jamie's and her future had been wrenched from her. How could the man be so cruel? She wondered if he could possibly drop his demand that they move to the farm. After all, it was unreasonable. She looked back up the hall, half hoping that Chase would come after her, begging her to reconsider, perhaps offering to drop his demands.

While she contemplated the possibility, an elevator car arrived. It was empty and Jessica stared into it for a moment, then back up the hall toward the law offices. When the elevator doors slid closed, she stepped to the button and pressed it again, looking once more toward Arthur Netley's office. It was idle to expect Chase to come after her. He was too stubborn for that. Besides, he had the upper hand.

Jessica sighed, feeling a wave of self-doubt. The thought of losing all that money, the opportunity it afforded her and Jamie, stabbed at her heart. Chase was right; the money was all that had mattered from the beginning. He had wounded her pride, but he still held the purse strings.

Another car arrived, but Jessica ignored it. She silently cursed him, trying to find a strategy to save face. The car left and she slowly began walking back up the hall toward Arthur Netley's private office. She knocked softly and entered. The two men were still seated where she had left them. They watched her walk across the room to the desk, where she leaned against the end of it, looking at Netley.

"I'll sign if you put in a clause that I can leave the farm if Mr. Hamilton misbehaves, or the environment is unwholesome for either me or my son."

The attorney looked at his client, who nodded. Then Netley took his legal pad and began writing. After a moment he turned the pad toward Jessica, who hadn't moved or looked at Chase. "Will that do, Mrs. Brandon?"

She read the two sentences the lawyer had written. "Yes."

Netley transcribed the clause onto the contract. Jessica read it, took the pen from him and signed at the bottom. "You can send me a copy." She glanced up at Chase, who sat calmly with his arms folded over his chest.

As Jessica walked away with determined strides, he watched the twitch of her nicely shaped rear end, remembering a spirited filly he had run at Keeneland for the Governor's Trophy three years before. She was his best brood mare now. It was a good omen.

TWO WEEKS LATER Jessica stood in front of the mirror on the back of the bathroom door. She could hear Mrs. Pantano, Jamie's baby-sitter, speaking with the boy in the kitchen.

Her neighbor was good-hearted, if a little excessive in making her feelings known about every aspect of Jessica and Jamie's life. Still she was trustworthy, very fond of the boy, and having her available gave Jessica freedom she wouldn't otherwise have. Half the time Mrs. Pantano refused her pay, saying she didn't need it as much as Jessica, and that was a welcome bonus.

The face in the mirror didn't betray the nervousness she felt at the moment. Jessica looked into her own eyes, feeling a little guilty about what she was going to do that day. The notion of going to a clinic to get pregnant seemed absurd, traitorous to her own body, and yet it was something she was determined to do.

At that moment Jessica's body was her own, and yet she had agreed to lend it to Chase Hamilton and his baby. The thought sent a wave of panic through her. In a way she was giving up control—her body wouldn't be exclusively hers any longer, nor would her life, for that matter. Pregnancy would mean moving to the farm, becoming a sort of hostage in the enemy camp.

Chase didn't see it that way, of course. He thought he was doing her a favor. But she couldn't help being resentful, even though her anger at his manipulation had abated during the past couple of weeks. At this point it wasn't Chase that concerned her so much as the ordeal she had to face at the clinic.

When the doctor had done his thing with the tubes and apparatus, she would—if things went well—be a different person from the woman in the mirror. She would look the same, but there would be a tiny germ growing inside her: Chase's baby. Jessica swallowed hard, trying to fight back the fear that welled up.

Think of Jamie! she implored the woman in the mirror. *Think of the future.* In a few short months it would be all over, her body would be hers again, and the baby would have disappeared from her life along with its father.

Harriet had talked ad nauseam about Jessica giving up her own child, but the baby implanted in her body would never be hers, except in a scientific sense. She would return from the clinic that afternoon, perhaps pregnant, but her heart and her soul would remain untouched. She knew what it meant to have a baby in the true sense, discovering that the love of a man and woman had produced another life. This, Jessica knew in her heart, was different.

The woman in the mirror looked as colorless as Jessica felt. She wore a resigned expression, a visage of duty. Jessica had put on only a minimum of makeup, had chosen a white silk blouse and a gray gabardine skirt to wear. This was business, the earning of a lifetime of security.

Jessica fluffed her hair with her fingertips, turned, took her purse from the bed and went into the kitchen to say goodbye to Jamie and Mrs. Pantano.

"It's nothin' serious I hope, Mrs. Brandon—you going to the doctor, I mean."

Jessica smiled at the heavyset, middle-aged woman. "No, it's not serious."

"Just a checkup?"

"In a way." Jessica saw no need to explain her situation to Mrs. Pantano until she began showing. No good would be served by making it public before it was necessary, and she would be spared the unpleasantness of getting undesired advice.

"Don't worry about Jamie. We'll be fine. In fact, if you want to stay out a while, don't bother over the money. I'll only charge you for three hours no matter how long it takes."

"Thank you, Mrs. Pantano, but I'll come right home after I finish at the clinic."

"Is it female problems?"

"Yes. I'm seeing my gynecologist."

Mrs. Pantano nodded knowingly.

"Well, I best be on my way. I'll miss my train if I don't get going." Jessica went over to Jamie in his high chair. "You be good."

The boy looked up at his mother, his mouth rimmed with grape jelly. She kissed him on the forehead and he took another bite of his toast.

Jessica smiled and headed for the door, then stopped to look at her son a final time.

"Hope everything goes well at the doctor, Mrs. Brandon," the baby-sitter called after her. "And don't let them talk you into taking something out. Never can tell when you might want another baby."

WALKING OUT of the train station, Jessica found New York the same as always: busy, distracted and indifferent. She battled the crowds until she finally managed to get a cab to the West Side.

When she entered the medical building, she was acutely aware of the impersonality of the facility. To the rest of the world it was just another day; no one seemed to care that Jessica Brandon had come to get pregnant.

The entrance to the fertility clinic was substantial yet inauspicious. The receptionist directed her to a small waiting room adjacent to the main reception area. Slowly opening the door, Jessica felt her heart pounding with dread and expectation.

The room was empty except for a man who looked up when she entered. It only took an instant before Jessica realized that the man was Chase Hamilton.

"Oh!" she exclaimed, shocked to see him.

"Right on time," he said as Jessica looked at him, remembering the unpleasant taste left in her mouth from their last encounter. Chase stood up. "What's the matter? Didn't you know I'd be here?"

"No... well, I hadn't thought about it...."

Chase smiled, gesturing for Jessica to sit. "They tell me this procedure requires the cooperation of both of us."

She flushed. "Well, yes, I realize... I guess I thought you'd be doing your part some other time—earlier, I mean." Jessica went to the far side of the small room and sat down, carefully avoiding Chase's eyes.

"Has something to do with freshness," he replied in a half whisper.

Jessica's cheeks burned with embarrassment. She risked a glance. He wore a dark suit and seemed rather formal to her, even a little uncomfortable—or was she projecting? She wondered if this was the way it was supposed to be when strangers made a baby. He didn't look as hard as he had at the lawyer's office. Maybe the weightiness of today's event had touched him, too.

Chase kept a discreet silence, maintaining the calm that seemed to be his trademark. She looked into his eyes, the eyes of the man who would father a child she was to carry. The notion struck her as ludicrous. She crushed her knees together and told herself that his body would never touch hers.

Chase had been watching her. "You all right?"

She nodded nervously. "Yes, fine. How are you?"

"Not liking the clinicalness of this very much." He grinned. "Seems like this ought to be done after some conversation and maybe a bottle of wine."

She managed a smile. "Is that the way you do it when you breed your horses?"

"Haven't lost your penchant for sarcasm, I see."

"Maybe you should have put something about that in your contract."

Chase laughed. "Do you suppose that would have done any good?"

"Probably not," she said, a smile touching her lips.

"Maybe it's time we start trying to be friends."

She was taken aback, unsure exactly what he was getting at. Looking around the room, she felt more uncomfortable than ever. "I wish they had put us in different rooms. I didn't realize it'd be like this."

"Not the way babies should be made, is it?"

"Considering the alternative, it's perfectly all right with me."

"That's right. You wouldn't go to bed with anyone for a million dollars."

"I said I wouldn't go to bed with *you* for a million dollars," she corrected.

Chase laughed.

Jessica was terribly uncomfortable with the course of the conversation, but she knew it was more than just the circumstances. She was acutely aware of Chase Hamilton's maleness and her own biological femininity. Never before had she been so aware of herself as a reproductive being. He was male and his function was to impregnate. Jessica could almost feel her ovaries throbbing. She tried not to squirm in her seat.

"How's Jamie?"

She acknowledged his politeness with a smile. "He's fine. The walking he did with you was really good for him."

"Good, good. He's a great little boy."

Jessica looked down at her folded hands on her lap. She remembered how wonderful and spontaneous it had been when she had gotten pregnant the first time. She and Alex hadn't really tried to have a child, nor had they tried to prevent it. They just let things occur naturally for a few months, then it happened. She had felt different, missed her period and there it was—she was pregnant.

"It's obvious how much he means to you, Jessica."

"What?" She looked up, perplexed.

"Jamie. It's obvious how important he is to you."

"Oh, yes. Sorry, I was thinking about something else." She saw the surprise in Chase's face. "I was thinking about my husband," she explained.

His expression grew sober. "You aren't having misgivings about this?"

"Oh, no."

"No guilt or anything?"

"No, nothing like that. I suppose getting pregnant is a rather emotional experience. Not the sort of thing a person does all the time."

"No, I guess not."

Jessica studied her long fingers on her lap and tried to recall the doctor's description of the procedure that would be used. The coldness of it was revolting, and yet, given the circumstances, it was the only way it could be done. She couldn't possibly be intimate with a man she didn't love, a stranger. And yet, despite everything, there was a part of her that would have preferred some kind of tenderness and human compassion.

Without looking at Chase, Jessica tried to imagine being intimate with him, picturing their bodies together. The thought sent a current of revulsion through her, not because she found him unattractive, but because it wasn't right.

She suddenly knew what the problem was. She would have preferred to have feelings for the man who was to father her child, but by the very nature of her relationship with Chase, that was impossible. This was for money. The man she loved was dead.

"What are you doing afterward, Jessica?" he asked in a low resonant voice. "Do you have plans for dinner?"

The invitation came as a surprise. She couldn't believe he would suggest socializing after having impregnated her. "Thanks, but I have to get home to Jamie."

"I didn't mean offense. I am serious about wanting to be friends, getting our relationship on a more constructive footing."

"Perhaps it's enough if we just try to be civil but keep it businesslike."

They sat in silence until a nurse opened the door.

"Mr. Hamilton, would you care to come in now?"

Jessica exchanged glances with him and her stomach clinched. She watched warily as he stood and walked quietly from the room.

JESSICA LAY on the examining table, staring at the print on the ceiling of a French impressionist painting advertising an exhibit at the Metropolitan Museum of Art. Alone in the room she had been trying to calm herself, but she kept seeing images of her body swollen with Chase's child. She fought the panic that kept threatening her, the voice that told her to get up and run.

Was it the notion of being pregnant by him that frightened her so? No, it wasn't that, she realized. It was the momentous implications of what was about to happen to her that had her heart thumping and her skin clammy. At that moment Chase Hamilton himself almost seemed irrelevant.

What terrified her was there would be no turning back, no escape. For months she would have no control over a situation the following minutes would create. Jessica closed her eyes and tried to think about Jamie, about what this would mean to his future. He was her only salvation.

In the midst of the swirl of emotion that had over-taken her, the door opened and Jessica looked up into the narrow bespectacled face of Dr. Duckett, a gray-haired man with kindly eyes. There was a half smile on his face, and for some reason Jessica focused on the stiffly starched collar and nondescript dark tie that the man wore under his white lab coat.

"How are you this afternoon, Mrs. Brandon?"

The nurse stepped into the room then and the two professionals began their work. Jessica listened to their words, responded to their questions and instructions, but she had entered a daze. Her mind shut out the stimuli, trying to protect her from the ordeal.

"Felt anything in your ovaries the past twenty-four hours or so?" the doctor asked.

"I think a twinge or two this morning."

"Hmm . . . and how was your temperature?"

"It dropped."

"Good, we might have hit it just right."

Jessica didn't know how long she lay there. She tried to ignore the tubes, instruments and other apparatus that were used to help effect the result they all wanted, but for very different reasons. *It's business,* she kept telling her-self. *It's for Jamie.*

Sometime later they left her. She had to stay on the ta-ble so that there was a better chance the procedure would be successful. As she stared at the print on the ceiling the doctor's last words kept running through her mind. "Just hold this position," he had said. "We need to give the donor's soldiers a chance to do their work."

HALF AN HOUR LATER when Jessica returned to the waiting room she was surprised to find Chase Hamilton still there. Slowly rising to his feet, he looked at her as though her face could tell him whether the insemination had been a success.

"What are you still doing here, Chase?"

"I wanted to make sure you're okay."

Jessica smiled through her embarrassment. "It's too early for a pregnancy test."

He gave a little laugh. "I know it's a little premature to sound like an expectant father, but somehow I couldn't just walk out the door."

There was a moment of awkwardness. "I've got to get back to my son," she said, starting to step past him.

Chase reached out to stop her, barely touching her arm. "Can I give you a lift?"

"No, thanks." She looked at him, trying to conjure up feelings of compassion, though it was hard to feel charitable toward anyone just then. "I'd really like to be alone."

He seemed a little annoyed, but withheld comment. "All right," he finally said, taking an envelope from his inside pocket. "I figured today wouldn't be very pleasant, so I wanted to give you a little something. Rather than flowers or more fruit, I decided a check would be more practical."

Jessica looked at him in surprise as he handed her the envelope.

"Maybe you can buy yourself a dress, get something for Jamie, or pay the utility bill—whatever is most pressing at the moment."

"That's very thoughtful of you, Chase, but really not necessary. I'm being well paid. There's no need—"

"Please don't object. I want to. Besides, if it didn't work today, you may not be getting any money for a long time." He pressed the envelope into her hand. "Take it for the boy."

Jessica acquiesced reluctantly.

"Sure I can't drive you home? The Bentley's out front."

"Thank you, but no." She felt badly turning him down, but it would really be impossible for her to be with him just then. He didn't seem to have the same appreciation of what had happened in the examining room as she had.

She looked up into the sapphire of his eyes, noticing the crinkles at the corners as he smiled at her a little sadly.

"I want you to know I appreciate what you did today," he said in a husky voice, barely more than a whisper.

"I know the baby means a lot to you. I hope it works out...." She heard the emotion in her own voice.

Then, to her surprise, he took her by the shoulders, leaned over and kissed her lightly on the cheek, his face touching her hair for a moment before he leaned back.

Jessica was overwhelmed with the tenderness of the gesture, the strong, masculine scent of him, the warmth of his body near hers. Still he lingered near her, almost embracing her, but not quite.

After a moment's hesitation she stepped back, searching his face and examining the confused jumble of her own feelings. Her eyes misted.

"Excuse me, Chase. I'm suddenly feeling emotional."

He stared at her in a curious sort of way, his jaw set, the emotion he was feeling repressed. Jessica wanted desperately to be alone, but for some reason she couldn't make herself leave.

"I'll go, then," he said softly, and went to the door.

Jessica watched as he stopped and looked back at her. She could barely see his face through a blur of tears.

Then, when he was finally gone, the air escaped from her lungs. She stared at the door, realizing for the first time what was wrong. In some perverse, inexplicable way, she had begun to care for Chase Hamilton.

CHAPTER FIVE

THE TRAIN RIDE back to Peekskill was a welcome interlude for Jessica. It had been an emotional afternoon and she was glad to be alone, to have time to get her thoughts and feelings sorted out. Her encounter with Chase Hamilton in the waiting room was troubling because of the feelings it had evoked, but it did give her another perspective of the man.

Jessica had to admit that he was kindhearted...and generous. He had already given her a lot, and now a check, too. The check! She had forgotten about the envelope completely, having stuck it in her purse without opening it. Quickly she fished it out and tore it open. Her eyes rounded. One thousand dollars!

She knew instantly that she couldn't accept that kind of a gift, but then she remembered his words: if she hadn't become pregnant, it might be months before she'd be receiving anything. Jessica decided she would keep the money only if Chase agreed that it would be an advance against the first installment. Dress money, indeed! She and Jamie could live for a long time on Chase's dress money.

She wondered, though, if it would be irresponsible of her to buy each of them a little treat of some sort. She could certainly use some new underwear, and another nightgown would be nice.

Since the bank was already closed by the time Jessica got back to Peekskill, she decided to return directly home, walking slowly in the hot afternoon air. She and Jamie could go shopping together the next day.

Mrs. Pantano and Jamie were sitting on the porch when Jessica finally dragged herself up the walk, exhausted by the day's events.

"Well, there you are, Mrs. Brandon!" The woman stood up, holding the child, who reached immediately for his mother. "How was everything at the doctor's?"

Jessica took Jamie, wrapping her arms around his little body. "Fine, I'm just fine."

"That's good news, isn't it?"

Jessica kissed the boy on the top of his head as he cuddled against her. Separations from her never pleased him.

"Were you a good boy for Mrs. Pantano?"

The boy thrust a couple of fingers into his mouth, lay his head on Jessica's shoulder and didn't bother to respond.

"He didn't have much of a nap, so I think he's a little tired, Mrs. Brandon."

"Maybe I'll give him some juice and put him down for a while now," Jessica said, pulling the screen door open.

The baby-sitter followed her into the house. "Oh, I nearly forgot," the woman said excitedly. "You had a telephone call while you were gone."

Jessica turned. "Oh? Who was it?"

"A Mr. Gessel or Jessel from New York."

"Mr. Geisel? Helmut Geisel?"

"Yes, that's the one. He said to tell you he sold one of your paintings this afternoon. Full price, he said."

Jessica's eyes rounded. "He sold a painting?" She spun around excitedly with the boy in her arms. "Jamie, did you hear that? Mommy sold a painting!"

The child laughed at his mother's antics. Mrs. Pantano beamed. "I thought you'd be pleased, Mrs. Brandon. It's your first, isn't it?"

"Yes! My first real sale, anyway." She squeezed Jamie until he protested, wiggling in her arms. "And you said full price?"

"Yes, that's what the man said. You'll be getting your check in a few days."

Jessica thought of Chase Hamilton's check in her purse and the fifteen hundred dollars or so she would net out of the sale of her painting. "I haven't felt so rich in my whole life!"

They went into the kitchen. Jessica got Jamie some juice and peered into the refrigerator. "I see half a bottle of white wine in here, Mrs. Pantano. Will you join me for a drink to celebrate my sale?"

"And the good news at the doctor's, too. Don't forget that."

Jessica turned from the refrigerator with the bottle of wine in her hand. "Yes, that, too. Let's hope that I don't have to go back again."

The baby-sitter got a couple of water glasses from the cupboard and Jessica pulled the cork from the bottle. She smiled to herself, wondering if indeed her life had really changed for the better.

THE FOLLOWING DAYS were a little like Christmas for Jessica and Jamie. They went shopping as she had planned, and Helmut Geisel's check came three days after his call. Jessica felt wonderful, and even worried that she might have been a little precipitous in rushing into the

surrogate mother thing, but knew without an inventory
of canvases and her own one-woman show, she'd never
be able to support herself and her child by painting.
Chase Hamilton's money was essential.

Though she kept busy, even getting in several succes-
sive days of painting, Jessica found herself listening to
her body, observing it for signs of pregnancy. She tried
to remember the last time—the way her breasts looked in
the early weeks, the way she felt.

Each day she wondered whether there was a child in
her womb, thought about the possibility of a baby, but
didn't discuss it with anyone. And the others involved
didn't intrude. Chase kept his distance. Harriet didn't
call, and Jessica decided not to phone her.

Toward the end of the second week, after the weather
turned hot and summery, Jamie had a bad spell. Jessica
noticed he was in pain a lot, refused to walk and re-
gressed emotionally, as he always seemed to when things
got rough. It bothered her more than it had in the past
because she had begun to hope that Jamie had made a
breakthrough during the past month. If nothing else, the
episode reminded her that money couldn't solve everything.

During the following week, on a hot afternoon while
Jamie was napping, Jessica sat in the living room in front
of an electric fan. She wore a T-shirt and shorts and was
feeling a little out of sorts. The telephone rang. She
groaned at the intrusive sound and crawled across the
couch to pick up the receiver. It was Chase Hamilton.

"How are you feeling, Jessica?"

She grinned at the solicitous voice coming over the line.
"You mean, do I feel pregnant?"

"Something like that."

"Well, the answer is no, not especially."

"But you don't feel *not* pregnant, do you?"

"I haven't had my period, if that's what you're getting at, Chase."

He cleared his throat. "It's a little difficult to be delicate about it, isn't it?"

"It's part of the process, I suppose. If it doesn't bother me, you shouldn't let it bother you."

Silence hung on the line.

"How's Jamie?" he asked after a while.

"Not very well. The heat has been bothering him. He's been cranky."

"Maybe he needs an outing. Why don't the two of you come over to my place? He can see Velvet again. That might raise his spirits."

Jessica looked at her slender bare legs and unconsciously ran her fingers through wisps of her tawny hair. "I think it'd be better if we didn't."

"Better for who? You or Jamie?"

"There's nothing wrong with thinking of myself, too," she said defensively.

"What is it you're afraid of, Jessica?"

You, she wanted to reply, but knew it would lead to a conversation she wasn't prepared to have. "Having your child is not exactly a casual social relationship. I'm trying to cope with it as best I can."

"Are you saying I'm making it difficult for you?"

Jessica could hear a little irritation in his voice and knew she had to turn the conversation in a different direction. "No, of course not. You've been very kind."

"You seemed to want space and I've given you that, haven't I?"

"Yes, you've been considerate."

"Well?"

She hesitated. "I don't mean to sound unkind, Chase, but I'd really like to stick to the contract, keep things professional and businesslike."

He didn't speak immediately, but Jessica imagined that his face was dour.

"All right. When are you scheduled to see the doctor again. It's this week, isn't it?"

"Yes. I'm a couple of days late already. The doctor said to come in when I was past due." She could almost see his expression lighten.

"You mean...you think it worked?" There was a hint of excitement in his voice.

"Maybe. I'm usually pretty regular."

"That's terrific!"

Jessica smiled. "Yes, it would be nice, wouldn't it?"

"Nice? God...."

"Chase, you sound like a schoolboy."

"Well, it's my first, I—"

"Let's not count our chickens yet," she cautioned.

"Will you go in tomorrow?"

"I thought I'd call for an appointment."

"Will you let me know?"

She laughed, feeling infected somewhat with his excitement. "I promise you'll be the first to know."

When she had hung up, Jessica lay on the couch, mildly amused at the conversation and Chase's boyish reaction. She rubbed her stomach distractedly through her T-shirt before she caught herself. It was a mannerism she had developed during her pregnancy with Jamie, her way of caressing and loving the baby while he was still in the womb. But this baby—if it was in there— was not hers to love. It was Chase's.

JESSICA HEARD the door to the waiting room click open and looked up from her magazine to see the nurse standing in the doorway. A brief smile touched the woman's lips.

"Mrs. Brandon, the test result was positive."

Jessica felt her stomach drop. "I'm pregnant?"

"We believe that you are. Dr. Duckett would like to examine you, if you'll wait a few minutes."

"Certainly." She smiled, but the corners of her mouth quivered. No matter how much she had prepared herself for it, the news seemed almost unexpected. She was pregnant!

Jessica looked down at the magazine on her lap. She had closed it in her excitement and couldn't even recall what she had been reading. She flipped through the pages for a moment, but abandoned the effort. Her mind was racing. Pregnant!

There were just nine months to delivery...no, less...barely more than eight. It would be over in no time. And this was what she wanted, what they all wanted.

WALKING FROM THE TRAIN STATION to her house in Peekskill, Jessica felt more exhausted than usual. It was undoubtedly the power of suggestion, because, in honesty, she couldn't say she'd felt a whole lot different before her visit to the clinic. Now she'd probably experience every possible symptom.

She thought about Chase and decided she'd better call him as soon as she got home. This was his big day and he was entitled to enjoy it. Heaven knows he was paying enough for it.

When Jessica finally made it to the house and pulled the screen door open, she was amazed to find her small living room overflowing with flowers. Mrs. Pantano and Jamie were sitting on the couch, surrounded by blossoms of every color.

"What's this?" Jessica exclaimed.

"The card's on the table." The plump woman smiled knowingly. "Maybe you've got an admirer, Mrs. Brandon."

Jessica nodded vacantly, wondering if Chase could have found out this quickly. She couldn't imagine who else might have sent them. She tore open the envelope. The card said, "Thank you, Jessica, for what you've given me. Chase."

"It *is* an admirer, then?" Mrs. Pantano said, fanning herself with a folded newspaper.

"Yes," Jessica replied simply.

Seeing no further comment was to follow, the woman got to her feet. "The heat's bothered me today. I think I'll be getting on home. Sal has the day off and he'll be wantin' an early dinner."

Jessica paid Mrs. Pantano and went to the credenza, where she took a box of chocolates from a drawer. "This is a little present from Jamie, for being so kind to him."

"Oh, Mrs. Brandon, that's really sweet. And thank you, Jamie," she added, turning to tousle the boy's hair. The baby-sitter made her way toward the door. "You might want to put away some of that money of yours for a wedding dress," she said, gesturing toward the flowers. "Whoever this man is, he seems awfully serious to me."

Jessica laughed. "Just a friend, Mrs. Pantano."

The woman gave a mocking little laugh. "If he's the one with the big fancy car Mrs. Elrich talks about, I wouldn't let him get away."

"My. I didn't know my relationships were so thoroughly discussed in the neighborhood."

"Everyone seems to worry about a young widow, Mrs. Brandon. There's not a woman on the block who doesn't wish good things for you."

"That's very reassuring. Thank you."

"And if these flowers mean what I think, we won't have to worry for long." Mrs. Pantano was on the porch. Jessica held the screen door open.

"He really is just a friend. There's no possibility of marriage."

The woman screwed up her chubby face. "He's married?"

"No, no. He's a bachelor. It's just that there's no prospect of a serious relationship, from either of our standpoints." Jessica was tempted to tell her the whole story, but she didn't have the energy or the courage just then.

"Don't let your late husband stand in the way of the future, Mrs. Brandon. That's a mistake too many woman make. If you were old, that'd be one thing. But don't let a hot one slip through your fingers. That's my advice."

When the baby-sitter had gone, Jessica turned to Jamie and Velvet. The boy looked so innocent, so oblivious to the monumental events of the day. She sat down next to him on the couch and stroked his head. "How do you feel today, honey?"

Jamie looked up at his mother.

"Better?"

He lifted his chin in a childish nod, and talked to the horse.

"Are you getting hungry?"

"I want pizza, Mommy," he said, and made Velvet bounce on his leg.

"Pizza? I don't think we have one in the freezer. Would you settle for a bowl of soup, some bread and fruit?"

Jamie shook his head. "No, I want pizza."

"Well, Mommy's too tired to go to the store. Maybe tomorrow. Why don't you come into the kitchen and help me fix dinner?"

Jamie looked at her, and though he didn't say anything, his expression spoke volumes.

"Would you like to walk into the kitchen the way you did for Mr. Hamilton?"

He shook his head and gave a little whimper, lifting his arms to be picked up.

She felt too tired to fight and followed the course of least resistance, taking him into her arms. Just then there was a knock at the door, and Jessica turned to see Chase Hamilton through the screen.

"You don't let flies light on you," she said, going to let him in.

"I wanted to see you."

She pushed the door open with one hand and Chase stepped inside.

He pinched the boy's cheek. "Well, how's the little horseman today?"

Jamie giggled, then turned and pointed over his mother's shoulder toward the couch. "Velvet," he exclaimed.

"Velvet wants to play, is that it?" Chase asked.

Jamie squirmed in Jessica's arms, unintentionally kicking her in the stomach.

"Careful, Jamie," she protested.

"Here, partner," Chase said, taking the boy from her, "you've got to be careful with your mother. Treat ladies gently. That's a lesson every young man needs to learn."

Jessica looked at her son in Chase's arms. He suddenly seemed energetic and robust, not the pathetic little waif he'd been only minutes ago. The child was pointing again at the toy horse, his other arm resting casually on Chase's shoulder.

Chase went to the couch and retrieved Velvet. Jamie took the horse and began running it up and down the man's arm. "I think we need to burn a little energy," Chase said with a wink.

"You two can go on a roundup if you want to," Jessica said. "I've had my excitement for the day."

Chase took her hand. "How are you feeling?"

"A little tired, but fine," She looked into his twinkling blue eyes.

"Good." He squeezed her fingers.

Jessica felt a little self-conscious at his affection. She turned away, noticing again the flowers spread around the room. "Oh, and the lovely flowers you sent." She gestured. "Obviously they arrived."

"Yes. A little overpowering, I see. I'd forgotten how cozy your place was."

"For a while I was afraid the doctor had told you something he didn't tell me...like there'd be triplets, maybe."

Chase laughed. "Perhaps that wouldn't be so bad. Counting Jamie and me, we could field a basketball team."

"Oh, God."

"Doesn't sound good to you?"

"It would be your problem, Mr. Hamilton. Your problem entirely."

He raised his eyebrows.

"I read the fine print on the contract, too. No splitting litters. I checked that out."

Chase grinned. "Any plans for dinner?"

"We were thinking of soup."

He looked at the boy in his arms. "Soup sound good to you, Jamie?"

The child shook his head. "Pizza."

"Ah, now there's a man after my own heart. How about if we all go out for pizza?"

"Velvet, too?" Jamie asked.

"Sure. Velvet, too." Chase looked at Jessica. "What do you say, Mom?"

She glanced at Jamie, than at Chase. "I think I've been roped into something."

He laughed. "We've got something to celebrate, don't we? Dinner out might be good for *all* of us."

He didn't say it, but Jessica knew by the way he glanced at her stomach that he meant all *four* of them.

CHASE TIGHTENED HIS GRIP on the waistband of Jamie's pants, reached over and dropped a quarter in the slot. The horse on which the child sat immediately began to rock in a slow undulating motion, and Jamie started shaking the reins enthusiastically, squealing with joy. The man grinned and looked over at Jessica, who sat in a booth across the restaurant, watching them.

She smiled, her pretty mouth indicating a mixture of pride and vicarious pleasure at her son's excitement. Chase studied her, trying to comprehend the fact that this lovely, unpretentious creature was carrying his child.

Though he had been looking forward to it for months, years even, now that it was happening he was having trouble believing it was really true. He felt differently than he would have expected. He was excited about the baby, but he was also very aware of the mother.

The other parent had never been a factor until now—just a faceless partner. But Jessica Brandon had changed that, and Chase wasn't sure how he felt about it.

Underlying his happiness was a sentimentality that was uncharacteristic of him. He felt affection for her, gratitude, perhaps, compassion for her son, but something more.... Jessica was wonderfully attractive, though at first that had been important only for genetic reasons, for the baby. Now she was no longer just breeding stock. He knew that because of the baby she would play a very important role in his life, though at the moment she was little more than a stranger.

Chase couldn't imagine feeling the same way toward the other women Harriet Thomas had proposed as surrogate mothers. Jessica was clearly different, and it troubled him.

He wondered if it was the circumstances: her need, the boy, their vulnerability. Could he explain away the feelings he had, or was there more? Perhaps it had been a mistake to choose a single woman. Had Jessica been married her husband would look out for her welfare and he would only have to concern himself with the child. But it was too late now. They had made a baby.

Without warning the mechanical horse groaned to a stop and Jamie looked up at Chase in dismay. The man and boy contemplated each other for a moment, then Chase fished another quarter from his pocket and joy returned to Jamie's face. The stationary gallop in the pizza parlor resumed.

After a while Jessica got up from the booth and made her way toward them. Chase admired the evocative femininity of her walk, his eye tracing the slender lines of her figure. There was no doubt she touched more than his compassion. She aroused him.

"You two going to ride all evening?" she said, a hint of loneliness in her voice.

Jamie interpreted her arrival as a sign the fun was about to end. He began bouncing in the saddle as though he might get the horse to take him safely out of his mother's range. Chase thwarted the boy's escape by lifting him by the pants partway out of the saddle.

"Slow down there, partner. We don't want any riding accidents."

"Ride the horsey, Mommy," Jamie protested.

Jessica smiled indulgently and folded her arms across her chest. "We'll wait until the horse gets tired. You mustn't spend all of Mr. Hamilton's quarters." She glanced up at Chase.

He suddenly realized she was like no other woman he had ever known. Chase liked her spirit—there was just enough independence in her soul to make a man want to conquer her.

"I can get some more change from the cashier," he said, coming to the boy's defense.

"Please, no," she said emphatically. "Jamie has to learn there are limits."

"Denial builds character. Is that it?"

She looked at him with her frothy beige eyes, seemingly uncertain whether his comment was meant critically. "You could put it that way, I suppose."

The horse stopped again and Jamie let out a wail of protest. Jessica reached for him, but Chase intervened. "I'll carry him. No sense in you lifting unnecessarily."

She gave a little laugh. "I'm pregnant Chase, not incapacitated."

He shot her a sideward glance and picked up the boy, who fell silent at his touch. "Well, I'm neither, so why take a chance?"

They walked to the booth and Chase put Jamie on the booster chair between them. The man smiled at her and Jessica felt both flattery and the urge to resist him. She glanced down at the glass of milk he had ordered for her along with Jamie's, then at the beer sitting before him. Jessica hadn't protested at the time, though she thought it presumptuous, but she decided a trend had set in that she shouldn't permit without protest.

"Chase, I know you mean well, but I'm not a child. And I don't need to be pampered. Just because a woman's pregnant doesn't mean she's fragile—certainly not at this stage, anyway."

His expression moved from surprise to skepticism to amusement. "I don't mean to offend you, Jessica. I guess I was just thinking of the baby."

"You needn't worry. I wouldn't do anything that'd hurt it."

"And maybe I was thinking of you, too," he added, ignoring her response.

Jessica looked at the man, uncertain what he was implying, but soon concluded from his expression that there was affection implicit in the comment. To her surprise, she felt herself blush.

JESSICA LEANED OVER the side of the crib, kissed Jamie, then stood looking down at him for a moment before stroking his head. She knew that all she had been through, and all she would go through in the coming months, would be worth it. Whispering good-night she returned to the living room, where Chase Hamilton sat waiting.

He looked especially attractive just then, his blue eyes midnight in the half-light, his dark hair and tanned features giving him an appealing, masculine look. Jessica walked toward him, knowing instinctively that such proximity was dangerous, but knowing also that she craved the nearness of a man.

"I didn't hear any signs of protest in there."

"No, Jamie's pretty good about going to bed."

He watched her sit on the couch beside him, half a cushion away. She stared ahead, seemingly nervous. Chase felt the tension, too.

"Do you want me to send Maggie over to help with the packing?" he asked after a while.

She turned to him. "Packing?"

"Yeah. I figure we might as well get the move over with. I'll pay for it, of course. I've made arrangements, but I don't know whether you wanted the movers to do everything, or if you'd want Maggie or someone else to help."

"Chase, I'm only a few weeks pregnant. I won't even begin to show for months. I know I agreed to live at the farm, but I was thinking in terms of the last few months, when the help will be important."

"That's not what I had in mind."

"Why would you want us there now? We'd just be underfoot."

"The preparations are just about complete. I've hired the governess for Jamie, a woman named Anne Bascom, and there're only a few days' work left on your studio. The contractor said it'd be ready at the end of the week."

"Contractor? What have you done?"

"Remodeled one of the outbuildings. I'd planned it all along."

Jessica shook her head. "Chase, that's really unnecessary. There's no reason for me to move in this early."

He was annoyed. "That's what I want. It's in the contract."

"But why?"

"I told you from the beginning, Jessica, I intend to have the entire experience."

She got up and walked across the room, looking out the window into the dark. "I signed up to be the mother of your child, not a surrogate wife. If what you want is to share the joys of pregnancy with someone, you really should have gotten married."

"Thanks for the advice, but I know what I want, and it's what I've done."

She turned around. "That's fine for you, and I'll endure what I have to, but what about my son?"

"What about him? He's well provided for in the arrangement."

"Materially, yes, but what about his feelings and emotional needs? Don't you think it's going to be hard for him to understand what this is all about? I thought that a few months at the end of the pregnancy would be something he could handle, but you're virtually suggesting we become a family."

"I don't see why that's necessarily bad for the boy. And I have no intention of doing anything that would hurt him. Look," he said, rising to his feet, "if it will help why don't you take a couple of weeks to prepare him and yourself for the move? We can schedule it for the first of August, if that's better."

"Yes, the more time I have the better." Her expression turned coy. "You wouldn't consider, say, the first of October, would you?"

"Do I seem like a soft touch? I'm losing the better part of a month as it is."

"Let's split the difference—September."

"You should have been a horse trader, Jessica. August first, that's my best offer."

She groused.

"Come on, cheer up. There are worse places to endure a confinement."

"You know, I'm beginning to see it's no accident you're single. Sometimes you act as though this were still the Middle Ages."

Chase smiled and walked over to her. He reached into his pocket, pulled out an envelope and placed it in her hand.

"I'm not as hard-nosed as you think," he said casually. "There are others anxious to see you in the household, like my sister, Meade."

"Your sister?"

"Yes, Meade and her husband, Roger, live in Connecticut, about ten miles from the farm. She's been kind of involved in this business from afar." He gave a little laugh. "Truth be known, Meade is just as excited about the baby as I am."

Jessica raised her eyebrows. "I hadn't realized anyone else was aware."

"My sister's the only one. I thought any public announcement should wait until the birth."

"Yes, that *is* more discreet."

"You'll like Meade. She's down-to-earth, straightforward like you."

Jessica could hear the warmth of sentiment in his voice. "Are you and your sister close?"

"She's a lot younger than I, more your age than mine. We really grew up separately because of the age difference, but as adults we've become quite close."

"It sounds that way."

"If you're referring to her interest in the baby, it's more than just an aunt's involvement. You see, she hasn't been able to have children and loves them. Meade's been waiting for years for me to marry so she can have a niece or nephew. When I told her about my plan, she was ecstatic. She's dying to meet you."

Jessica looked at the envelope Chase had handed her. "What's this?"

"Your paycheck." He grinned. "As I recall the only reason you tolerate me is for the money." Chase reached up and pinched her on the cheek. "I'd better let you get to bed. You're eating and sleeping for two, you know."

He went to the door, stopping partway out.

"Thanks, Jessica," he said, looking a touch self-satisfied. "You've made me a very happy man."

When he had gone Jessica looked at the plain white envelope. She hesitated, then tore it open. Inside she found a check for fifty thousand dollars.

Jessica stared at it, feeling confused. He'd said she only tolerated him for the money, and that had been true, at first. Now she wasn't sure how she felt. Her relationship with the man was becoming very complicated... and something told her that was precisely what he had in mind.

CHAPTER SIX

JESSICA'S CHECK had spent the night folded in half, secreted under her bedside lamp. The first thing she did the next morning was to make sure it was still there. Peering at the scrap of paper through blinking eyes, she couldn't believe her good fortune. Fifty thousand dollars!

Jessica felt giddy, unable to remember when she had been so lighthearted. The check had lifted the weight of the world.

The first order of business was to get the money in the bank. Then she would spend a little of it—not much, just enough to bring home the reality of her newfound wealth. She had denied herself for so long that some deferred spending and a few treats would not really be irresponsible.

After breakfast she and Jamie went to the bank, then to a toy store, where she let him pick out one item himself while she selected another. They settled on a spaceship with flashing lights and a box of finger paints.

Afterward they went by the art store, where Jessica bought so many things that a delivery was arranged. When the equipment and supplies arrived that afternoon, Jessica was thrilled. The sight of a new easel, canvases, paints and brushes stacked in the corner of the living room made her want to get to work immediately. Instead she contended herself with unpacking and organizing things.

The next day she began painting with a vengeance. Jamie was set up with his finger paints on the floor next to her, with an old plastic tablecloth under him to protect the carpet. He cooperated and they worked happily for most of the day.

Though in the following days Jamie got restless at times, Jessica did manage to finish a canvas by the end of the week. It was an impressionistic portrait of a small boy in a flower garden. She knew Helmut Geisel would have to look everything over when the portfolio was complete, but she was satisfied that it was a good start.

On Friday morning Jamie played with his finger paints again, doing a picture of Velvet, while Jessica applied a wash to her next canvas. She had thought about Chase off and on during the week, about the move that was looming, and half regretted that she had so easily capitulated.

It was pretty silly to move into his place when any real signs of her pregnancy were still months away. It would have been so much easier if he had just let her stay at home until the fifth or sixth month. Then she wouldn't have to give up her house, just in case buying or renting a nicer place didn't seem practical after they left the farm.

The way Chase had things fixed, the move seemed more than just a temporary stay. Jessica wondered if he might be persuaded to reconsider. Remembering his intractable nature, she decided the prospects were not good.

After lunch Jamie went down for his nap quietly, and Jessica hoped to get in a nice long session at her easel, undisturbed. For a while she worked, but for some reason the paint fumes made her feel light-headed and vaguely nauseous.

For July the weather had been fairly mild, but it had warmed up considerably that day and Jessica decided that the heat was getting to her, as well. Taking off her painting smock, she went into the bedroom to lie down.

For a while she lay on the bed listening to her body, wondering if what she felt could have anything to do with the pregnancy. With Jamie she had had virtually no morning sickness, so there wasn't much to compare.

By the time she started feeling a little better Jamie was awake. He looked over at her from his crib, surprised to see his mother there.

"Want to come over here and lie down with Mommy?" she asked as he sat rubbing his eyes.

The boy nodded and Jessica got up, lifted him over the railing and carried him to her bed. For a while he lay quietly next to her, his head on her shoulder. Jessica thought again about the move.

"Do you remember Mr. Hamilton's farm, Jamie, where you rode the horse?"

"Big Velvet."

"Yes, Big Velvet. Did you like the farm, honey?"

He had slipped his fingers into his mouth. "Uh-huh."

Jessica gently pulled his hand away. "Do you think it would be fun to live there?"

Jamie's eyes rounded. "With Velvet? Would we live with Velvet?"

"Maybe we could live at the farm with Mr. Hamilton and Maggie. But Velvet would be there, too."

"I like that man," Jamie said thoughtfully.

Jessica stroked his head.

"Mommy..."

"Yes, darling?"

"Would that man be my new daddy?"

Jessica hadn't expected the question. "Why, no, Jamie. Mr. Hamilton is just a friend. He's Mommy's friend, and your friend, too."

Jamie sighed and looked a little perplexed. "Does he have a little boy?"

"No, darling, he doesn't." Jessica could see that Jamie's little mind was hard at work on the situation. She agonized, sorry that she had brought up the subject. It was apparent, though, that the matter would have to be dealt with, and it wouldn't be easy. "It would be just a visit, Jamie. A long vacation. We wouldn't live there forever."

"Why?"

"So Mommy could paint in a special studio there, and also so you could get some physical therapy every day. It would be easier if we stayed there for a while, honey."

"Would we sleep here?"

"No, we would sleep there." Jessica was feeling worse and worse about the conversation. "But right now I'm just thinking about the move. I haven't decided."

"Why can't we live there all the time with Velvet?"

"That would be nice for you and Velvet, Jamie, but that's not what Mommy wants."

"Does that man with Velvet want to be my daddy?"

Jessica squeezed Jamie against her, feeling her heart wrench. "No, darling, he wants to be your friend, your very special friend."

The boy looked up at her, sensing her emotion. He didn't say anything; he just put his little hand against her face.

JESSICA AGONIZED the rest of the afternoon about the move. When she finally picked up the phone to call Chase, she was frustrated to learn he was in California, watching one of his horses race. Disappointed, she spent a rare evening watching television with Jamie, then fed him a light supper. The boy had just been put down for the night, when the phone rang.

"Jessica, it's Chase. Maggie said you'd called. Is something wrong?"

"No, no, of course not. It's nothing important."

"Are you sure?"

"Yes... I probably shouldn't even have phoned." Jessica had been caught off guard, and now she was bungling her opportunity to discuss the move.

"I take it you didn't call to pass the time of day. How's the packing coming?"

"Uh, that's what I called you about."

"I had an inkling it was."

Jessica had the feeling she was already up to her knees in quicksand. "I wanted to ask you to reconsider."

"Jessica, we've settled this already."

"I know, but I'm concerned about Jamie. Frankly I'm not so sure moving out there for seven or eight months is in his interest."

"I've agreed to take care of his needs—"

"It's not that. It's the emotional side that concerns me. I discussed the move with him today and he's upset."

There was silence for a moment. "*He's* upset, or *you're* upset?"

Chase's ability to cut right to the heart of the matter never ceased to amaze her. "Perhaps we both are."

"I don't see any cause for alarm. Personally, I'm confident Jamie will be just fine. But I realized long ago I'll have my hands full with you."

"Thanks a lot. You're not exactly Mr. Congeniality yourself when it comes to getting along with people."

Chase chuckled. "Our kid's going to be dynamite."

"I didn't call to discuss *your* baby. I called to discuss *my* son."

"What exactly is the problem, Jessica?"

She sighed. "He asked me if you were going to be his new daddy."

For a moment Chase didn't respond. "Well, that's normal enough. I don't see any problem."

"That's because it's not your problem. When Jamie and I pack up to leave after the baby is born, then it's going to be *my* problem. How am I going to explain that the nice man who came into his life is just passing through? I'll have to live with that, Chase. You won't."

"Aren't we overdramatizing this a little, Jessica?"

"No *we* aren't," she snapped. "*You're* just being insensitive."

"Look, just because Jamie and I spend some time together does not mean he's going to be traumatized for life. Kids get attached to favorite teachers, but they can't spend their lives in the same grade. If they go away to summer camp and love it, that doesn't mean they're going to develop neuroses just because they've got to go home."

"You don't understand."

"Of course I understand. I'm very fond of Jamie and I wouldn't want to do anything to hurt him. Besides, there's nothing that says I can't continue to be friends with him."

"Oh, yes, there is! After this baby is born I'm never going to see it or you again. That means Jamie never will, either."

Now Chase sighed. "Look, we're not getting anywhere. Why don't we get together to discuss this? As a matter of fact I'd planned to have you over for dinner this weekend to meet Meade and Roger, but they're spending a couple of weeks at their place in Vermont, so we'll have to do that later. But I think it'd still be a good idea if you and Jamie came over to the farm to see the setup, meet the staff, and so forth. I'm sure both of you will feel better after a visit.''

"I've no doubt the arrangements you've made are lovely, but that's not the issue.''

"Maybe not for you, but for Jamie it matters. Tell you what, if after the two of you come over he's not pleased, I'll let you delay the move till later in the pregnancy.''

Jessica's expression brightened, but something told her not to take heart. "You obviously feel you have a safe bet.''

"You've very perceptive, Jessica. I think I do.''

She felt defeated, but strangely pleased.

"I'll come by and pick you up late Sunday morning. We'll make it for lunch. How's, say, eleven-thirty?''

JAMIE SAT ON THE COUCH, playing with Velvet. Jessica stood at the front window in a pale yellow cotton dress with white piping, watching for the Bentley. It was already a scorching day so her legs were bare. Her one concession to the occasion was her new pair of white sandals.

Chase, she kept telling herself, was her employer, but that fact didn't deter her from being nervous about seeing him. Ever since his call she had felt unsettled, wary. And she knew it wasn't so much Chase who worried her as her own feelings.

When she saw his car coming down the street she sat in Alex's chair, taking momentary comfort in the security it represented. She soon got to her feet and paced across the room before retreating to the couch and sitting next to Jamie. She was stroking his head, when she heard Chase's footsteps on the porch.

He rapped lightly on the screen door.

"Come in, Chase."

He stepped inside, looking relaxed in a green polo shirt and buff cotton twill pants. "Hi." He smiled at them both, but his attention was mostly directed at Jamie.

Jessica rose as Chase walked over and picked up the boy. "Hey, partner, ready for a surprise?"

Jamie looked at him with wonder on his face.

"You don't waste any time getting out of the starting gates, do you?" Jessica said wryly.

He gave her a grin. "How you doin', Mom?"

The corners of her mouth twisted a little with amusement, but Jessica turned immediately and walked over to the table. She picked up a white envelope and carried it back to him.

"What's this?"

"The money you loaned me that day at the clinic."

"Money?"

"The 'dress money.' Remember?"

He handed back the envelope. "That was a gift, not a loan."

Jessica refused to accept the envelope. "It was a loan."

His grimace was mocking.

"I always pay my debts," Jessica said flatly.

Chase tore open the envelope and examined the check for a thousand dollars. "No interest?"

"How much would you like?"

He laughed. "Just kidding."

"I had the use of your money. I'll be glad to pay interest."

"Don't be silly." He looked at Jamie, who seemed rather pleased to be in Chase's arms. "This will be my interest."

"Your confidence never ceases to amaze me, Chase Hamilton."

THEY DROVE DOWN the long driveway leading to the estate, past grazing horses in the field, past the house to the barn. "We'll start with Jamie's surprise," Chase announced.

"Another horseback ride?" Jessica asked. She could see he was making it very difficult for her to change his plans.

"Not exactly." He got out of the car, walked around to the passenger side and opened the door. "Come to think of it, you and Jamie might be more comfortable here. I'll be right back." He left them sitting in the Bentley and went into the barn.

Several minutes later Chase returned. "Watch over there, Jamie," he said, pointing to the barn door. "Okay, Mack, bring him out!" he called.

The barn door swung open and a pony and cart appeared, led by the farmhand. Jamie's eyes rounded and he began bouncing enthusiastically.

"Mommy, Mommy! Horsey!"

Jessica looked up at Chase, her own face full of excitement.

"It's Jamie's," he explained. "A present from me."

"A present?"

"You can keep the pony here at the farm free of charge, so you won't have boarding expenses."

"We can't accept something like that."

Jamie was trying to climb down off Jessica's lap. The man laughed.

"I think it's too late."

"This is out and out bribery. Low blow!" she protested.

He grinned and took the squirming boy. "Mind if we go for a ride, Mom?"

She gave him a disapproving look. "You're really not playing fair."

"This was planned long before our conversation the other evening. The pony's been here a week."

"No wonder you were so sure about Jamie."

The child was wriggling. "Mommy!" he complained, trying to walk right out of Chase's arms.

"May we?" the man asked again.

"Be careful."

"Don't worry. Jamie's a natural horseman. I can tell."

The man and boy went to the cart and climbed in. Jessica watched as they rode up and down the driveway, Jamie giggling with glee all the while. It pleased her to see her son so happy, but it worried her, too. What about tomorrow? Chase wasn't thinking about tomorrow.

After twenty minutes the riders returned to the car, where Jessica had been trying to sort out the jumble of emotions she felt. She smiled hesitantly, shaking her head at Chase. He playfully tweaked her cheek, a self-satisfied expression on his face.

"There's a little surprise for you, too. Want to see it before lunch?"

She looked skeptical. "It had better not be a coach and four white horses."

"No, but you're close. It's a pumpkin and four white mice."

Jessica laughed. "I suppose I have to provide my own fairy godmother?"

"There *are* limits to my generosity." He winked and extended his hand to help her out of the car. "Come on, we can walk."

They headed toward the house, but Jessica was confounded when they went past it and toward what appeared to be an old carriage house nestled among a copse of maples.

"Where are we going?" she asked as they walked around the building.

"You'll see."

The carriage house seemed freshly painted. The shutters and windows were open, and a peek inside revealed an empty expanse of polished floor. Chase opened the door and gestured for her to enter.

Shooting him an uncertain glance, Jessica stepped inside. A single room made up most of the building. It was empty except for a large studio easel at one end, a padded stool and a chest. On the wall near the chest was a telephone. Overhead was a large skylight.

"Your studio," he proudly announced.

"Chase..." She tried to protest, but the place was beautiful.

"There's a cot in the little room back there for you to rest when you're tired. And a half bath to save you a run back to the house."

She turned to him, her mouth partway open. She didn't know what to say.

"The purpose of you having my baby was to be able to paint, wasn't it? You might as well be productive while Jamie is riding in his pony cart."

"I want my horsey," Jamie said, squirming a bit in Chase's arms.

"Hold on, partner. There's another surprise for you and your mom, but first she has to check out the studio."

She turned to him, her expression imploring. "Chase, I—"

"Come on," he said, taking her arm, "tell me if I got the right supplies."

They went to the chest, where Jessica pulled open a drawer. It was packed with dozens of tubes of oil paints and brushes of every description: white bristle flats, rounds, filberts and even a box of red sables, the last surely costing the equivalent of half a month's rent on her house. There were pallet knives, cans of turpentine and oil, and several kinds of varnish.

"I had an exhaust fan installed," Chase said, pointing to the ceiling, "in case the fumes bother you."

"Oh, Chase. You shouldn't have done all this. It's too much. It really is."

"There are some canvases in the closet," he added, "but I didn't get many because I wasn't sure of the sizes you like to work with."

Jessica was speechless.

"Go have a look at the little rest area behind that door and see if it's all right."

Jessica looked where he had indicated. There was a single bed, a side table and lamp, and a straight-backed chair. A small window opened onto a vista of the rolling hills. She turned back to the man.

"It's lovely, but—"

Chase held up his hand. "Before you say anything let's look at the last surprise."

"How can there be more?" she lamented, and followed Chase and Jamie out of the studio.

As they walked back to the house no one spoke, but Jessica's head was spinning. The studio was an artist's dream. Chase obviously considered the matter of the move resolved, but she felt an obligation to offer some resistance.

They entered the house through the kitchen. Maggie turned from the sink, where she was washing vegetables. "Afternoon, ma'am," she said, beaming.

"Hello, Maggie."

They continued on through the house and Chase led the way up the stairway to the second floor, Jamie still happily in his arms. He stopped at the head of the stairs. "My rooms are up that way," he said, pointing toward one wing of the house. Turning, he walked in the other direction.

At the end of the hallway he opened double doors leading to a large suite. "This is for you," he said. "Have a look around."

She walked through the rooms, peeking into the opulent, mirrored bath. Jessica felt like a kid in a candy store—she couldn't resist looking at everything. Returning to where he and Jamie waited, she gave him an anxious look.

"Now come this way." He opened a door off the bedroom and they entered another smaller bedchamber, decorated and furnished for a child.

Jessica glanced around and turned to Chase. "It's lovely. More than I could reasonably expect. But there's still the concern I expressed to you on the phone."

"I'll be glad to try to reassure you on that score. But I'm really confident it will work out just fine. For everyone," he said, glancing at the boy in his arms.

Jessica gently took Jamie's hand and pulled away the fingers that had slipped into his mouth. She studied his little face with motherly concern.

"Given your attitude, I decided to present you with a fait accompli," Chase admitted.

"It's not accompli, yet."

He grinned. "I'm optimistic by nature. Besides, there's more. Come on."

"Oh, my God..." Jessica sighed and followed him back down the hallway.

They stopped at a door and Chase knocked. A moment later a woman in a nurse's uniform appeared.

"Jessica, I'd like for you to meet Anne Bascom, the nurse who'll be assisting you with Jamie. This is Mrs. Brandon and her son, Jamie," Chase said to the amiable-looking woman, who was about Jessica's age and also blond, though bigger boned and taller than Jessica.

The women shook hands and Anne said a few words of greeting to Jamie before the trio continued on down the hall. Halfway to the stairs they stopped, and Chase opened the door to a large tiled bath. Inside was a man dressed in white, and various types of physical therapy equipment.

"Jessica," Chase said, "I'd like you to meet Mr. Valticos, a physical therapist. He will be coming in two hours a day to work with Jamie." He turned to the man. "This is Mrs. Brandon, and Jamie."

"Nice to meet you," he said.

"Mr. Valticos assures me that this equipment is adequate for Jamie's needs," Chase explained.

"Oh, yes, ma'am. This is the finest equipment available."

Jessica nodded agreeably. Chase took her by the arm and they retreated downstairs. "I know it's presumptuous to have hired them without consulting you," he began as they walked along, "but I conferred with an orthopedic specialist and she assured me that thorough and frequent therapy will speed Jamie's recovery. Frankly, it's just too unmanageable to oversee a program with you in Peekskill."

"What about me, Chase? Aren't you forgetting my preferences and needs?"

"No. To the contrary, they were a prime consideration. That's why we started in the studio."

"I don't need such an elaborate setup to work."

"No, but it can't hurt."

They were in the sitting room. Chase and Jamie sat down on one couch, Jessica the other.

"I think Jamie's pleased with what he's seen. Don't you?"

"I'm sure he is," Jessica replied dryly.

"Can I rest my case?"

"When do I get to give my arguments against?"

He smiled wryly, his handsome face and cerulean eyes brimming with confidence. "How about now?"

Jessica blinked, not expecting to be thrust onstage so abruptly. But he had challenged her, so she had to carry through. "Okay..."

Chase leaned back and crossed his legs, his arm around Jamie's shoulders. Jessica hated him just then, but she couldn't resist him, either.

"Before you start," Chase interjected, "let me just say that the pony and cart are Jamie's regardless of whether it's the first of August or later. I don't want to use that as a lever against you."

Jessica nodded. "That's very considerate."

"Okay," he said, gesturing, "the floor is yours."

She looked at the two of them and suddenly felt like a heel. In all probability he had planned it that way, but it was no less effective for the knowledge. "Look," she began, trying to be both forceful and reasonable, "you know what my concern is."

His expression was open, waiting. He looked down at the boy and tousled his hair. Jamie giggled. Jessica felt terrible—like an executioner. But there was basis for her concern, she wasn't fabricating it.

"How about if I take Jamie upstairs?" Chase asked. "Since Valticos is here we might as well make use of him."

"Is he familiar with Jamie's case?"

"The staff has been thoroughly briefed. Miss Bascom and Valticos both have talked to the specialist."

"I see." It was obvious that Chase had seen to every detail. "Go ahead and take him up, then."

He and the boy left and Jessica waited, trying to shore up her determination. She looked around the room, knowing that eventually she would be living there, and wondering whether it was really worth the fight to delay the move.

Chase came back down in a few minutes, his step lively, energetic. "Jamie took to it like a fish to water," he said, dropping down opposite her.

"Yes, he's never minded the therapy."

"So, you were saying it would be bad for Jamie to be here."

"Not bad for him... I just mean it wouldn't be...good for him."

The man grinned with amusement. "Sort of like purgatory, is that what you mean?"

"No, that's not what I mean at all."

"Well?"

"Chase, Jamie and I have been alone since Alex died. He's had no father that he's ever known. He's very fond of you. What happens if he gets really attached to you? How can I let him have something like that, then take it away?"

He contemplated her. "I still don't see why Jamie shouldn't benefit all he can from the next seven or eight months. Kids have to learn to adjust to change. As long as I'm sensitive to your concern and act accordingly, he and I can be friends, and keep it limited to that.''

"Easy for you to say.''

"Not a very telling argument.''

"It's convincing to me.''

"Look, Jessica, I've thought this through very carefully, and I've set it up so that we all benefit. Yes, I'll admit that it's as much for me as for you and Jamie. I'll have peace of mind knowing that you—and the baby— are well cared for. And I'll have the opportunity to experience a little more of the pregnancy.''

"It's really essential that we be here the whole time?''

"Well, as you know from the contract, I'm obligated to provide an apartment near the hospital during the last few weeks before the delivery.''

"Yes, but that's at the end. It's now I'm concerned about.''

"If it's my presence that's a problem, you may as well know that I won't be here all that much. I'll be spending a great deal of time in Kentucky. Plus I'm going to Europe this fall for a month to buy some blood stock. The house'll be empty much of the time. You may as well enjoy it. I didn't buy the place to house the staff.''

Jessica shook her head plaintively.

Chase looked at his watch. "Lunch should be ready soon. Why don't you go up and get Jamie? I'll check with Maggie.''

Jessica sighed and got to her feet, sensing that she had lost the battle. Chase stood opposite her, his face noncommittal, though she knew he had to be savoring his victory. She felt as though they were two once hardened adversaries who had lost the will to fight. And if that weren't bad enough, she was beginning to feel charitable toward him. Jessica could see he was making it a habit of having his way. It was a trend she figured she'd have to stop before they were headed down a path she didn't want to take.

CHAPTER SEVEN

JESSICA'S MIND was so muddled, her feelings so mired by confusion, that she didn't notice the painting until they were seated. But there it was on the wall of the sun-room, where Chase had elected to have Maggie serve the meal. She dropped her napkin on her plate at the sight of it.

"Chase! My painting!" She whipped her head toward him. "Where did you get . . ."

The startled expression on his face slowly dissolved into a smile.

"You were the one! You bought my painting from Helmut Geisel!"

"Yes, doesn't that please you? I'm rather fond of it, actually."

Jessica felt her shock boiling into anger. "Is it the painting you're fond of, or your act of charity?"

Chase looked surprised. "What are you saying? I saw the painting, liked it and bought it. What's wrong with that? It was for sale, wasn't it?"

"Of course it was for sale. But I thought it had been bought by a legitimate buyer, not a . . . philanthropist!"

"Hey, that's unfair. I bought that painting because it pleased me."

"Oh, sure, out of the hundreds of galleries in New York and the thousands of paintings, you just happened to buy mine. And on the very day we . . . we . . ." She glanced at Jamie. "On the very day we went to the clinic!"

Chase calmly picked up his napkin. "No, as a matter of fact I was curious about your work. You had mentioned Geisel the day we met and I went over to his place after I left the clinic to have a look. I saw the painting and bought it because I liked it. I did hang it, as you can see."

Jessica glared at him, unsure what to believe.

"Would it have been better if a stranger bought it?"

"Yes."

"Why?"

"Because then I'd have known it was the painting and not me that was being bought."

"I didn't buy you, Jessica. I bought *it*."

She tried to control her anger in front of Jamie. "It's just more of your manipulation. I may as well be your concubine for all the privacy and independence I have."

Chase, too, was trying to remain calm. "That's hyperbole if I've ever heard it."

Jessica's eyes flashed. "The trouble with you is you can't distinguish between horses and people. You think everybody can be bought and sold."

"Oh, come on now."

She saw that she had struck a nerve, but his building anger didn't frighten her. "How would you like it if you were trying to get a career started and you discovered suddenly that your big breakthrough wasn't what it seemed, after all. That someone was just meddling in your business?"

Chase bristled. "Is that what it is—meddling? All the money I'm paying you, all the benefits you're realizing are just meddling?"

"That's right! And I know I'm going to have to earn every cent. Probably two times over."

Jamie had been listening to the rising voices of the adults and gave a little whimper of concern. Jessica and Chase both looked at him. Then the boy's face began to crumple. "Mommy..."

Jessica got up, stepped around the table and lifted him from the pillow-lined chair Maggie had fixed for him. She shot Chase a hostile glance and held the boy against her. When the man rose to his feet, Jessica felt a sudden urge to get away. Turning on her heel, she headed for the door.

Chase, with hands on hips, watched her go, his face flushed with anger. "Damned woman," he muttered just as Maggie came in from the kitchen with their soup platters.

"Is there anything wrong, sir?"

"Nothing but an ungrateful woman who's more stubborn than a mule."

Maggie looked down at the tray in her hands. "Should I be holdin' the lunch a wee bit, then, Mr. Hamilton?"

"Just give me a few minutes to cool her down and get her back in here," he said, and headed out the door.

He found Jessica sitting on the front steps, Jamie on her lap. She didn't look up until he was standing beside her.

"Look, I'm sorry," he said after a minute. "I didn't intend to upset you."

"This whole thing has been a mistake," she mumbled. "Harriet was right. I never should have done it."

Chase felt his gut wrench. Hostility between them was the last thing he needed. And he felt badly for having upset her. As he joined them on the step, Jamie looked at him, his eyes a little round, though he was otherwise calm. "Guess you don't have much opportunity to see big people get into scraps, do you, Jamie?"

The boy looked at him blankly, not understanding what was going on.

"Let me give you some advice, son. Never underestimate a woman's capacity for anger. And never try to do a good deed unless you're absolutely sure it's what she wants."

"I'm bringing up my son to be considerate. Your advice is unnecessary," Jessica said, without looking at him.

"And if one form of apology doesn't work," Chase continued, "try another. You'll succeed eventually."

There was a long silence.

"When I looked up and saw my painting on your wall," Jessica finally said, "my heart sank. It was the same as when I was a little girl and I set up a lemonade stand in front of our house. My father was my only customer. Do you suppose that made me feel like a runaway success in the lemonade business?"

Chase looked over at her, noticing the soft texture of her skin, the delicate lines of her profile. "Did you hate him for his patronage?"

"At least there were no surprises. He just walked right up and plunked down his nickel. I had to come here to discover my painting on your wall."

"I should have told you before. But you ought to at least take heart in the fact that I hung it. I may have a charitable spirit, but I don't hang paintings I don't like."

Jessica looked at him. He could see her anger had abated. "I suppose I overreacted," she said, showing a touch of embarrassment.

"Maybe I didn't think the situation through very clearly."

She smiled at him a little sheepishly. "You didn't even pick the best of the two."

"Geisel told me he thought the other one was a better piece, but I wasn't buying it for him *or* you. I was buying it for myself."

Jessica put Jamie down on the step between them.

"Listen, if it really bothers you that I have it, I can give it back to Geisel on consignment. I'd probably make a profit, particularly if I asked him to hold it back until after your show."

"Now you're humoring me."

"All right, then, just tell me what you want me to do."

"Never mind. Just forget it. If you're not telling the truth, you're the one who'll have to live with the damn thing, not me."

His expression turned whimsical. "I have every confidence that the foresight to buy that painting will make me a very rich man someday."

"You'll have to wait until I'm dead, I'm afraid. With few exceptions, values go up only when the supply is cut off."

He grinned. "I'm a patient man. I'll just have to wait."

Jessica laughed in spite of herself. "I hope I live to be a hundred."

"Imagine. Me, the owner of a Grandma Brandon!"

"Oh, shut up!"

Chase began laughing. He got to his feet and stood before her. Jessica couldn't help smiling herself.

"Come back inside. Soup's on." He leaned down and picked up Jamie. "I'll bet I can count on you being hungry, partner." He started toward the door as Jessica got to her feet to follow them.

"Let me explain something about women, my man," she heard him say to the boy. "Never count on anything until you're safely in the winner's circle. Fillies have the darnedest way of surprising you."

Jessica looked at Chase's broad shoulders and at her son's face as he listened intently. The boy *was* missing something by not having a father, just as she was missing something by not having a man.

DURING THE BALANCE of the lunch Jessica felt closer to Chase, yet more troubled than ever by what he represented. She decided that he must have sensed something, as well, because he seemed to look at her now and then a little differently. What did he *really* think of her?

After Jamie had referred to his pony for the fourth or fifth time, Chase turned to Jessica.

"How would you like to take a walk around the farm? Jamie can ride in his pony cart and you and I can get some exercise."

"All right."

They left the house and headed toward the barn, Jessica walking alongside Chase, feeling his presence acutely. Even if brash, he had a generous spirit, and he was so good with Jamie. Something about the chemistry of them all together made her feel womanly, vulnerable. She felt protected, and she liked it.

While the boy and man were getting the pony ready in the barn, Jessica leaned over the top board of the fence and stared across the paddock. Chase had made it all so pleasant, so comfortable—and so difficult to resist. And yet she knew there was danger.

The amenities he offered them were one thing, but the emotional pitfalls were quite another. He had succeeded in quashing her arguments regarding Jamie's well-being, but the concerns were still there. Her fears for herself were another matter entirely. How could she ever tell Chase she was afraid of becoming too fond of him?

A little smile crossed her face. Of course, the way she behaved around him he'd never believe her. And she couldn't give him the wrong idea. Except for the mutual awareness that plagued their every encounter, there was really nothing to indicate how Chase felt.

It would be idle fancy to think that she could be anything special to him, other than the surrogate mother of his child. If there was a basis for his interest, that was obviously it. Jessica smiled into the warm, gentle wind, feeling a little melancholy.

At the far side of the field a half-grown colt frolicked in the summer air, carefree and oblivious to the short weeks until fall. The new season would soon be upon them, then winter, and at the beginning of spring the baby would come. Then Chase would leave their life. In one sense it seemed like such a brief time. In another, it was a cruel and painful eternity.

CHASE HELD JAMIE while Mack rigged up the pony and cart. Looking outside the barn, he saw Jessica leaning against the fence, gazing wistfully across the field.

She was slender and her beauty was more radiant than ever. Even at a distance she seemed to give off that healthy glow that came with carrying a child. The pride Chase felt at knowing it was his was overwhelming.

He wondered, though, about his feelings for her. She was attractive—there was no denying that. But how much of what he felt was for the woman, and how much for the role she had come to play in his life? Chase had tried to treat the surrogate thing as business, but there was no doubt in his mind that he had let his emotions get involved with Jessica Brandon.

He knew it was foolish. There were simply too many traps, too many ways to go wrong. By impregnating her, he had made Jessica virtually untouchable. She was not just another woman now, she was the mother of his child, but one who swore never to see it, or him, after the birth. And yet, despite all that, there was the fascination, the allure....

Jamie squirmed in Chase's arms and he gave the boy a playful slap on the bottom. He was genuinely fond of the child. Yet it was ironic that that, too, probably damned him in Jessica's eyes. For the first time in his life Chase had a sense of how impotent his power could be. The more he was able to do for the woman, the worse off he was.

"Will this do, Mr. Hamilton?" the farmhand asked, indicating the makeshift backrest and safety belt he had rigged for Jamie.

"I think it will do nicely, Mack. Maybe we ought to soften it some with a couple of pillows, though. Would you mind going up to the house and getting two or three from Maggie?"

"Yes, sir."

"I'll take the pony and cart into the yard," Chase said, and climbed up into the little seat with Jamie.

When they came out of the barn into the bright sunlight Jessica was waiting. As she strolled over to them, Chase took in her slender figure and the yellow cotton dress. The wispy curls of her tawny hair moved in the breeze, making him want her just then. Knowing she was carrying his child made it seem criminal that they had never made love.

"Are you two going to make me walk?" Jessica asked with a little laugh.

"No, Jamie's going to ride along after Mack brings some pillows from the house."

Chase stepped down from the cart, keeping a grip on Jamie's shirt so he wouldn't slip off the seat. Jessica moved closer to them and Chase's eyes settled on her lips. His physical awareness of her was almost painful. He felt an aching in his loins and it took a determined effort not to touch her.

"Oh, and a little seat belt, too!" She looked up at him, her face open, innocent. "You're so thoughtful."

He gazed into her soft beige eyes. "He's your son."

Jessica seemed to hear something in his voice, gazed back at him for a moment and then reached past him to touch the boy's cheek. "You ready for a ride around the farm, honey?" She glanced at Chase again, her face a mixture of uncertainty and curiosity. She smiled tentatively, then looked away.

Chase chafed at his dilemma, not sure whether he was wiser to try to forget his attraction for her, or rail at the injustice of it. He drew a deep breath and looked at the nearly cloudless sky. "It's a wonderful day, isn't it?"

Jessica was holding Jamie's hand. "Yes, it's a beautiful day."

When Mack returned a few minutes later with the pillows they secured the boy carefully in the cart and headed down a lane toward a stream that meandered through the valley. Chase led the pony and Jessica walked beside him. They didn't speak for a long time.

She looked over at Jamie's beaming face. The pony and cart, the verdant countryside had to be paradise on earth for a child.

"You really outfoxed me, Chase."

"All with good intent."

The lush grass waved in the breeze. Swallows darted from tree to tree. Jessica felt the therapeutic balm of the nature around her.

"I suppose if Jamie and I are going to live here with you, it's best we're friends."

"I agree."

Jessica stopped and Chase did, too. She looked up at him, her exquisite face harmoniously beautiful—her nose, cheekbones, mouth a delicate composite. He studied her, intrigued by her beauty.

"I guess it'll be the first of August, then," she said simply.

"I guess it will."

Jessica extended her slender hand. "Shall we make it official?" she asked softly, her voice not much more than a whisper over the hum of insects in the summer fields.

He took her hand.

She seemed to read something in his eyes and turned her face away, into the breeze. Chase took her chin and turned her back to him, then leaned over and lightly kissed her lips.

CHASE HAMILTON PUT the telephone receiver back into its cradle and stared across the study at his Gainsborough. The conversation he'd just had with Dan Meecham, the manager of his twelve-hundred-acre farm in Kentucky, had not been satisfying.

The tone of Meecham's voice had said everything there was to say. The races at Keeneland were coming up in October; here it was nearly August and he hadn't been back to look over his horses in two months. Chase knew that he had been neglecting his business and his love—horses.

After the disastrous outing of Knight's Honor at Golden Gate Fields a couple of weeks before, he had decided that his trainer, Ben Shadel, had to go. But because of Keeneland, he'd have to wait. There just wasn't time.

Chase knew that his absentee image wasn't being helped by his neglect of the Kentucky operation. But that didn't bother him nearly so much as the pitiful results on the track of late. He could almost hear the tongues wagging all the way from Lexington.

"The Gentleman from New York" was what the old families in the Bluegrass called him, and it wasn't exactly with admiration. Chase was fairly new to horse breeding, having taken the money he had inherited from his father and bought his Kentucky farm ten years before. Other breeders spent part of their time elsewhere, too, but the serious ones considered Woodford, Scott, Bourbon or Fayette counties home. Chase Hamilton liked the Bluegrass, but Kentucky was—after all was said and done—only the place where his business was conducted.

Sighing, he turned his desk chair toward the window and looked across the paddock at the gentle undulation of the Westchester County landscape. By all rights he should get on a plane and fly down to Lexington, but there was Jessica's move to the farm at the end of the week. The past few months it had been one little thing after another. The truth was, the baby was more important to him than anything in his life just then.

When Chase thought about the child a warm, happy feeling came over him. During the past six months, while planning the birth, he had always thought in terms of a son—one who looked like him, though that was more by default than ego. Until Jessica Brandon, the mother had been a remote and faceless partner. But now he pictured the child as a girl, even a little blond one.

While the prospect of the baby warmed him, the thought of Jessica was troubling. He had virtually forced her to move onto the farm, rationalizing it as his due for the hundred-thousand-dollar fee, but deep down Chase was suspicious of his own zeal. A touch of guilt nagged at him.

He knew there was mutuality in the attraction, but he also knew that whatever she felt for him was a problem to her. Chase sensed that her husband's ghost was very much in the picture, though she herself may not have realized just how much. Her feelings for Jamie, on the other hand, seemed normal enough, but she was over-protective—undoubtedly as a result of what the family had been through.

And here, in the midst of it all, he found himself: a threat to Jessica's memories of her husband, perceived by her as a potential danger to her son and, on top of everything else, the father of her unborn, yet already disinherited, child. Ironically the two of them were inextricably bound, but only for the moment. Force of circumstance destined them to part, for how could they hope to have a normal man-woman relationship, even if they wished it?

Chase rose from his chair and went to the window. The old mare that Jamie had ridden was standing in the field under the warm rays of the morning sun. Chase remembered the tears in Jessica's eyes when he'd handed Jamie back to her after the ride that first time they had come to the farm. She was a devoted mother—there was no denying that. And yet the baby they shared meant nothing to her. Was it simply the way she had chosen to protect herself, or was there more to it than that?

The telephone rang on the desk behind him and he looked at it with irritation before answering.

"Hi, Chase." It was his sister, Meade. "I hope I'm not interrupting anything."

"No, I don't seem to do much work these days, anyway. How was everything in Vermont?"

"Peaceful, relaxing."

"And how are *you*, Meade?"

"I'm not pregnant, of course, though God knows we tried. I always hope that getting away might make a difference...."

"They're a number of things they can do these days, Meade. You haven't tried most of them."

"Yes, that's true. I was sure the fertility pills would do the trick, but they haven't. I guess that surgical procedure to check me out inside, the laparoscopy, is next."

"You'll have your baby eventually."

Meade sighed. "Well, enough about me. What's the latest on young Master or Mistress Hamilton? I had a note you'd called. I assume it was to gossip about my prospective niece or nephew."

"No, actually it was to invite you and Roger over for dinner Saturday. Jessica and her son will be moving in Friday, and I wanted you to meet her."

"She agreed to live with you, then? Or did you twist her arm?"

"I didn't kidnap her."

"No, but I know how determined you can be."

"Meade, I'm paying Jessica an awful lot of money for her trouble."

"I should hope so! You should make it as easy for her as you possibly can."

"That's exactly what I'm doing."

"It'd be a mistake to push her, though. Let things develop at their own pace."

"What things?"

"Well…your relationship. Despite everything, Chase, there's more to what you two share than just the doctor and his test tubes."

"It's Jessica who is having problems coming to terms with that, not I."

"Well, it wouldn't be easy for any woman to have a baby by a man she didn't love."

Chase started to ask what that had to do with it, then remembered Meade wasn't just his sister, she was a woman. They could be so disdainful when logic was used to question conclusions based on emotion. "Don't forget," he said gently, "Jessica and I have a business relationship."

"Oh, poppycock!" she replied. "Babies can't be reduced to a simple matter of dollars and cents. Certainly not for the one bearing the child."

"That's exactly what it is. For Jessica more than me."

"I don't believe that, Chase."

"You don't know her."

Meade didn't reply for a moment. "Now that you've gotten to know her…is she what you were looking for?"

"Yes. Why?"

"I'm just curious. You said she's attractive."

"She is."

"Are you fond of her?"

"What is this, the grand inquisition?"

"No, sisterly concern—plus a heavy dose of curiosity. I wouldn't have thought you'd mind."

Chase had to smile. It was like dozens of conversations he had had with their mother. During the last years of her life, Marion Hamilton had pressured her son to marry. He'd eventually get upset with the needling and she'd let him know she was hurt by his reaction. Meade had clearly become his mother's self-appointed successor.

"Of course I don't mind. That's why I'm having you over for dinner."

"Well, I'm looking forward to meeting Jessica, but I hope being family we don't just compound the poor girl's problems."

"What are you talking about?"

"She's in a very difficult situation. How she's going to be able to hand the baby over to you and leave is absolutely beyond me."

"Fortunately it's not your problem, Sis."

They ended the conversation with Meade accepting Chase's invitation to dinner. Putting down the phone, he returned to the window. What was it about a woman's advice that always left a man with self-doubt? He could have had the same conversation with Roger, and unless a flaw had been found in his logic, there would have been no effect at all.

What Meade had managed to do was to stir up the feelings of guilt that had been smoldering. Perhaps he had an obligation to Jessica beyond providing for her and Jamie, an obligation to see to her emotional well-being and her happiness.

Chase looked at the phone, paused for a moment and dialed Jessica's number. It was busy, so he replaced the receiver.

He pictured her in his mind, remembering her stubborn independence and defiant spirit as much as her physical attractiveness. Maybe it was that fire in her that had touched him in particular. She was clearly a challenge, and some men thrived on that.

Whatever it was, he desired her. He had kissed her because of it and had considered doing more, but his sense of responsibility had prevented it. Meade was right; he couldn't take advantage of her.

Chase picked up the phone and dialed again. Still busy. He hung up, frustrated. If he was going to do the right thing, he'd start out by giving her the space she wanted. There was work that needed tending to in Kentucky. He'd leave Maggie to help Jessica with the packing and the move and come back for the dinner with Meade and Roger on Saturday. All that remained was to inform Jessica.

CHAPTER EIGHT

WEARING AN OLD PAIR of shorts and a tank top, Jessica sat amid half a dozen packing boxes on the living room floor. One was filled with painting supplies, another with books. Protruding from the top of a large box nearby was Jamie's tousled hair. At the moment his spaceship and Velvet were engaged in some horrible combat. His mother couldn't see the action, but the sounds of warfare were unmistakable.

It was a sweltering day, and Jessica thought off and on about the lovely, air-conditioned ambience of Chase's home. Though she had declined his offer to have Maggie help with the packing, having accepted Harriet's offer, instead, she was looking forward to being at the farm, relieved of much of the burden she had been carrying alone.

Jessica reached for her glass of lemonade on the coffee table and took a long drink. "Want some more lemonade, Jamie?"

But he was busy with his battle and paid her no attention. She smiled and wondered if Chase would be getting the boy she assumed he wanted. They hadn't talked about that. She decided to ask him sometime if he had a preference.

Whenever she thought of the baby, her mind invariably turned to Chase and, during the past few days, to that kiss with which he had sealed their bargain. Jessica knew in her heart there was more than simple friendship in that kiss, but she tried not to think about it. She just hoped and prayed it would stop there.

"Anybody home?" There was a tapping on the door and Jessica looked up to see Harriet Thomas through the screen.

"Harriet," she said, rising to her feet, "I was afraid you got lost."

"Sorry to be late. Tony didn't bring his car by until eleven-thirty."

Jessica opened the door, glancing past her friend at the Ford compact parked at the curb. Harriet, in jeans and a cotton blouse, stepped inside. They briefly embraced. "It was nice of your friend to let you borrow his car."

"Lord, you can't imagine how horrendous it is to have to decide which man you're going to owe a favor to. For the next six months every time he brings you to the door, you know he's thinking about the time he let you borrow his car."

"Poor Harriet. You should have taken the train."

"Are you kidding? Every girl needs an excuse. The trick is borrowing the right car!"

Jessica laughed. "How about a glass of lemonade?"

"Sounds fabulous."

Jessica went into the kitchen to get a glass and the pitcher. Harriet bent down to say a few words to Jamie.

When Jessica returned with the refreshments Harriet took a long drink. "Ah. Tastes wonderful!" She smiled at her friend. "Have you two had lunch?"

"No, but I can whip up a snack if you're hungry."

"I had planned to pick something up for all of us on the way, but when I was running late I thought I'd better come here directly. Why don't I go out and pick up some sandwiches?"

"No point in doing that, Harriet. I can fix something."

"Nonsense. You can use a break from cooking. Besides, I've had the pastrami crazies all morning. Is there a deli nearby?"

"There's a nice one downtown, about six or seven blocks up the street."

"Great. You two want to come along?"

Jessica looked down at herself. "I'm not dressed and I was thinking of letting Jamie play on the lawn with the hose for a while to cool off."

"Great. Why don't you two have your swim. I'll cater."

"Under one condition," Jessica said, going to her purse on the table. "I'm buying."

"No, my treat."

"No, it's mine, Harriet. You took a day off work and drove all the way out here to help me pack. The least I can do is feed you. Besides, I'm not a pauper anymore."

Harriet gave her a mischievous grin. "No, that's true. You're on the verge of becoming Lady Hamilton."

"I am not," Jessica snapped.

Harriet laughed, taking the ten-dollar bill that was handed her. "I'll accept this, but only because it's Chase's money."

"Whose money's paying *your* rent the next few months, dear lady?"

"Touché. But, then, I'm not becoming a live-in!" She shrieked gleefully as Jessica chased her toward the door and out onto the porch.

"You got me into this mess, Harriet Thomas!" Jessica called after her.

"Not on your life. You'll never pin that bit of foolishness on me." She was halfway to the car. "Of course it may turn out to be the best stroke of luck you've ever had!''

JAMIE SAT ON THE GRASS at the shady end of the lawn with a dribbling hose. Jessica was on the porch watching him. The boy was having a ball soaking himself from head to toe, swinging the hose over his head like a lasso and squealing with joy at the feel of the water. Unable to resist, Jessica walked down onto the lawn to join him.

Seeing her, he began waving the nozzle in her direction, but the feeble trickle was no threat. Jessica laughed, got down on her hands and knees and began crawling toward him. Jamie giggled excitedly. He dropped the hose and tried to crawl away, but his braces prevented him from moving very far.

"I'm going to get you! I'm going to get you!" she growled in her lowest voice. And Jamie tried to scramble away, laughing with glee.

Just when his mother was almost upon him, he picked up the hose and pressed his fingers over the end, spraying both of them. Jessica shrieked and Jamie laughed.

She jumped to her feet, but he continued spraying so that she was forced to dash out of range. Jessica looked down at the front of her soaked shirt and was brushing a tendril of wet hair from her face, when she glanced up and saw Chase Hamilton's Bentley sitting at the curb.

"Good Lord," she muttered under her breath as he got out of the car.

"Sorry to drop by at such an impropitious moment," he called out good-naturedly, "but your phone seems to be out of order. I tried calling, but couldn't get through."

Jessica felt like fleeing and Chase's news gave her the excuse she needed. She turned and dashed for the house, stopping on the porch. "Would you watch Jamie for a second?'' she called back to him. Without waiting for a reply, she scampered into the house.

Inside she found the telephone receiver askew, apparently knocked ajar during the packing. She righted it, then headed straight for the bathroom. A quick look in the mirror confirmed her worst fears. She peeled off the soaked tank top and shorts.

Riffling through her dresser drawers and the partially packed boxes and suitcases, she was unable to find the powder blue polo shirt she wanted. It was times like this Jessica hated her messiness.

Annoyed, she went to the closet, hoping to find her short-sleeved pink cotton blouse. Thankfully it was on a hanger, but her white pants were wadded up on the floor. She picked them up, and the jelly stain on the front reminded her why they were there in the first place.

Jessica grabbed her jeans and quickly put them on. To her surprise it was a struggle to fasten the waistband. Could she have gained that much weight already?

She put on the blouse, ran a comb through her wet hair and went back outside onto the porch. Chase and Jamie were walking across the lawn, with Velvet waiting for them at the far end. She noticed for the first time that he was wearing a navy polo shirt and white slacks. Chase looked up at her and grinned.

''I kind of liked the other outfit.''

Jessica fought the fire in her cheeks. ''Did you come by to walk Jamie?'' she asked, ignoring his comment.

''Not exactly. I'm leaving for Kentucky tomorrow morning. I'll be gone when you move in, so I wanted you to know before you arrived.''

''That's very considerate. Thank you.''

"I also wanted to let you know that my sister, Meade, and her husband, Roger, will be coming over for dinner Saturday night."

"Thoughtful of you to give me a day to unpack," she chided.

Jamie was unrelentingly taking Chase down the lawn and he had to turn to look back at her.

"I'd feel better if you took it easy on this move. No reason in the world you should be doing any lifting."

"I'm taking care of myself. Besides, Harriet's here to help with the packing. She just ran down to the deli. Have you had lunch?"

"Yes. I had a bite before I left the farm."

Jamie had almost reached Velvet, and Jessica watched them take the final steps to their goal, noticing how crisp and fresh Chase looked. His lean, muscular firmness and tender demeanor with her child made him especially appealing. She had a sudden urge to inhale his cologne, to be close to him.

Chase picked up Jamie and Velvet and walked slowly back to the porch. Standing below her with her son under his arm, he gave her a languorous, approving look. "But, then, I like this outfit, too."

Jessica self-consciously touched her wet hair. "It's just a cotton blouse and an old pair of jeans."

"Maybe it's the way you wear them, then." Chase saw her bottom lip drop slightly open, a response forming, before vanishing unsaid. The lip seemed to tremble, then she forced a smile.

The exquisite contours of her face were all the more apparent with her hair wet and slicked back. Chase felt his loins warm, and despite his resolve to keep his distance, he had an urge to take her into his arms.

"Would you and Jamie like a glass of lemonade?" she asked evenly, oblivious to the turmoil she had wrought.

He looked at the boy. "What do you think, partner?"

"Yeah," Jamie replied agreeably.

Chase carried him up the steps and stood him on the porch. "If you want some lemonade, my man, you'll have to walk in and get it. Let's see if we can walk to the kitchen before your mom get's it poured. What do you say?"

"Okay," Jamie agreed.

Jessica held the door for them. "I don't know how you do it, Chase."

"Maybe it's just part of being a man."

His cologne enveloped her, filling her lungs, and at that moment Jessica understood his meaning . . . much better than he ever would have guessed.

BY THE TIME THE MOVERS ARRIVED on Friday Jessica had everything ready. It was another hot day and she had awakened feeling queasy. There was no time for feeling ill, however—whether real or imagined—so she got Jamie dressed, fed him breakfast and packed the last of the dishes and food in a small carton.

The boxes had been divided between those going into storage and those that were to go to the farm. The furniture, meager as it was, all was to go to the warehouse. In little more than an hour everything had been loaded onto the truck and a driver arrived with the Bentley to take Jessica and Jamie to Chase's place.

Jessica held her son close during the ride, feeling that she was undertaking a much more momentous journey than the fifteen miles would indicate. In a way it was almost as big a step as the pregnancy itself.

Maggie was waiting when they arrived. She had prepared a lunch for the two of them and Anne Bascom. The nurse, who was to act as governess, felt it was important to gain Jamie's confidence gradually, though he had never balked at being cared for by a sitter. Jessica could see immediately that the nurse was a professional through and through.

During lunch they chatted mostly about Jamie, Anne being careful to include the boy in the discussion whenever appropriate. After they had finished eating, the nurse took Jamie up for a nap in his new room. She returned just as the movers arrived.

"I'll oversee the moving men," Maggie said to Jessica. "You and Miss Bascom just sit and enjoy your tea."

When the good-natured housekeeper had left the sunroom, Jessica smiled at Anne. "Maggie's quite a woman, isn't she?"

"She really runs this place, Mrs. Brandon. I've only been around a few days now, but there's no doubt who's in charge."

"I certainly hope she doesn't resent us coming."

"I think she's positively thrilled about it."

Jessica contemplated her companion. "How much, exactly, has Mr. Hamilton told you about the reason for our moving here?"

"He explained you were surrogate mother to his child."

"I expected he had, but I wanted to make sure."

"Since there's no Mrs. Hamilton, you're not really a surrogate, though, are you? You're the only mother the baby will have."

"I hadn't thought of it that way, but I suppose you're right."

"I admire what you're doing, Mrs. Brandon. I didn't want you to worry about that."

"Thanks, Anne. I appreciate you saying that. But truth be known, I'm not really in a very different position from you. Chase...Mr. Hamilton...hired me to perform a service. That's all."

"Oh, I wasn't implying there was anything else."

"I know you weren't. I just wanted you to know I regard what I'm doing as a job, nothing more."

Anne nodded. "I understand."

"He has struck me with some extra duties, however. Tomorrow I've got to meet his sister and brother-in-law. I think they're actually coming to see the baby, but for the moment that means me."

The nurse laughed. "It is a rather strange job you have, isn't it?"

Jessica nodded. "Yes, it is." She looked up at her painting on the wall, remembering how it had caused a fight. She thought again about Chase's kiss during their walk and wondered if her comment to Anne that what she was doing was just a job was accurate or just wishful thinking.

The nurse was pouring more tea, when a sudden wave of nausea came over Jessica. Anne noticed the look on her face and appeared concerned. "Are you feeling all right, Mrs. Brandon?"

"Yes, just a little queasy."

"Has it happened before?"

"In the past, when it's been hot, there's been a little. This morning when I got up I felt a touch, but it's nice and cool here. I don't understand it."

"Could be morning sickness. Time of day means nothing, of course. Normally it doesn't happen after you've eaten, though. Perhaps you've worked a little too hard. Why don't you go upstairs and lie down for a while?"

"Yes, maybe I will." Jessica started to get up and then remembered the quandary she had been in about what to wear the next evening for the dinner party. "By the way, Anne, do you know where the nearest shopping is around here?"

"What sort of shopping?"

"Clothes. I don't really have anything appropriate for tomorrow night, so I thought I'd try to find a dress."

Anne Bascom suppressed a little smile. "There's Mount Kisco, or White Plains if you want to go farther."

Jessica realized how incongruous her plan seemed in light of her earlier remarks. She wondered if there could possibly be a significance. After all, what woman didn't want to look her best, regardless of the circumstances?

MEADE PHILLIPS WAS VERY TALL, broad shouldered and strikingly attractive—a feminine version of her brother, though her eyes were chocolate brown and her dark hair had been lightened. Her white silk coat-dress was understated, yet elegant. She was both sophisticated and down-to-earth, completely without pretense.

She turned back to Jessica, having watched her husband and brother walk from the elegant sitting room toward Chase's study.

"Isn't that sweet, Chase finding some excuse to take Roger into the other room so we can talk? Sometimes men in their innocence can be so endearing."

Jessica smiled, turning the glass of bubbly mineral water nervously in her hand. "Chase *is* sweet. He's very kind."

"And you're brave, Jessica. I really admire what you're doing."

"I'm no philanthropist. Chase is paying me very well."

"Still, I'm impressed. There has to be a side of you that's deeply humanitarian. Money alone couldn't be the motive."

Jessica gave a half shrug and sipped her mineral water.

"Perhaps I'm projecting," Meade said. "Babies are such an emotional subject for me."

"Yes, Chase mentioned you wanted a child."

Meade laughed. "Wanted? I'm afraid it's become an obsession." She took her cocktail from the coffee table. "But it's entirely my own fault. I let the issue get completely out of hand. Better I accept facts."

"It's only natural," Jessica replied, feeling truly sympathetic.

"Yes, but we Hamiltons never stop with an excuse. We keep going until we get what we want."

"I have noticed a certain...determination...in Chase."

"Lord, he's the worst of the lot, though I suppose I'm a close second."

"Do the doctors say there's no hope of a child?"

"It's looking doubtful. Fertility drugs definitely won't do the trick. But I guess it's that tiny possibility that keeps me going."

Jessica watched Meade sip her drink. "Have you considered adoption?"

"Yes, but it's truly a last resort. Roger's not real keen on the idea, the wait's so long, and I really want our child, or at least his." A wry smile crossed her face. "I don't suppose you'd be interested in producing another baby next year?"

"Lord!" Jessica gasped. "This one will more than fill my quota."

Meade glanced over Jessica's honey silk dress. "I do hope you'll forgive me if I act a little jealous once you begin to show. It's the hardest thing...seeing other women pregnant or with a baby."

"I'll understand," Jessica said, feeling genuinely sorry for her.

"Now that you're here, I guess we'll be seeing a lot of you."

Jessica hesitated. "I suppose so."

"This is not what you want—living here on the farm—is it?"

"It would be easier for me if I didn't. Let me put it that way."

Meade nodded.

"It's nothing against Chase, of course," Jessica added hastily. "It's just my way of dealing with it."

"Is the idea of giving up the baby a difficult one for you?"

"Oh, no, that's not what I'm referring to."

Meade looked at her, perplexed.

"What I mean is, going through a pregnancy is the sort of thing you only do with a husband." Jessica paused. "It's Chase's baby, not mine, so it'd be easier for me if I'm not involved, if I stay emotionally clear of the whole business."

"I understand. You don't want Chase's enthusiasm and attachment to rub off."

"Right. We've been at odds over arrangements, and I haven't been able to explain how I feel. He interprets my attitude as unfriendly, when I'm really only trying to protect myself."

"Knowing my big brother as I do, I can understand your problem. He believes if he wants something good for someone, they ought to want it, too. He can't understand when they resist."

Jessica studied her. "Do you really think it's that important to him to experience the whole pregnancy minute by minute?"

"He means well. I'm sure there's no ill intent."

"Oh, I know. I've never doubted his motives." As soon as she said it, Jessica realized she wasn't sure it was true. In fact, she didn't know with certainty how Chase Hamilton felt about her. And more important, she wasn't sure what her feelings were toward him.

"He's like a protective animal with its young, that's all. Chase is the same way with his horses—and believe me, that's a compliment. You're like one of his treasured Thoroughbreds. The only difference is *they* don't resist his loving care."

The women looked at each other.

"If he gets to be a problem, Jessica, let me know. I'll do what I can to intercede. Our mother used to be the only one he'd ever listen to, and now that she's gone, he sometimes listens to me."

"Thanks, Meade, but I'm sure that won't be necessary. I've pretty well made it clear that my moving here didn't imply any obligation except being under his watchful eye." Jessica lifted her glass to her lips just as a queasy feeling came over her. She blanched.

"You all right?"

"Yes, just a little nausea. It'll pass."

Meade scooted to the edge of her chair. "Can I get you something?"

"No, thank you." Jessica looked down at the tray of hors d'oeuvres that she had been avoiding because of their richness. "Well, maybe something bland. A cracker—that sort of thing."

"I'll see what Maggie has. There must be something in the kitchen. I'll go find her."

Fighting her nausea, Jessica looked around the room. It was a fine house, very comfortable, but it wasn't hers. She could never be more than a guest. She thought of her little place in Peekskill, picturing the old worn couch and her husband's chair. Alex.

His world—their world—had been a very different one from this. His life might have been modest alongside Chase's, but Alex was a decent person. Jessica bit her lip, feeling defensive for her husband, for herself. Why were this house and Chase Hamilton so threatening?

Meade returned with the housekeeper in tow. "I think Maggie has found something suitable," she said, seating herself opposite Jessica on the couch.

"Yes, ma'am, there be some soda crackers, grams and a few sweet biscuits, if you like," the woman said, placing a plate before Jessica. Then, still leaning over the table, she lowered her voice discreetly. "If the problem be that you're in a family way, ma'am, you might take a wee bit of warm milk. It'll settle your stomach. I guarantee it will."

"Oh, thank you, but no, Maggie. The crackers will be just fine."

"Yes, ma'am." The woman nodded and left the room.

Jessica picked up a saltine and took a bite from the corner of the cracker, then she took another. "Hmm. Amazing how pregnancy makes a person redefine their pleasures."

Chase and Roger Phillips, a thin, blond man in his late thirties, entered the room. "Pleasures?" Chase said good-naturedly. He looked devastating in a steel-gray three piece suit and burgundy tie. "Did I hear someone mention pleasures?"

Meade turned to view the men. "Women do discuss those things from time to time," she said pointedly.

"What are the pleasures of which you speak? Or is it a secret?"

"They must have been talking about sex," Roger said, adjusting his rimless glasses.

Everyone laughed.

"As a matter of fact," Meade rejoined, "we were talking about food."

Chase, unbuttoning his suit coat, sat down beside Meade. Smiling at Jessica, he leaned forward and took an hors d'oeuvre. He gestured toward her plate of crackers. "Bring your own?"

"Meade had Maggie bring them," she replied evenly. "Rich foods don't agree with me."

"The graham crackers have less sodium than the saltines," he said, popping an hors d'oeuvre in his mouth.

"Chase, let the poor thing enjoy her cracker, for heaven's sake," Meade protested.

"Sorry, didn't mean to pontificate. But sodium's not good for anyone, pregnant or not."

Jessica looked at him. "How about hay?"

Roger laughed loudly and Meade winked at Jessica.

"Touché," Chase mumbled, smiling at her. He leaned back and put his arm behind his sister, crossing his legs. "By the way, I like your dress." His eyes drifted down her.

"Thank you," Jessica replied, smoothing her honey silk skirt.

"Is it new?"

"As a matter of fact, I bought it for tonight."

Chase's smile grew, and Jessica found herself staring at his wide mouth, so full of vainglory. Her stomach tightened. They each held their gaze as the energy flowed between them. A glance at Meade told Jessica she was aware.

Roger leaned forward during the ensuing silence and took a cracker from Jessica's plate. "When's dinner, anyway?"

CHAPTER NINE

DURING DINNER JESSICA LISTENED to the conversation and watched the others more than she participated. The dining room and the service were formal, though it wasn't really like a dinner party. It was a family meal; the mood and conversation had that feel. Jessica felt a little alien and out of place.

As Maggie served dessert, Roger, a senior account executive with a Madison Avenue advertising firm, told them about some of the funny things that had come out of a campaign he was running for a client. Chase and Meade were listening with rapt attention, commenting and laughing.

Jessica tried to follow the patter, but her mind wandered back to the conversation with Harriet in the salad bar that day she first heard about Chase Hamilton. How naive she had been, and how wise Harriet was. Jessica didn't realize it at the time, but what she had done was sell not only her body, but her freedom, as well. The thought was a dismal one, and the more she dwelled on it, the more depressed she became.

"Jessica, are you all right?"

She looked into the concerned face of Meade Phillips. "Oh...yes, I'm okay."

Chase and Roger had fallen silent and were also looking at her with concern.

"I was afraid you might not be feeling well again," Meade said in a gentle voice.

The attention brought up a well of emotion, and Jessica was embarrassed. She felt a sudden need to get away, to be by herself. Putting her napkin on the table, she glanced toward the door. "Perhaps I'll just step to the powder room," she said in a half whisper, and began scooting back her chair.

Chase quickly got up and helped her. Ignoring him, she began moving briskly across the room, almost at a run. She passed through the sitting room and went to the entry hall. Seeing several doors, she pulled one open but it was a coat closet. Crying out in exasperation, she slammed it closed and went to the next. It was the powder room. Stepping inside, she locked the door.

Taking a towel from the countertop, Jessica moistened the corner and carefully dabbed her eyes, trying to cool the sting of tears that threatened to flow. The face she saw in the mirror was flushed and strangely unfamiliar. She took a deep breath, and felt a little better. As she was beginning to calm down, there was a light knock on the door.

"Jessica, are you all right?" It was Meade. "Can I get you something?"

"No, thank you, I'm fine now. It was just a little nausea. It's passed." Jessica could hear footsteps outside the door and Chase's voice.

"Is she okay?"

"Yes, just a little nausea. I think she'll be fine," Meade replied. "Pregnancy isn't a picnic, you know. Amazing what havoc you men can wreak with a little pleasure, isn't it?"

"It wasn't exactly pleasure, remember?"

Behind the door, listening, Jessica smiled. His comment made her forget herself and she felt sorry for him—more even than for herself. Considering all the inconvenience she was going through, somebody ought to have gotten a little pleasure out of it. Jessica looked again in the mirror and decided she was all right, that she ought to go out.

Chase and Meade were standing together in the hall. They looked up at her with concern as she stepped out of the powder room.

"I'm fine now," she reassured them. "I'm sorry to disrupt the dinner."

They went to the sitting room. Chase turned to Meade. "Why don't you go on back and finish your dessert with Roger? I'll stay with Jessica."

Meade silently assented and left the room. Jessica sat and Chase dropped down on the couch opposite her.

"What ill have I wrought, Jessica?"

"No ill, just the usual tribulations of pregnancy."

"Was it like this the first time, or is there something fundamentally incompatible about us?"

"Maybe that *is* the problem," she replied with a little smile.

"Then again, maybe the doctor got his test tubes mixed up."

"Lord, don't even say that!"

Chase grinned sardonically. "Why? Would it matter?"

She felt her stomach clinch at the thought of an unknown man's baby inside her, but she kept her expression composed. "No, I suppose it wouldn't matter—to me. I was thinking of you."

He looked at her for a long time, and Jessica felt him as strongly as if she were in his arms. The moment hung. Then Maggie entered the room, breaking the spell.

"Would you and the lady be wantin' some tea, sir?"

He glanced at the housekeeper, then at Jessica. "What do you think, m'lady? Would you care for some tea?"

His voice was low and rich and his mouth seemed especially appealing. A little tremor went through her. It wasn't at all the queasiness she had been feeling, nor was it fear or displeasure. It was a warm, inviting sensation. It was the woman in her responding to the man in him.

In the shadowed darkness of her bedroom Jessica unbuttoned her dress, stepped out of it and draped it carefully across a chair. Moments later she looked down at her naked body, barely able to see her swollen breasts, the lines of her hips and legs in the darkness.

The trim figure of which she was so proud would be spoiled for a time, but she would regain it. She ran her hand over the plane of her stomach, liking the flatness, but feeling the tiniest bit of softness under her skin. It wouldn't be long, she knew, before Chase could see the evidence of his child.

The thought of Chase Hamilton was equally pleasurable and troubling. Jessica was gradually coming to accept the fact that she was fond of him, but she was uneasy because his feelings weren't clear to her. She suspected they were really for the baby.

The sexual tension between them couldn't be what it appeared. She wasn't just another woman to him—she was the mother of his child. And given his obsession, he probably couldn't separate her from the baby.

What it meant was that Chase Hamilton was off-limits. The child who had brought them together would keep them apart. The solution was always to keep her child, Jamie, in the forefront of her mind.

Stealing to the door separating their rooms, Jessica opened it and looked inside. In the soft moonlight coming in the window she saw his little face amid the large bed, pillows surrounding him on every side. The joy he added to her life brought a smile to Jessica's lips. Quietly she closed the door.

CHASE HAD ALREADY LEFT for the city on business by the time Jessica came down for breakfast. Jamie was at the kitchen table with Anne Bascom, a large bowl of cereal in front of him, splashes of milk and a couple of cornflakes adorning the front of his shirt. It was strange to awaken and already find him having his breakfast.

"We thought you might like to sleep," Anne explained.

"Thank you. That's the first time I've managed that in a long time."

"Jamie and I did quite well this morning, so if you like we can make it routine."

Jessica smiled gratefully and sat down. She wasn't quite sure how she liked being so thoroughly relieved of responsibility for her son. Maggie came into the kitchen.

"Mornin', Mrs. Brandon. Did you sleep well?"

"Yes, thank you."

"You'll be wantin' breakfast, will you, then?"

"Please."

Jamie was splashing at his cereal, but before Jessica could say anything, Anne gently stopped him. All the help was nice in a way, but she was beginning to feel superfluous.

"Are you goin' to paint today?" Maggie asked as she moved around the kitchen.

"Yes, I thought I'd go out and organize the studio."

"Your pictures are so pretty, or at least the one I've seen is. Did you know, Anne," she said to the nurse, "that Mrs. Brandon did the one in the sun-room?"

Anne looked at Jessica with surprise. "No, I didn't realize. You're very talented."

Jessica was a little embarrassed by all the compliments. "Thank you."

Maggie walked over to the table and handed her a sheet of paper. "Here's the list of foods Mr. Hamilton says you may choose from, ma'am. I'll fix whatever you like."

Jessica looked up with surprise. "Mr. Hamilton?"

"Yes, ma'am. He had the doctor prepare a diet for you. I'm to keep a record of what you eat."

Jessica turned red. Chase's gall astounded her. One would think she was a child, not a responsible woman. Barely disguising her anger, she looked over the typed list. Knowing there was no reason to raise a fuss with Maggie, she quietly requested fresh fruit and whole wheat toast.

Jessica wondered how many other little surprises were in store for her. She instantly decided to rebel by establishing a stash of jelly beans in the studio. Regardless of Chase's preferences, the baby would have to make do with a human mother—not a breeding mare.

Of course she wouldn't do anything irresponsible, but she wasn't about to regard her body as a machine, either. Lord Hamilton would just have to accept that, whether he liked it or not.

AFTER BREAKFAST Jessica went to the studio to take her measure of the place. Her boxes of supplies were stacked against the wall, her canvases neatly leaning beside them. The room had a barren, if orderly, feel that she didn't like. She decided to unpack her things, combine them with what Chase had bought and make the place feel lived in.

Working alone, she gradually began to gain a sense of identity. The carriage house would have her stamp on it. She could be comfortable, do her work, create, express herself. She was already beginning to feel a sense of purpose and dedication. Perhaps, she thought, the move to the farm would turn out to be more beneficial than she had at first realized.

After the studio had been set up to her satisfaction, Jessica took out her sketch pad and reviewed some ideas she had worked out. Feeling inspired, she propped a canvas on her easel and began painting. Suffering no interruptions, she worked away, losing all track of time.

She was only vaguely aware of the falling darkness outside when Maggie rapped at the door.

"Excuse me for interruptin', Mrs. Brandon, but I was wonderin' if you would be interested in some supper. We've fed the little one, and Mr. Hamilton called to say he was stayin' in town for his meal."

Jessica looked at her watch, shocked that the time had gotten away from her. "Oh, I hadn't realized it was so late. Where is Jamie?"

"Anne is readin' to him in his room."

Jessica quickly wiped her hands with a cloth and removed her smock. "Was he all right today?" she asked, going to the sink to wash up.

"Oh, yes, ma'am. He was a regular little gentleman. Mr. Valticos came and he had two hours of therapy this mornin'. He had a good lunch. I would have come for you, but I figured if you wished to eat you'd come to the house on your own."

Lunch. Jessica had forgotten about eating entirely. Now that she thought about it, she *was* hungry. And the light nausea was there, lingering in the background. She dried her hands and went with Maggie back to the house.

"I got a little worried," the housekeeper said as they walked along the path in the twilight, "when you didn't come up this evening. I hope it's okay by you that I come for you, ma'am."

"Of course it's okay, Maggie. It's the first long stretch I've had to myself in years. I just got wrapped up in my painting."

She went to Jamie's room, where the boy greeted her enthusiastically, though he seemed quite content with Anne. While the nurse read the last few lines of the story, Jessica sat on the edge of the bed.

"Thank you, Anne," she said. "I appreciate your extra kindness. I'll tuck Jamie in if you want to retire. It's been a long day, I know."

"He's had a good time," the woman said, stepping to the door.

"In the future you can bring him out to the studio for a break, if I get involved the way I did today." She turned to the boy. "Would you like that, honey, to come out and visit Mommy sometimes while I'm working?"

Jamie nodded.

Anne smiled. "Well good night, then," she said, and stepped from the room.

Jessica stroked the boy's head, thinking how much she had enjoyed working that day... yet how very much she had missed her son.

THOUGH THERE WERE BOUTS of morning sickness in the days that followed, Jessica managed to settle into a routine, making tremendous progress in the studio. She usually went to the house for lunch, and Jamie and Anne Bascom came out to visit her at least once each day.

Chase was frequently gone by the time she rose, but they did have breakfast together once. He made several short business trips and so was often not around during the evenings. When he was he played with Jamie and they practiced walking a lot, going from one end of the sitting room to the other, just as they had in her front yard in Peekskill.

For a few days in a row Chase was home, but Jessica was busy in the studio most of the time. Maggie thoughtfully brought her out a little lunch, which she ate alone, her mind preoccupied with her work. She was in a prolific stage—had finished three more canvases and was feeling quite pleased with the results.

During a break one afternoon she wandered over to the window and looked out to see Chase with Jamie in the pony cart. They were just leaving the barn and were heading down the lane. Though it was a sight she'd expected to see a great deal of once they had moved to the farm, somehow there was a touch of sadness to the scene. Or was it just her own state of mind?

Jessica realized she had been avoiding Chase, if only subconsciously. And while she couldn't exactly say he had been avoiding her, she knew he hadn't gone out of his way to see her, either. She frequently found herself thinking about him, wondering where he was and what he was doing.

She started skipping breakfast, going directly to the studio from her room each morning. It apparently didn't go unnoticed, because one day Maggie brought out a bowl of fruit and an assortment of breads and cheeses without comment. Jessica was pretty sure it was done on Chase's orders.

That day Maggie told Jessica that Chase had gone to Lexington for a few days. The news was received with relief. She felt it was pretty silly that so much tension had developed between them, but she was still glad for the respite afforded by his absence.

The first day Chase was gone Meade Phillips called to invite Jessica and Jamie to lunch. She quickly accepted and decided to put aside her work and spend the whole day with Jamie. It was Anne Bascom's day off, so it worked out well. Mr. Valticos came late morning as usual and Jessica spent the session with him.

"He's a good kid, Mrs. Brandon. A good patient," the man said reassuringly.

"What do you think of the long-term prospects?"

"Five years or so from now nobody will ever know there was a problem. If you keep up the regular therapy for at least a couple of years," he added.

Though the man couldn't have intended it, he was stating still another reason that it would be difficult to leave the farm. When the session was over, Jessica thanked the physical therapist for all he had done for Jamie and took her son in to get dressed for lunch.

THE PHILLIPSES' STATION WAGON pulled up at the door right on time and Meade came up the steps, a little gift for Jamie in hand.

"Meade, that wasn't necessary," Jessica said as the woman took Jamie's hand. The fondness for children was obviously a Hamilton family trait.

"I so rarely have an excuse," Meade replied, patting Jamie's cheek. She looked at mother and son, smiling. "Is anybody hungry?"

They drove to a pleasant little country inn not far away in Connecticut. Most of the patrons were women having lunch with friends. The three of them settled in a corner table, Meade making a particular fuss about Jamie's comfort.

Jessica watched her pampering and making friends with her son, detecting a maternal quality in the woman's manner that rivaled Chase's paternalism.

"So my big brother has deserted you already," Meade said, turning her attention to Jessica.

"It's okay by me. I cherish my independence and privacy, Meade. One of the reasons I accepted his offer to live on the farm was that he said he'd be traveling a lot during the pregnancy."

Meade smiled wryly. "Does he know that?"

Jessica laughed. "I didn't mean that quite how it sounded. I don't mind Chase's company. I just like the idea of time alone. Too much togetherness would only make it harder."

"You've said that before, Jessica, but I just wonder if you aren't forcing this distance."

Jessica was surprised at the woman's directness, and it showed on her face.

Meade quickly added, "I'm sorry. It's none of my business, I know. I'm a little like my brother, I suppose—feeling an obligation to try to create paradise wherever I see the opportunity."

Jessica shrugged indifferently, but Meade's comment was a little troubling.

"In case Chase hasn't mentioned it to you," Meade said, "this baby's going to be getting a heavy dose of Auntie Meade."

Jessica smiled. "I'm sure both he and the baby will be glad."

Meade looked at her. "You know, you're remarkable. You really are." She glanced over at Jamie, who was busy playing with the toy she had given him and paying them no notice. Still, she lowered her voice a little. "An eavesdropper would never guess it's *your* baby we're talking about. Whether you admit it or not, Jessica, you've got a very big heart."

Jessica knew the words were well intended, but somehow they hurt. She felt awful just then—and not over Meade's comment about the baby. What bothered her was that she didn't feel anything toward it at all. Nothing. Not love, not sacrifice, not generosity, not guilt nor even regret. If she felt anything, she felt heartless. The thought brought tears to her eyes and she looked at Jamie, wanting reassurance.

ON THE DAY Chase was due back Jessica donned the T-shirt and jeans that had become her work uniform and retreated to the studio. She began a new canvas, eager to throw herself into her work. In all she had six completed paintings counting the one she had done in Peekskill. It was a good start, but she knew it was better to be ahead of schedule than behind because the last months of the pregnancy would be more difficult.

It was late afternoon, and though she had looked out the window from time to time during the day, she had seen no signs of Chase. Relieved, she decided that he might not return until evening, and she began cleaning up for the day.

Jessica removed her smock and was rubbing down her hands with turpentine, when the phone rang. She picked up the receiver.

"Jessica? It's Helmut Geisel here."

"Mr. Geisel! This is certainly a surprise. How good to hear from you."

"Yes, indeed, my dear." There was a little laugh. "I see you have found yourself a patron."

"A patron?"

"This is Chase Hamilton's residence where I call you, is it not?"

"Oh, yes. I have the use of a vacant studio here." Jessica colored, wondering how much the man knew. "How did you find me?"

"I had a call last week from Mr. Hamilton. He inquired about the value of your painting that he purchased a couple of months ago."

"Yes..."

"It was fortunate he called, because I told him I might have sold your other one. It was then that he gave me this number and said you were under his employ temporarily." Geisel laughed. "Does he have you painting the ceiling of his dining room, Jessica?"

She smirked at the innuendo, but held her tongue. His comment about selling her painting was still playing in her mind. "*Have* you sold the other painting?" she asked expectantly.

"Yes, yes, that's why I am calling. I've sold it to a very important collector of contemporary works from Miami. Julius Feldman. He left just now with it. He couldn't wait to have it shipped to him in Florida."

"That's wonderful!"

"Yes, it is, and I congratulate you, Jessica. It is an important sale for you. These people talk to one another, you know."

Jessica felt her heart soar. She covered the mouthpiece of the phone and let out a little squeal of joy. As she did, the door to the studio opened and Chase Hamilton appeared. There was an inquisitive look on his face.

Seeing him, Jessica blanched. She stared at him for a moment, then turned her attention again to Helmut Geisel.

"How is the painting coming, Jessica?" he asked in his high accented voice. "How many canvases do you have for me?"

She glanced over at the wall where the finished pieces were propped up. "Six."

"That's all? I'd hoped you'd have a dozen by now."

Jessica looked at Chase, who was leaning against the wall by the door, watching her. He was in shirt sleeves, his tie was loosened and the top button of his shirt unfastened. Though his presence was disconcerting, Jessica was aware how sexy and ruggedly male he looked.

"I would have more done, but...I've been sick off and on during the past month or so."

"Nothing serious, I hope."

"No, it's pretty well passed." She looked at Chase and saw the tiniest smile at the corners of his mouth.

"Well, I hope you have some things for me soon, Jessica. This sale to Julius Feldman is a good start, but I would like to follow it with a show. When will you have ten or fifteen canvases for me?"

Jessica tried to think, feeling at once the excitement of the conversation and the vague touch of fear engendered by Chase Hamilton's presence. "Oh, perhaps in a few months."

"That's good. I would like to have a look then. Naturally we need more than that for your show, but I want a feel for what you are doing. Do you understand?"

Again her eyes wandered to Chase, who seemed to be enjoying the sight of her in jeans and the skimpy T-shirt. She forced herself to concentrate on her conversation with the art dealer. "Yes, that would be fine."

"Good. Will you still be living at Mr. Hamilton's home?"

"I'm not sure, perhaps. Probably."

"Well, I'll want to contact you. Next time let me know if you go away, please."

"Yes, certainly. I intended to call. I've been so wrapped up in my work, it just escaped me. But my son and I have only been here a short time."

"I see." There was a knowing little laugh. "A new...relationship, then, I take it."

Jessica could almost hear the evil thoughts turning in his mind.

"This reminds me, Jessica. The maid told me when I called earlier for Mr. Hamilton that he was away on business and wouldn't be back till this evening."

"Yes..."

"If you see him would you tell him I would be happy to take that painting of yours on consignment. After today, I may be able to sell it for him at a profit."

Jessica looked at Chase, whose deep blue eyes were locked on her intently. "Yes, I'd be happy to pass that on to Mr. Hamilton."

"Why he wants to sell now, I don't know." There was an evil little laugh again. "Unless it could be that he gets Brandons free?"

Her eyes flashed, but she bit her tongue. "I assure you, Mr. Geisel, our relationship is strictly business."

Chase had folded his arms and was obviously listening with interest. She glanced at him and saw his grin, then flushed.

"If you'll tell him to call me..." Geisel was saying, then he paused. "Hmm...maybe I should come sooner and have a look-see at the work you've done. Would you mind? It might be good, you know, to keep one or two Brandon's on my walls.''

Jessica couldn't help a smile. Helmut Geisel's tone was so very different from the last time she had seen him. ''Whatever you wish, *Helmut*.'' She couldn't resist the familiarity.

Chase Hamilton began walking slowly toward her.

''All right, then,'' she said into the phone, ''just let me know what you decide. Goodbye.''

By the time she had replaced the receiver, Chase was beside her. ''Did you sell another painting?''

She was momentarily distracted by the faint scent of his cologne. Though she was ready to burst with joy at the news, she felt equally ready to run from Chase.

''Yes,'' she said, forcing calmness.

''Who's the fortunate buyer?''

''Somebody from Miami. Feldman, I think the name was.''

''Julius? It doesn't surprise me. He's never far from whatever's hot.'' Chase turned and walked to where Jessica's paintings were lined up along the wall. He studied them.

''Do you know him?''

''Not well, but we've met.''

''Geisel said it was an important sale.''

He turned and looked at her. ''Yes, *Helmut* was right.''

Jessica knew he was teasing her. ''He's started taking me seriously, I think.''

Chase turned back to the paintings without comment.

She watched him studying her work, wondering what he was thinking. ''How was your trip?''

''Fine.'' He stepped along the line of canvases. ''You're really quite good, you know.''

She was pleased. "Thank you."

He looked at her, his eyes equally curious and critical. "Are you going to hole up out here the whole seven months that are left?"

The question was unexpected. It struck her as strange, a touch angry. "That was the idea, wasn't it?"

"I didn't expect you to hide out here."

"Hide? I work here, Chase."

"You're skipping meals, neglecting your son—"

"Now just a minute!" Jessica's anger flared. "I'm not neglecting my son. I'm doing exactly what you proposed when you set this arrangement up. You were the one who chastised me for sitting on my rear, taking care of Jamie, instead of getting a job, remember?"

Chase looked annoyed at her counterattack.

She hardly paused. "Just who do you think you are, anyway? My father? Or my trainer?"

"Jessica—"

"No, come to think of it you can't even make that claim," she went on furiously. "This time you're just the stud!"

"Jessica, that's not what I meant at all. I was just concerned about you, about the baby. I'm sorry."

She could see contrition in his eyes and instantly realized that she had overreacted. Embarrassed, she turned away, walking slowly to the window.

Chase followed her. She felt him come up behind her.

"You've been working too hard," he said softly. "And this tension that's developed isn't doing either of us any good." He turned her around, letting his hands rest on her shoulders. "It's a lovely evening," he whispered, his eyes boring right into her.

Jessica felt goose bumps rising. She found herself trapped between the urge to flee and the urge to sink into his arms.

"Let's take a walk before dinner," he said, his fingertips gently caressing the soft flesh of her arms. "The air will be good for you."

Taking her hand, Chase led Jessica to the door.

CHAPTER TEN

IT WAS ONE OF THOSE rare evenings when the air was not too hot or too cool and seemed to lie on the land, still and rich with the perfumes of nature. The rose, orange and lemon hews of sunset were awash in the liquid sky to the west as Jessica walked beside Chase toward the highest hill on the farm. The grassy carpet of the lane, the stillness in the trees, and most of all the sensuous caress of the air enticed her to follow him into the slowly falling darkness.

He hardly spoke, but she felt the intimacy of his presence. Jessica was acutely aware of her body, the sensations that surrounded her, the earth. She knew that some things happen in life without will, and she sensed that this moment was one of them.

She glanced at Chase, more curious about his thoughts than she was concerned about the dangers of a solitary walk with him. After all the tension it seemed just that they go someplace and have it out, whether in a friendly or hostile way.

He held her hand firmly, possessively, as they walked, and she liked it that he gave her no choice but to go along with him. At the base of the hill they left the lane and climbed the grassy slope toward the empyreal sky above. The first stars began piercing the atmosphere as they reached the crest of the hill.

They stopped, both breathing deeply. A light hush of air rose, touching Jessica's hair and moist skin. He slipped his hand around her waist, and she let herself lean into his body, melding her softness with his strength.

Jessica hadn't forgotten their circumstances—the child she was carrying, the way Chase had virtually forced her to live with him—but it all seemed unimportant in the face of her needs. She wanted it to be all right to be with him and to need him.

Chase's arm tightened and Jessica felt his muscle hard against her. She looked up at him and knew they would kiss.

Chase eagerly took her lips, consuming their soft moistness as he crushed her in his arms. He would have inhaled her entirely, merged her into himself, if he were able.

Jessica quivered, then opened her mouth to accept him, moaning her desire through his warm lips. The sudden hunger in her was so great, so intense, that she wanted to cry out.

His fingers slipped under the tail of her skimpy T-shirt and began working the flesh of her back. She was startled by his strength, but in her desire she submitted, wanting to feel his force, wanting to be caressed. She opened her mouth wider, holding him against her tightly.

Chase's fingers went to the clasp of her bra and it gave way, sending a little wave of apprehension through her. His hands began roaming her back and sides and she stiffened, her desire waning momentarily. But the magic in his touch, the erotic friction of his body, ignited her again and she responded, her inner core warming and beginning to throb. Against the warmth of his chest her nipples hardened and she felt her body's desire.

So long had the physical woman lain dormant that her arousal seemed almost frenetic, choking her with its force. Her heart, her lungs, her throat, her loins ached to be taken. In spite of the silent, screaming doubts inside of her, she wanted him.

Jessica let the sensation mount, wanting the feel of him more than she wanted to think, or even care what it meant. She kissed him, liking the feel of his tongue trailing the edges of her teeth, the sensation of his mouth caressing hers.

When their lips finally parted his breath spilled over her cheeks and throat, his tongue raking her neck and exploring the delicate shell of her ear. Anxiously his hands slipped around her torso to her breasts, and he took them in his palms, kneading their ripe fullness.

Jessica gasped, then felt weak with excitement as he lightly touched her buds with feathery strokes of his thumbs. It was the first such intimacy with a man in years, and she trembled.

"Oh, Chase. My God . . . oh . . ." she moaned, gasping at the force of her craving.

He lowered her slowly to the carpet of grass. She lay on her back, staring up at him in the half-light, her eyes round with awe. Chase lowered himself to one knee beside her. Then he pulled up the front of her shirt to expose her breasts.

Her eyes closed as she felt the caress of the air on her naked skin. When his lips touched her erect nipples, she moaned again. When he gently sucked on them, caressing them with his tongue, she whispered his name, barely forming the sounds before they were lost.

As his tongue swirled around her bud, teasing it to pulsing erection, his hand slipped across her stomach to her jeans, moving over the coarse fabric and down her front. Jessica's body shook with surprise at his intimate touch, her legs stiffening.

Instinctively she grasped his wrist, but he held firm and warm against her private place, all the while his tongue provoking her to irresistible heights of excitement. Jessica pulled at his hand but only halfheartedly, liking the feel of him, yet fearing it. She began pulsing at his touch, her feminine reservoir growing dewy.

Spontaneously her pelvis lurched, seeking more intimate contact, penetration. Waves began to build deep inside her and Jessica, disbelieving, realized she was on the verge of climax. Her heart stumbled with excitement and she gasped as waves coursed from her breasts to her womb.

Suddenly her breathing grew short and she gasped for air. The night began to close in.

"No," she murmured, "please stop." Her heart was racing like a trip-hammer. She tried to lift her head but felt too weak. The sensation, the night, the fear, all combined against her and she gave a little cry of desperation.

Chase realized something was wrong. He moved his face near hers. "Jessica, are you okay?"

She only half heard the question, her mind wavering between the man beside her and the void. She forced open her eyes and saw the faint cyan sky above, an instant before the light melted into darkness.

JESSICA WAS FIRST AWARE of the cool grass against one cheek and Chase's warm fingers on the other. She felt the hard ground beneath her and opened her eyes. Hovering over her in the twilight, he looked down with concern and fear etched on his face.

"Jessica, are you all right?"

"What happened?" she murmured.

"Oh, thank God!" he whispered. "You're all right."

"Chase, did I faint?"

He smiled at her, relieved. "Yes, dead away. It must have been the climb up the hill and being pregnant."

Jessica touched her stomach and felt the fullness of her flesh through her clothing. Then she felt the twisted lump of her bra askew under her T-shirt. She examined his face, remembering the wild passion before she fainted.

Chase kissed her forehead. "You aren't hurt, are you?"

She shook her head. "No, I guess I just blacked out."

"Fortunately you were lying down." He lowered himself to his elbow beside her and looked into her eyes, relief having replaced the fear. Then he reached across and gathered her close against him, hugging her, sharing his warmth.

"Are you cold? Do you want to sit up?"

"I'm all right. Let me just rest for a minute."

He stroked her head.

"Were you worried about the baby?" she asked, her voice not much more than a whisper.

"I was worried about you."

She smiled weakly. After a moment her head felt clearer and she got up on her elbows. Below them in the falling darkness were the lights of the house, warm and inviting. Though the air was still comfortable, Jessica shivered, feeling their isolation. "Jamie's down there," she murmured. "He may be upset. I'd better get back."

THE WALK TO THE HOUSE was not difficult, but Chase never let go of her arm. Jessica felt fine physically, but her emotions were a maelstrom of confusion. She was a little tired by the time they climbed the steps and she used it as an excuse to go straight upstairs.

Jamie had already had his dinner and was quietly playing in his room when she looked in on him. Anne Bascom was happy to see her and quickly told the boy good-night.

Jamie was tired, too, so Jessica put him in his bed and read him a story from a large book of fairy tales, her mind completely oblivious to what she was reading. After three or four pages he fell asleep, and she thankfully turned out the light and crept from the room.

She had gotten into her nightgown and pulled back the bed covers, when there was a knock at her door.

"Who is it?"

"Chase."

"I was just getting into bed."

"I want to talk to you, Jessica."

The tone was commanding, insistent, and she decided she'd better hear what he had to say. She slipped on her old tattered bathrobe and went to the door. He stood outside, his expression strangely determined.

"How are you feeling?"

She stepped back to admit him. "I'm fine, really." Jessica felt anxious, knowing what had happened had been a terrible mistake. And she sensed he knew it, too.

"You fainted, though. That's not normal."

"It was just the exertion and the . . . excitement."

"I think we should call the doctor in the morning."

"It's nothing, really. Besides, I'm scheduled to go in for a checkup in a few days."

"Let's not take any chances." His voice was gentle, but firm.

Jessica was inclined to object to his insistence, but decided that what mattered at the moment was to end the conversation. Taking the course of least resistance, she acquiesced by nodding.

Chase was silent, letting his eyes slowly drift down her body. She felt uncomfortable.

"Don't be concerned about me. I'm okay."

"Are you?" His look was penetrating. "I don't mean physically."

She looked down, embarrassed. "Look, I'm awfully tired. I'd really like to go to bed."

"All right, if that's what you want."

She heard irritation in his voice and glanced up at him, but he had turned toward the door.

"I'll make the appointment with the doctor for as soon as he can take you." He stopped in the hall and looked back, his eyes raking her possessively. "See you in the morning."

JESSICA LAY IN BED, staring into the darkness for a long time after Chase had gone. She couldn't believe what had happened, but in another sense it seemed almost inevitable. The sexual tension between them had been so intense—it was like a good fight that needed to occur. And now that it was over, it could be forgotten. She was determined to forget. But could Chase?

They hadn't made love, and that undoubtedly left him frustrated. But he had succeeded in arousing her passion, in making her want him—and that was, after all, what a man really needed emotionally. Now that he had gotten it, maybe he would leave her be.

Jessica sighed. It was not an easy situation—being virtually locked up with a man whom she found attractive and who had designs on her. It was not a position a woman ought to be in, unless she was prepared to do something about it.

And if nothing else was clear, Jessica knew full well that she couldn't become emotionally involved with Chase Hamilton, not seriously. To do so would be disastrous.

She was bound to him more closely, in a way, than a wife to a husband. Divorce was impossible, at least until the baby was delivered and her body was free.

And her son was like a hostage to Chase's generosity. Jamie could live without the benefits Chase offered, just as before, but to take him away from the farm now would be to deny him. She could only do that if there were no other choice.

Most troubling of all were her own feelings for the man. To love Chase would be to love the baby. And that, her emotional sanity wouldn't permit.

They were all bound together, each needing the other. Jessica needed to be loved for herself, not her role as a surrogate mother. Jamie needed a real father, not one who would pass with the season. Chase needed a surrogate wife, not just a surrogate mother for his child. And none of them was truly free to walk away, not—at least—for another seven months.

Jessica fantasized about running away. If she could go somewhere, have the baby and bring it to him, it would be so much easier. If only he would accept that. But she knew he wouldn't—willingly.

She tossed in her bed, her thoughts making her more and more anxious. One moment Chase was a demon, the next her lover, kissing her, making love to her on the hilltop.

If only she weren't pregnant. If only she were just herself in Chase's eyes. If only he didn't so fiercely love the other being inside of her. If only...

And then gradually, uneasily, Jessica slipped into a troubled sleep.

THE SKIES WERE LEADEN as Chase helped her into the Bentley. Jessica watched him walk around to the driver's side, feeling wary. Off in the distance there was a faint roll of thunder.

They hadn't really spoken yet that morning. Anne Bascom and Jamie had eaten breakfast with them, so there hadn't been much of an opportunity for Jessica to gauge his attitude. He was polite to a fault, which she had come to realize was his manner, but he betrayed no indication of his thinking. By the time they were to leave for the clinic, Jessica had grown quite nervous.

Without a word Chase drove out the long driveway to the road, then headed south for the trip into Manhattan. After a few minutes he turned to her.

"Since we'll be tied up at the clinic until nearly noon, I thought we might as well have lunch in the city."

"Thanks, Chase, but I've got plans."

He was surprised. "Oh?"

"Yes, Harriet and I were going to meet when I came in for my checkup. It's been sort of a standing date."

"I don't imagine Harriet would be upset if you missed it, would she?"

"I'd really like to see her."

Chase didn't reply. He just stared straight ahead at the road.

"Now that I'm living at the farm, I hardly have any life of my own," she explained. "It's important to me."

"Is that what it is?"

"What do you mean?"

"Are you sure it isn't what happened last night?"

Jessica didn't look at him. She watched the lightning flash in the distance. "Last night was a mistake. I thought that was obvious enough."

"There was nothing wrong in what happened."

"It's the sort of thing neither of us can afford."

"What's that supposed to mean?"

"I don't have to explain the nature of our relationship—you wrote the contract. What happened was just a loss of control on both our parts. I take my share of the blame."

"Loss of control? Is that what you think it was?" His voice had become angry.

"Well, I'm certainly mature enough to know the difference between sexual arousal and something more profound. I let myself get carried away like a silly teenager. I assume it was the same with you."

Chase gave an incredulous laugh. "I can't believe this."

"You can't believe what? That just because I slipped once I'm not ready to jump into bed with you and profess my undying love?"

"I don't see any need to degrade it."

"What are you trying to say—that it's just another aspect of my job? That I'm supposed to take it in stride that you tried to seduce me?"

"Now just a minute. What happened was as much your doing as it was mine. Don't try to make it sound like I took advantage of you. You wanted me every bit as much as I wanted you."

"You're right. I admitted my share of the blame. I gave you the wrong impression. You had no way of knowing that I'd separated you from your body, that it wasn't you I was making love with."

Chase shot her a withering look. "So that's what it is. You're the surrogate mother for the wife I've never had, and I'm the surrogate lover for your dead husband?"

Jessica looked back at him equally angrily. "No, Chase Hamilton, you'll never be a surrogate lover and you could never replace my husband. I'm human and I failed. I let you arouse me, but I'll never make that mistake again."

A hostile silence settled over them. They drove under threatening skies, neither of them speaking until they reached the clinic. After Jessica had her exam, Chase joined her in Dr. Duckett's office.

"I don't think the fainting spell is anything to be concerned about, Mr. Hamilton," the doctor said. "Chances are it was just a simple case of syncope—an oxygen deficiency in the brain. Mrs. Brandon said you'd just climbed a hill and that she was experiencing temporary dyspnea—difficulty breathing."

Chase and Jessica exchanged looks.

"So unless there's an unwarranted reoccurrence, I wouldn't be concerned." The doctor looked at her. "Exercise is good for you, but be careful not to overdo it."

The doctor proceeded to inform Chase that everything was progressing well and that the pregnancy seemed normal. They briefly discussed diet, and then Chase and Jessica got up to leave.

In the hallway he took her arm. "I suppose you didn't explain in detail what we were doing before you fainted."

"Of course not."

He cleared his throat. "It might have been a good idea to be candid with him in case there's a medical concern."

She gave him a sideward glance. "Exercise is exercise. You heard what he said. And I'm definitely not going to

be overdoing it, because I'm not going to be doing it
again—period."

Chase groaned with annoyance. They waited at the
elevator.

"I don't see why you're complaining. Our contract
states that I'm not to have intercourse during the pregnancy, and the prohibition didn't exclude you."

"There's no reason you have to be so gleeful about it."

The elevator came and they stepped inside the empty
car.

"Chase, sometimes I don't understand you at all.
What is it you want out of this deal—a sex partner as a
bonus free gift?"

"For one thing I'd like to avoid the hostility that sur-
rounds everything we seem to do."

"You're beginning to see why I didn't want to live with
you," Jessica said coldly.

The car arrived at the ground floor.

"Perhaps I am."

Outside it was raining heavily, the downpour so intense that the street was veiled in a curtain of rain.

"I'll drop you off wherever you're meeting Harriet,"
Chase said matter-of-factly.

"That won't be necessary."

"Jessica, don't be silly. You'll have trouble getting a
cab in this weather, and probably get soaked in the process."

She pushed on through the doors to the sidewalk.
Chase stepped out behind her just as a taxi pulled up at
the curb and disgorged a very pregnant woman.

"Here's my cab now," Jessica said with a little laugh,
and ran to the vehicle, helping the passenger out before
sliding into the dry interior. She looked out the rain-
streaked window at Chase Hamilton's glum face, feeling

sorry for him and taking pleasure in her triumph at the same time.

As they whisked away Jessica tried to forget her argument with the man, tried to think about her own life and her own needs. Seeing her one good friend was one of the few pleasures left to her. She wasn't going to spoil the occasion by worrying about Chase Hamilton.

THE TAXI TURNED DOWN west Fifty-first Street and, coming to a flooded area, slowed to a crawl. When they arrived at the bistro-style restaurant the driver pulled closer to the curb than was usual, and stopped.

"Watch your feet, miss," the cabbie said. "That ain't the East River out there—it just looks like it."

Jessica tipped the man an extra dollar and dashed inside Café des Sports. Harriet arrived five minutes later, her hair and face damp. They embraced.

"Lousy weather," Jessica said, "but it beats going to the salad bar."

"Thank God for wealthy clients!"

They laughed and followed the captain to their table.

"So," Harriet said, sitting down, "still have your girlish figure, I see."

"Not for long, I'm afraid."

"It seems your matron days are almost upon you, Jessica."

"Lord, don't make it sound so glamorous."

"Don't chastise *me*, love," Harriet teased. "I was the one who advised you to go back into modeling, remember? It was you who opted for muumuus and support stockings."

"I opted for a hundred thousand dollars, and you know it."

Say YES to free gifts worth over $20.00

Say YES to a rendezvous with romance, and you'll get 4 classic love stories—FREE! You'll get a lighted makeup mirror and brush kit—FREE! And you'll get a delightful surprise—FREE! These gifts carry a total value of over $20.00—but you can have them without spending even a penny!

MONEY-SAVING HOME DELIVERY!

Say YES to Harlequin's Reader Service, and you'll enjoy the convenience of previewing four brand-new books delivered right to your home months before they appear in stores. Each book is yours for only $2.50—25¢ less than the retail price.

SPECIAL EXTRAS—FREE!

You'll get our monthly newsletter, *Heart to Heart*—the indispensable insider's look at our most popular writers and their upcoming novels. Now you can have a behind-the-scenes look at the fascinating world of Harlequin! You'll also get additional free gifts from time to time as a token of our appreciation for being a home subscriber.

Say YES to a Harlequin love affair. Complete, detach and mail your Free Offer Card today!

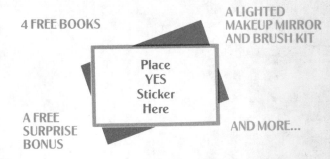

YOUR "NO RISK GUARANTEE"

- There's no obligation to buy—and the free books and gifts are yours to keep forever.
- You pay the lowest price possible and receive books before they appear in stores.
- You may end your subscription anytime—just write and let us know.

If offer card below is missing, write to Harlequin Reader Service,
901 Fuhrmann Blvd., P.O. Box 1394, Buffalo, NY 14240-9963

Just then the waiter arrived to take their drink orders. Harriet asked for a glass of white wine, and Jessica requested mineral water.

Harriet leaned back and studied Jessica for a moment. "So, how's it going?"

"Fine."

"Oh, come on, love. You know I'm dying to hear," Harriet coaxed. "Let's have it from the top."

Jessica smiled at the no-nonsense expression on her friend's face and told her about the walk in the evening air and the seduction.

"My God, Jessica, the man's in love."

"Oh, Harriet, he is not. He's completely taken up with his baby. I'm a favorite brood mare, that's all. He just got carried away, let himself get excited. Any affection he feels is for the mother of his child, not me."

"How can you be sure? Maybe you're not looking at it with an open mind."

"I am so. It's obvious."

The waiter appeared with their drinks, and Harriet sipped her wine. "How about you? How do you feel about him?"

Jessica hesitated. "I'm determined not to let my feelings develop into anything I'll regret."

"But that's not answering the question. Obviously you wouldn't have let him get as far as he did if you didn't care for him."

"It was just a physical thing. It meant nothing."

"I don't believe that for a minute."

"What makes *you* so sure?"

Harriet lowered her eyes. Jessica reached out and touched her friend's hand.

"I'm sorry. I didn't mean to snap. I'm afraid I've been testy with everyone lately." She bit her lip. "I hope to God I don't fall in love with him."

"But that would be wonderful!"

"No, it wouldn't. I'd suffer."

"Suffer? The man's obviously interested in you, too. For all you know he may be considering marriage."

"Even if he was that foolish, it could only be for the wrong reasons. Life for Chase Hamilton *is* breeding and nurturing. He's discovered that the mother of a baby is a little more special than the mother of a colt, and he's thinking it would be nice to have one of them, too. Besides, he's a man. When there's a woman to conquer, he can't pass up the challenge."

"Jessica," Harriet admonished, "don't be so cynical, for pete's sake."

She sighed. "Well, maybe I'm exaggerating. At best he's deceiving himself and I'm suffering because of it. Any affection or love he expresses is directed toward my *role*, not toward me."

"That's fear talking. I can't believe a man that sophisticated is unable to distinguish between you and your role. Obviously he wouldn't feel the same about *any* woman carrying his child."

"No, I suppose that's true," Jessica admitted. "But what woman wants to be loved because she's the mother of a man's child? Not me, Harriet. Thanks, but no, thanks."

"Well, even if the man is in love with the idea of a family, so what? You could do a lot worse."

Jessica sipped her water. "I may have been desperate enough to sell myself to Chase for nine months, but marriage is a whole different kettle of fish. You're talking lifetime, Harriet."

Jessica's friend gave her a disapproving look as the waiter approached again. "Whether you see it or not, that's your insecurity talking. You're just afraid he cares for you because of the baby—afraid you'll lose him when the luster of motherhood is gone."

"That's not true!"

They ordered and Harriet asked for another glass of wine. When the waiter had gone she looked slyly at her companion. "If I were in your shoes, love, I wouldn't give a damn one way or the other. I'd go for it."

Jessica looked at her, seeing the logic but knowing Harriet wasn't considering all the issues. "What about the baby? Aren't you forgetting him...her...it? I'm a surrogate mother, Harriet. My sanity depends on keeping this baby at a distance. How am I supposed to pursue the father and forget the child? That just makes no sense."

"What about later, after the birth?"

"I've thought of it, I'll admit. But can you imagine a relationship with a man who's living with a child you've emotionally carved out of your life? I can't."

Harriet looked forlorn. "If I'd known this would happen, I'd never have let you do it."

Jessica reached over and took her hand. "No, my goal is still valid. I'm going to paint my heart out, take his money and run. I just hope and pray he stays away and makes it easy for me."

Harriet picked up her fresh glass of wine when it was delivered and took a long drink. Putting it down, she looked at Jessica, started to say something, then thought better of it. She turned instead to the window and the pouring rain.

CHAPTER ELEVEN

FRESH MORNING AIR and a dappled sky had replaced the rain of the previous day when Jessica made her way along the muddy path leading to the carriage house. All morning and half the night she had wrestled with the events of the past two days, but despite her best efforts she was not able to put it all into perspective.

She had awakened early, even before Maggie was up, had fixed herself breakfast and decided to try to escape from it all in the studio. But the normally relaxing environment did nothing to quell the storm of anxiety that had been plaguing her.

Nevertheless, Jessica decided to plunge into her work and began preparing a fresh canvas. After securing it on her easel, she squeezed generous amounts of primary colors on her palette, then took a painting knife in hand. She stood for a long time just looking at the canvas, trying to summon up creative inspiration, though her mind refused to cooperate.

At the main house, Chase Hamilton descended the back steps, inhaling the fresh smells of moist earth and vegetation. On the path he saw Jessica's footprints in the soft soil, and smiled to himself at the thought of her fleeing.

When he came to the carriage house Chase looked in a window and saw Jessica at her easel. She was motionless, her feet positioned as though she were preparing for some sort of bold assault on the canvas. As he watched her, she scraped up two colors at once and extended her hand to the top right corner of the blank canvas, then pulled the knife diagonally to the lower left.

She stepped back, studied the result, then made several more bold strokes, seemingly with as much concern for emotional expression as for visual effect. Fascinated, Chase observed as she continued, stopping occasionally to examine the results before attacking the canvas again.

Jessica had applied much more paint than Chase thought warranted, but she didn't appear satisfied. After watching her make another slash at the canvas, he decided to go inside.

She glanced up as he entered, then turned back to her work. Smearing in an offending blob of paint, she refused to look at him again.

"I've been watching you work," he volunteered.

No reply.

"Unusual technique you have."

"This is my therapy as well as my work," she said dryly.

"It would seem so."

Jessica spread more paint over the canvas.

"I'll be leaving for the city in a while and thought I'd come out and see you before I left."

"Why's that?"

"I had dinner with some people last night and it occurred to me I didn't know what to tell them about you."

She looked at him. "What do you mean?"

"We haven't discussed how we're representing our relationship to the outside world—that sort of thing."

"There's no great mystery, is there? I'm the surrogate mother to your child."

"Well, yes. It's just that I didn't want to embarrass you if I introduced you that way."

"Do you expect to be introducing me to anyone?"

Chase looked at her in profile, examining her slender figure. Recollections of her half-naked in the grass flashed through his mind. A pang of desire followed by regret washed over him.

It had been stupid to be intimate with her, to kiss her, to let his natural feelings rule him, but the impulse wasn't an easy one to ignore. Although her desire for him had been as strong as his, he did feel guilty. Her distress over the incident was apparent.

When he didn't answer, Jessica glanced at him.

"I was invited to a gallery opening last night and I didn't know how to explain I'd be bringing you as my guest."

"There's no need to take me, and therefore no reason to explain."

"Since art is your business—your career—I thought it would be a good opportunity for you. It wasn't for selfish reasons, Jessica."

She turned to him and sighed. "I'm sorry. I didn't mean to sound ungrateful. It's just that it's difficult to live this way."

"I know. That's why I wanted to talk to you. It won't be long before you begin to show. If we're out together, like at this gallery opening, or if I have people over, an explanation may be called for. I didn't want to say anything without conferring with you first—make sure you're comfortable with the way it's presented."

"How do you want to present it?"

"Unless you have an objection, I thought we ought to announce the baby."

She turned to him. "You don't really mean announce, do you . . . as in announcement?"

Chase grinned. "Not in the sense of printed up and sent to everyone we know. I just thought I'd let it be known so that you aren't subjected to embarrassment. We can't pretend I'm running a home for unwed mothers, can we?"

She gave him a disapproving look. "That wasn't funny."

Chase shrugged. "Sorry." He watched her, feeling the distance between them, not liking the way things had gone in the past couple of days.

"Say whatever you want. The people that matter to me already know. If I'm an embarrassment to you, I can certainly stay in the closet."

He stepped closer to her. "I don't give a damn about appearances or what anybody thinks. What we do is our business. As a matter of fact, I'm rather proud of what we've done. It's just that I'm not the only one concerned. That's why I wanted to talk to you."

Jessica could see that he was sincere and it made her feel good in a funny sort of way. But she could see another emotion on his face, as well—the sort of thing that had preceded their walk up the hill. Wanting to nip it in the bud, she moved past him to the window, putting a little more space between them.

Chase didn't say anything, but she felt his presence intensely. Still, she looked out at the green hills, not wanting to face him. "I'll leave whatever is said entirely up to you," she finally volunteered.

"Good. I've already accepted the invitation to the opening of Carlos Cordena's gallery. It'll be in October, right after I get back from the races at Keeneland. You probably won't be showing much by then, but if the matter comes up, the baby's mine.''

Jessica turned around slowly. Chase had made his pronouncement with such assurance that she knew he had intended the outcome from the beginning of the conversation.

He was looking at her canvas. ''There'll be lots of people there you ought to meet, and probably a number you already know. It wouldn't hurt to do a little networking. There's politics involved in being a commercially successful artist, you know.''

She watched Chase's face as he contemplated her work, and wondered if he realized that it was just an expression of emotion, not a painting. After several moments he left her easel and walked toward the door, pausing to tweak her cheek.

''I think I prefer your other style, Jessica.''

THE REST OF THE MORNING was a virtual loss. Jessica couldn't get Chase Hamilton out of her mind. He was constantly there, whether as villain, friend, employer or lover.

At noon she had a quiet lunch with Jamie, who told her all about the new therapy program Mr. Valticos had started, though much was lost in the telling. Maggie informed them that Chase was staying in town on business and wouldn't be home for dinner. Jessica was glad for the reprieve.

After lunch she took Jamie out to see his pony. Supplied with some sugar cubes Maggie had given them, they managed to lure the animal to the fence, where the boy was able to pet him. Jamie begged Jessica to take him for a ride, but she didn't feel comfortable with the idea. She resolved to have Chase teach her how to drive the cart.

When it came time for Jamie's nap Jessica took him into the house, then went back out to her studio to try to find inspiration. She hadn't been there long, when Helmut Geisel called to ask if he might come out the next day to have a look at her work. A wave of panic rushed through her, but she knew he would have to see her paintings eventually. If for any reason her work was unsatisfactory, better she know now than later, after she had put months into the effort.

"What's a good time, Jessica?"

The lilt to his voice always made her feel uncomfortable. "At your convenience. I'll be here all day."

"I have an early appointment here at my salon, but I could be up there by late morning."

"That would be fine. In fact, why not come for lunch?"

"Mr. Hamilton wouldn't mind?"

The question struck Jessica as strange, then she wondered if he was interpreting the invitation as some sort of improper suggestion. It made no sense, but she decided to quash any doubt. "I have the use of the facilities here for my business needs, Mr. Geisel. Chase doesn't mind if I have a business lunch. Besides, there are no public restaurants nearby." She'd never discussed the matter with Chase, but she was sure he wouldn't mind, and Maggie was too good-natured to object to the extra work.

"Lunch would be most enjoyable, Jessica. Next time, though, you will be my guest."

"Yes, thank you." She realized now that what pleased him was the excuse to reciprocate. She rolled her eyes, hoping Helmut Geisel wouldn't be a problem to her in *that* regard. She wondered whether there was any chance Chase would be around the next day and might join them.

They ended the conversation, and Jessica went to her finished paintings and began examining them with a critical eye. Doubts started assaulting her. She removed the canvas she had used for her artistic tantrum that morning and placed it in the closet, out of sight. Then she took a fresh one and fastened it on the easel.

As she stared at it for a time, her worst fears were realized. No inspiration whatsoever came. Near panic seized her. Jessica knew she couldn't possibly finish another piece by the next day when Geisel arrived, but it would be nice to have something in progress. Nervously she went to her sketchbook and began thumbing through the pages.

IT WAS AFTER TEN by the time Chase came in the front door that night. Everyone seemed to be in bed and he was tired himself. The business dinner he had had that evening was dull and the food uninspired. Though he didn't normally have late-night snacks he was hungry, and went to the kitchen.

He was rummaging around in the refrigerator, when Maggie came in from her adjoining rooms.

"Oh, Mr. Hamilton, it's you. I was wonderin' who'd be in the kitchen this time of night."

"Hope I didn't disturb you, Maggie. I just got home and was hungry. Thought I'd see what I could dig up. Any interesting leftovers?"

"There's always somethin', sir. But why don't you let me fix you a proper meal?"

"No need for that. Besides, I'm perfectly capable of fixing something for myself."

"Yes, sir, you are, indeed. But I wouldn't feel right sittin' at the telly while you're here in my kitchen."

Chase could see he had been outmaneuvered, so he went to the table and sat down.

"There's cream of broccoli soup left over from dinner and some fresh baked bread, or some of that coconut cake you like so well, if you'd prefer a dessert, Mr. Hamilton."

"The cake sounds good."

The housekeeper smiled knowingly. Chase grinned to himself. He liked pleasing her, and her coconut cake was fabulous.

"Would you like a cup of coffee with your cake, then?" she asked as she began bustling about the kitchen.

"If you'll join me, I will. Otherwise it's not worth the trouble."

Maggie looked at him with surprise.

Chase had always maintained a very formal relationship with the housekeeper. They never ate together, but with Jessica in the house he felt the need to keep the lines of communication open. "I thought we might chat for a while," he explained.

"About Mrs. Brandon and the boy?"

Chase hadn't realized he was so transparent. "I was hoping you could give me the benefit of your insights."

Maggie nodded. She was getting cups and saucers from the cupboard. "Would you care to wait for me to brew you a pot of coffee, Mr. Hamilton?"

"Not for me, no. Instant's fine, unless you'd prefer the brewed."

"I'll be havin' tea myself, sir."

Chase waited until Maggie brought the coffee and cake to the table. She sat down opposite him, obviously feeling a little uncomfortable at being with her employer in such informal circumstances.

"How do you think Mrs. Brandon and Jamie are doing, Maggie? Are they adjusting well?"

"Oh, yes, sir. She works in her studio like a demon, she does. And the boy seems real content with Anne."

"No problems you've noted?"

Maggie looked a little embarrassed. "To be honest, sir, I don't think she's pleased with the list of foods you've given her to choose from. Resents it, I believe, sir."

Chase smiled. "I'm not surprised."

"She asked me to do something a little special for her lunch tomorrow with the gentleman art dealer, but apart from that she's agreed to eat what's on your list."

"Art dealer?"

"Oh, I thought you were aware, sir. Mrs. Brandon is having the gentleman to lunch. He's coming to see her paintings tomorrow."

"Geisel?"

"I think that's his name." Maggie put her hand to her mouth. "I hope I didn't say somethin' I wasn't supposed to be talkin' of, Mr. Hamilton."

"No, no. I'm sure Mrs. Brandon intended to speak to me about it. When was this arranged? Do you know?"

"Just today, sir. She spoke with me about it at supper."

Chase nodded and took a big bite of Maggie's coconut cake. He ate enthusiastically, but his mind was on Jessica and Geisel. Surprisingly, he felt a pang of jealousy.

The housekeeper was watching him closely.

"You make damned good cake, Maggie."

Her cheeks turned red. Chase grinned at her, but he was already thinking about Jessica again. He had intended to go into town the next morning, but now he considered changing his plans and staying at the farm.

JESSICA DIDN'T COME DOWN for breakfast the next morning, so Chase ate alone with Jamie. As usual the boy talked about the pony cart, so Chase promised him they'd go for a ride after his physical therapy session with Mr. Valticos.

While Jamie was upstairs, Chase worked in his study, making calls and reviewing financial reports. He glanced out the window from time to time, hoping to see Jessica going out to her studio, but he didn't. He wondered if she was spending the entire morning getting herself ready for Geisel's visit.

Though the dealer was highly respected, Chase had never cared much for him. Something about the man did not inspire confidence. And he did have a reputation for preying on women, particularly young attractive ones, though Chase saw no reason that he ought to succeed, apart from his money.

Jessica did not seem like the type who would be impressed by Geisel, but the man was an important figure in the art world. Perhaps that would create an interest that his "charm" failed to evoke.

He stared at the page of figures before him, then got up from his desk and went to the window. Though he had no real justification, he felt a little angry with Jessica. What was it about her that kept pulling him off the course he had set? Every time he'd put her in the compartment of his mind he wanted her in, she'd slip out and present him with a fresh dilemma. Maybe he was the one who'd been naive about wanting her to live with him on the farm....

There was a knock at his door, and Chase turned to see Anne Bascom. Jamie was in her arms. "Young Master Brandon is ready for the pony ride if you are, Mr. Hamilton."

Chase looked at his watch. "Yes, Anne, that would be fine." He walked to the door and took the boy from her. "Well, my friend, what do you say we go for a ride?"

"Oh, boy!" Jamie exclaimed.

Chase and Miss Bascom laughed.

A moment later the man and boy were headed for the back door, when Chase heard the doorbell. Maggie came running out of the kitchen past them.

"That'll be Mrs. Brandon's guest," she said, puffing.

Chase paused, considered going to the front hall to chat with Geisel until Jessica came down, then changed his mind and headed out the back door.

HELMUT GEISEL WALKED SLOWLY along the wall of the studio where Jessica's paintings stood, pausing to contemplate each canvas for a moment. He had been at it for what seemed an eternity and Jessica was so nervous she felt faint. She had hardly eaten a bite of lunch, barely able to await his verdict. Standing behind him, she was mouthing a silent prayer, watching the man's stubby body for signs of a reaction. She saw none.

Jessica glanced out the window and saw Chase astride one of his horses, apparently heading out for a ride. Anne had said he had stayed home that day, but somehow she hadn't expected to see him.

He looked good to her just then. And rather than seeming a danger as he frequently did, he struck her as a very friendly force. She wished he would come into the studio and be with her as she dealt with Geisel. Yet even as she wished it, she saw the irony in the desire.

"Very interesting," Geisel said, more to himself than to Jessica. He pointed at one of the canvases, his diamond ring sparkling in the sunlight streaming in the window. "This one in particular I like. It's a marvelous piece."

Jessica let out a sigh of relief. A ray of hope.

"That one," he said, pointing to another, "and the one on the end should be on my walls, too. But these others are not of the same quality."

She felt her heart sink.

"Of course that is only my opinion." He turned to her, a smile on his fat lips. "But some people say my opinion is worth noting."

Jessica nodded. "Of course it is." She glanced out the window again, but Chase had disappeared.

The art dealer looked her up and down, much as he had the paintings.

"What do you think, then?"

Geisel gestured with his ring. "For a show you have a long way to go—in numbers, I mean. But I am encouraged with what I see. Twenty more like your five best and you will have a very important premier exhibit."

"Twenty?"

"Twenty good ones, my dear. I suggest you aim for thirty-five."

"I don't think I can do that many. Not before . . ."

Geisel moved toward her, his expression avaricious. He reached up to caress her cheek with his fingers. "Not before what?"

Jessica shivered at his touch. She remembered her conversation with Chase about announcing the baby. He did say he had nothing to hide. She looked squarely at the art dealer. "Not before I have my baby."

"Baby?" Geisel's hand dropped immediately, his face contorting with surprise.

"Yes, Helmut. I'm pregnant."

The man stood for a moment in stunned silence. "It would be indiscreet of me to inquire as to the father, I would imagine."

"No. I think it's obvious enough. It's Chase Hamilton."

Geisel looked at her blankly. "Chase is a man of many talents. And like me, he has a good eye."

Jessica started to explain that she was just a surrogate mother to Chase's baby, but on an impulse she decided not to say anything.

After another pointed examination of her body, the dealer turned again to the canvases against the wall. "If you are unable to have a show ready before your...baby, you can always complete the necessary work afterward, no?"

"I would really prefer to finish before the birth."

"Well, I suppose that is up to you. All I can do is render a judgment on what you offer me."

"Yes, I plan to get as much accomplished as possible in the next few months."

Geisel smiled. "I understand the last weeks can be difficult." He looked at his watch. "Well, I've had a delightful lunch and you've shown me some impressive paintings." He glanced once more at his favorite. "It's time I be on my way."

Jessica followed him to the door. She looked out the window toward the barnyard as she walked, but Chase was nowhere in sight.

Outside it was warm but the fast-approaching days of autumn were clearly in the air. They walked along the path toward the house.

"When is your baby due, if I may ask, Jessica?"

"The end of March."

"You have a long time to go, then."

"Yes."

They walked in silence for a while.

"Would it be indiscreet of me to ask whether there is a prospect of marriage?"

They came to Geisel's car.

"No, there won't be any marriage."

"I see."

The art dealer turned to her, extending his hand. "Again, thank you for a delightful afternoon." Pulling Jessica's fingers to his mouth, he kissed them with exaggerated ceremony. He grinned at her. "Please extend my congratulations to Chase, my dear."

She nodded and watched the man open the car door and slide onto the seat. Geisel started the engine, waved and was gone.

Jessica turned away, a terribly empty feeling in the pit of her stomach. As she started back the way she had come, she glanced up and saw Chase astride his horse. One look at the man's face and she realized he had been watching.

DURING THE NEXT FEW WEEKS Jessica did not see much of Chase. They never talked about Helmut Geisel's visit, and a strange sort of formality pervaded their every encounter. The two of them and Jamie were sometimes together in the evenings, they took meals together when the occasion arose, but Chase was often gone, and Jessica devoted as much time as possible to her work.

September came and went, ushering in the shorter days of fall, the brisk mornings and the first of the autumn colors in the leaves. At the beginning of October Chase left for Kentucky to prepare for the races at Keeneland.

Several days after Chase's departure, Jessica decided to do a few portraits to add variety to her collection for the show. She chose Jamie as her first subject.

She took him out to the studio with her, propped him up on a chest and began a portrait of him, Jessica had brought along his horse, Velvet, and several other toys for distraction, and Jamie cooperated, playing quietly without being overly active.

They had only been at work for half an hour or so, when Meade Phillips tapped on the door and stepped into the studio.

"Hope I'm not interrupting, Jessica."

"Hi, Meade. No, come on in. I could use a little break." She pushed up the sleeves of her painting smock and looked at the woman. Meade was wearing a beige jersey dress and matching pumps. A forest-green scarf was draped around her neck.

"Ooo...the fumes, how do you stand them?" Meade asked, wrinkling her nose. "Didn't Chase install a fan? I had suggested it."

Jessica's eyebrows rose. "Oh, that was your idea." She gestured toward the ceiling. "There's a fan. I just didn't bother to turn it on this morning."

Meade walked over to the switch on the wall and flipped it. Then she went to where Jamie sat on the chest.

"How's the little man today?" She stroked the child's cheek as he looked at her with a smile. "So, did my brother run off and leave you again?" Meade asked, turning to Jessica.

"He's in Lexington for the races."

"Why didn't he take you? Heaven knows you could have used a change of scene."

"Meade, I'm not his wife. He didn't take me for the same reason he didn't take Maggie."

"I'm not so sure you're right about that. Chase is a lot more fond of you than you realize. Not that he's told me so," she quickly added, "but I can tell."

"Neither of us wants or needs encouragement in that regard."

"Oh, there I go again." Meade walked over to where Jessica stood at her easel. She touched her shoulder. "I'm as bad as a meddling in-law, aren't I? I hope you can forgive me. I've really tried to stay away and not interfere, but believe me, it's not easy."

"There's no reason to stay away, Meade."

"To be honest, it's not just because of my big mouth that I say that. If I'm around you much, I'll get addicted to this pregnancy business and want to be over all the time to get a vicarious fix of premotherhood."

"As far as I'm concerned, you're always welcome."

Meade patted Jessica's arm. "I promise not to be too doting, but if I do get out of line just let me know."

"That's very sweet." She contemplated the woman, wondering just how much Chase had told her about recent events, exactly what she knew.

Meade studied Jessica's canvas for a moment.

"Incidentally," Meade said, gesturing toward the paintings against the wall, "I like your work a lot. You're really very talented. Very prolific—in more ways than one."

Meade laughed, but Jessica heard a subtle touch of jealousy in her voice. She wondered whether that might not end up being a problem between them. "Any word on your own situation, Meade?"

"I'm having the laparoscopy in a couple weeks. Needless to say that will be my moment of truth."

Jessica looked at her questioningly.

"It's where they make a tiny incision in your abdomen and look inside with a microscope. Scary, isn't it," Meade said, "how one little thing like that can become so pivotal to your whole life?"

"I'm sure it will work out all right for you."

Meade smiled. "I wish I had your confidence."

They were looking at each other, the emotion playing on their faces, when they heard a little cry from Jamie, then a thump. Jessica whirled around and saw her son crumpled on the floor, motionless.

"My God!" Meade cried. They both rushed to the boy.

Jessica bent over him, stifling a little cry of anguish. "Jamie," she whispered, "where does it hurt? Tell Mommy where it hurts."

He sobbed a little in response, but didn't speak.

"He may be hurt badly," Meade said, "maybe you shouldn't move him. I'll call an ambulance."

As Meade ran to the phone Jessica knelt over her son, wringing her hands. She drew her mouth close to his ear.

"Jamie, Mommy is going to call the doctor. You rest and hold real still." She stroked his cheek. "Don't try to move, darling. Don't try to move."

Seeing her son's crumpled body, Jessica felt nauseous. She heard Meade imploring that an ambulance be sent. The fright in her voice made Jessica feel faint.

It was just like that evening with Chase on the hilltop. But this time she couldn't pass out. The glassy look in Jamie's eyes told her how important it was that she be there for him. Willing away the darkness that was threatening, she fought off her tears. For his sake she knew she mustn't cry.

CHAPTER TWELVE

JESSICA SAT IN THE WAITING ROOM of the hospital in Mount Kisco, staring blankly at the wall. It was late afternoon and Meade had been with her all day. The attending physician in the emergency room didn't know what was wrong with Jamie, except that it wasn't a fracture. His back and neck—which Jessica had been sure were broken—were okay. For the past hour the boy had been undergoing tests with a specialist.

There were tear streaks on Jessica's cheeks, and every once in a while a fresh tear would spill over and run down until she dabbed it with a tissue. She was sure Jamie was terribly injured. It was entirely her fault; she never should have put him on the chest.

"Jessica," Meade said softly, "I really think you ought to have something to eat. You've missed lunch and it will be a while before Jamie's out. You can't do anything here."

"No, I've got to stay. I can't leave."

Meade sighed. "Don't torture yourself. Jamie will be all right. I'm sure of it."

Jessica shook her head. "It's all my fault."

"No, if it's anybody's fault, it's mine. I interrupted you. I interfered. It wouldn't have happened if I hadn't come in and distracted you."

"I'm responsible, Meade. It was stupid to put him on that chest."

"You had no way of knowing."

Jessica looked at her hands in her lap.

"Come on. Let's get something to eat."

She just shook her head in reply.

"Can I bring you something, then?"

"I'm not hungry."

"Well, I'm bringing you something, anyway." Meade rose to her feet, looked at Jessica sympathetically and left.

Ten minutes later Jessica was still staring down at her hands, when she sensed someone in the doorway. She turned, expecting to see the doctor, but instead saw Chase Hamilton. She slowly stood.

In an instant he was there, taking her into his arms, holding her.

She began crying, the emotion spilling out spontaneously. Chase stroked her head.

"How did you know?" she sobbed.

"Meade called this morning. I got on the first flight."

Jessica rested her head on his shoulder, feeling protected. He kissed her forehead. "You didn't have to come, Chase."

"Of course I did. How is he?"

"They don't know what's wrong yet. He's having tests."

Chase led her to the couch and they sat down side by side, his arm around her shoulders. "Where's Meade?"

"She went out to eat."

"Have you eaten?"

"No, Meade's bringing me something."

He brushed wisps of hair off her face.

"I've hurt Jamie, Chase. I've hurt my son."

"Of course you haven't hurt him. It was an accident."

"I was foolish."

"It was an accident." He took out his handkerchief and dabbed her cheeks.

Jessica looked up at him. "Do you think he'll be all right?"

"I don't know, we'll have to wait and see."

"I'm so glad you're here," she said simply. "I'm glad you came back."

A moment later a doctor came into the waiting room and walked toward them. As they rose, the doctor looked at Chase, who had put his arm around Jessica.

"Oh, are you Mr. Brandon?"

"No, I'm a friend of the family."

The doctor glanced at Jessica.

"My husband's dead," she explained.

"I see. Well, the news about your son seems to be good. He suffered a concussion, but there doesn't appear to be major damage. Head injuries in children can be very tricky, though, so I'd like to keep him in the hospital overnight for observation."

"It's not serious, then?"

"It doesn't appear to be, but we want to make sure."

Jessica made a little joyful sound, then turned and hugged Chase.

"Would you like to see your son before we send him up to pediatrics?" the doctor asked.

"Oh, yes, please."

He looked at Chase. "You can come in, too, if you like."

They followed the doctor to the ward, where he directed them to Jamie and left.

The boy was lying down, an ice pack against the side of his head. The nurse at his side smiled as they approached. "He's got a bad bump and a headache," she explained. "Doctor ordered a sedative, so he may seem a little groggy."

Jamie lifted his arms to Jessica and shook his hands feebly, conveying his eagerness to touch her.

"Mommy..."

She leaned over and pressed her face against his. Seeing them together, Chase felt a lump in his throat. He stood at the foot of the bed as mother and son whispered endearments. Finally Jessica stood upright, a fresh gloss of tears in her eyes. She looked relieved, grateful.

"Mrs. Brandon," the nurse said, "you can go with him up to pediatrics if you like."

Jessica nodded her gratitude and looked at Chase.

"You go on with Jamie. Meade and I'll come and say hello after you've settled him in."

CHASE HANDED THE CLERK a large bill and looked at the giant stuffed panda while he waited for his change. When the woman had counted out the money he put the over-size beast under his arm and turned to Meade, who stood behind him, smiling. They headed for the elevator.

Jessica and Jamie were chatting when they stepped into the room. The boy's eyes rounded at the sight of the panda. Chase stopped at the foot of the bed and held the bear up in front of his face. With a funny voice he said, "Is this Jamie Brandon's room?"

"Yeah!" came the reply.

"Is there a place for me in the bed, too?"

Jamie giggled and Chase peeked out from behind the toy. He handed it to the boy.

"He's bigger than Jamie," Jessica exclaimed, smiling happily at Meade.

The child squeezed the stuffed animal with enthusiasm.

"Aren't you going to thank Chase, Jamie?"

"Thank you," he said in a little singsong voice.

"You're welcome."

Chase put his arm around Jessica's shoulders. "Do you suppose the patient will live?"

"I believe his prospects just improved dramatically."

Chase put his hand on Jamie's shoulder. "Do you like your bear?"

The child nodded and patted the stuffed animal.

"He's a present from Auntie Meade and me. We hope you feel better and that your head stops hurting."

"Okay," Jamie said compliantly.

They all laughed.

Just then a nurse came in the room. "Doctor doesn't want Jamie to get too excited," she said in a kind but firm voice. "He should get some rest, Mrs. Brandon. You can come back and see him this evening, but to tell you the truth, I think he'll sleep right through to morning. You might be better off to rest yourself and come back bright and early. He'll be having breakfast at about eight." The nurse touched Jessica's arm. "Jamie will be just fine."

While Chase and Meade waited, Jessica kissed her son again, then hesitantly started across the room, pausing at the door to look back. Seeing him hugging his bear, she felt better. It was as though the entire weight of the world had been lifted in a single stroke.

WHEN THEY GOT BACK to the farm Meade declined Chase's offer to come in for a drink, saying she had to get home to Roger. The house was dark when they went inside.

"Where is everyone?" Jessica asked.

"It's Anne's day off, of course, and I called Maggie from the airport and told her to take off, too, if she wanted. Apparently she decided to take me up on it." They made their way back to the kitchen.

"Who'll fix your dinner?" Jessica chided.

"*I* plan on fixing dinner for both of us."

"You?"

"I'm not the unenlightened man I appear."

She laughed. "Do you know how to cook bean curds and tofu?"

Chase grimaced. "I suppose that's a comment on my dietary plan."

"It's a comment on your unrelenting paternalism."

"Well, maybe an occasional traditional meal wouldn't hurt," he conceded.

"Like when you have to eat it, too?"

Chase shrugged sheepishly.

"I can see you're of the 'do as I say, not as I do' school."

"If *I* were pregnant, Jessica—"

"Ha! That one was nicely planned."

He slipped his arms around her waist and looked down into her eyes. "Can I help it if I'm a man?"

Suddenly filled with awareness of him, Jessica didn't bother to answer the question.

He broke the long silence. "You look tired."

"I am."

He took her to the table and pulled out a chair for her. When she was seated, he moved behind her, put his hands on her shoulders and began massaging. Jessica gave a soft moan of pleasure as his thumbs eased into the corded muscles of her back.

"You're really tense."

"I was scared to death when Jamie fell. It's as if I didn't take a breath all afternoon." It was true, but the tension she felt just then was more a result of his fingers on her flesh than the day's events.

"Does this feel good?"

"Mmm. Wonderful."

Chase continued his rhythmic manipulations and Jessica began realizing what she had been missing during their recent estrangement. It felt good—too good—because she knew that with the passage of each delicious second the danger increased.

Reaching up, she grasped his wrists and gently pulled his hands away. "You'd better stop, or I'll fall asleep." She smiled up at him. "Wouldn't it be a shame if you had to eat all the tofu by yourself?"

He chuckled. "My intentions were good in arranging that diet."

"I think there's a saying about good intentions," she said, rising.

Chase furrowed his brow, trying to remember.

"Something about the road to hell . . ."

He grinned. "Surely you don't see me as that sinister."

"You may not be sinister, but you don't make it easy for me."

He didn't respond. He just stood there, unspoken thoughts and emotions tugging at the corners of his mouth. After a long moment he spoke.

"Tell you what, while I start dinner why don't you go upstairs and get into something comfortable?"

"You're as stubborn as a mule, Chase Hamilton. Are you sure it's horses you breed?"

He threw back his head and laughed. "Go on upstairs. I'm going to make you my famous tortellini."

Jessica left, sensing somehow that wasn't all he had in mind.

JESSICA WEARILY STEPPED into her nightgown. Outside twilight had fallen and the house was strangely silent. With Jamie in the hospital she felt alone and vulnerable. Without her son to care for and love there was no reason to be strong. For the first time in a long time, she focused on her own needs.

As she slipped on the new bathrobe she had bought to replace her tattered old one, she wondered about Chase's feelings for her. What did he really feel? Pity? Desire? Did he see her as a woman and sense *her* needs? Or did he just feel concern for the vessel that was carrying his child?

Wondering about him made Jessica anxious, desirous. In a way she felt empty—incomplete without his company and comfort. Seeing him at the hospital in her moment of need brought that home to her, more even than the estrangement. The feeling was not unfamiliar, though. It had been a similar craving that had caused her to marry Alex, a similar need.

She reflected on the emotions swirling inside, thought of Chase Hamilton's arms around her at the hospital, the feel of his warm, strong body. She realized that the desire she felt was not a result of weakness, and yet it was no less to be feared. Needing him, she knew, robbed her of her control. It was dangerous to want a man. And yet she did.

Jessica descended the stairs to the kitchen, where Chase was hard at work. He had put on one of Maggie's aprons and looked rather silly in a tie and dress shirt with the flowered fabric wrapped around him. But in a way the incongruity was appropriate. Chase Hamilton was a web of incongruities.

He didn't see her for a moment, enabling her to study him, to admire his attractive masculine countenance. His broad shoulders brought to mind their lovemaking and her heart began beating heavily in response. As she looked at him, she was unsure of her feelings and what they meant.

"Well, there you are!" he said, noticing her at last. "Feeling better?"

She nodded. "Yes. Much." She went to the counter to watch him dump spinach tortellini into a pan of boiling water. "Can I help?"

"No, you take it easy. I'm cooking tonight."

Chase stepped over to the table and pulled out a chair for her, obviously wanting her to rest. With an ironic little grin on her face Jessica sat down.

"I'll bet you're like this with your horses when they're expecting."

"My horses are strictly business, and the only emotion involved is pride," he said, returning to the stove.

"What emotion is involved here?"

He half turned, contemplating her. "Concern," he said, after a moment.

Jessica felt embarrassed over having asked the question. What was it that always made her want to provoke and challenge him?

"Does that bother you?" he asked.

"What?"

"That I'm concerned about you."

"No, I'd be surprised if you weren't. After all, you've invested a lot in this baby of yours."

"Ours."

"Yours. I'm just a temporary participant."

Chase stared at her, but said nothing.

Jessica noticed a bottle on the counter next to him. "Is that wine?"

"Alcohol-free wine. It's only grape juice, but they've managed to make it taste fairly authentic," he replied.

"Aren't you going to have some of the real thing? After all, *you*'re not pregnant."

"I couldn't let you sacrifice alone, could I?"

Jessica suddenly felt wicked. "But Chase, there are so many things I have to do without because of this baby. You don't plan on depriving yourself of *everything*, do you?"

His wide mouth twisted in amusement. "If that's an oblique reference to sex, Mrs. Brandon, as you've pointed out, our contract calls for your abstinence, not mine. What I do is my business."

Jessica's eyebrows rose. "But my sex life is your business? Is that it?"

Chase seemed even more amused. He shrugged. "That was our deal, as I recall."

"Well, damn our deal!" Her temper had flared, even though she knew he was teasing her. And the pleasure he was taking in it made her even more angry.

"Are you feeling deprived? Is that the problem?"

"Deprived? Me?" Jessica forced herself to remain calm. "I think your arrogance has blinded you, Mr. Hamilton. I'm sure most women will tell you they can get along a lot better without a man than the reverse."

Chase turned to look at her and she could see by his expression that he was thinking about their lovemaking. "I don't think you're at all suited for celibacy, Jessica. At least not for the longer term."

"The longer term is *my* business. You only bought me for nine months."

He looked at her calmly, his eyes telling her he wanted to end the tension. "I apologize if I offended you. That's the last thing I want to do."

She trembled in response to the intimacy of his tone. Turning, she looked at the clock on the wall. "Jamie should be asleep by now. Maybe I'll call the hospital and make sure he's all right."

AFTER FINISHING DESSERT, they wandered into the sitting room.

"It's not exactly cold yet," Chase said, "but it is fall. How about having the first fire of the season?"

"That would be nice." Jessica sat on one of the twin couches as he knelt to build the fire. "You know, I've never lived in a house with a fireplace before."

He glanced over his shoulder. "Oh? Well, it's not as common in Manhattan as in the country."

"It's not just that. I've never had the money to afford a place with that sort of amenity."

"Not even during your marriage?"

"No, Alex and I were never rich. We lived from month to month." She chuckled. "When Jamie came along it just about broke our budget."

"You've never really talked about your husband. What did he do?"

"Alex was a free-lance writer. He paid the bills by writing articles for magazines, but that wasn't what he wanted to do. He saw himself as a playwright, at least that was his dream. Unfortunately he didn't live to prove he could do it."

Chase was just about finished building the fire. "Would he have made it?"

"Funny thing is, I don't know. I'd like to say yes, that I believed in him totally, but the truth is I wasn't sure."

"You weren't sure of him as a person or as a writer?"

Jessica looked at him, wondering if he knew how profound his question was. "Why did you ask that?"

"What do you mean?"

"Was there something in what I said about Alex that made you ask whether I believed in him as a person?"

Chase struck a match, then watched for a moment as the flames flared. When it looked as though the fire had caught, he rose and sat on the couch opposite Jessica. "I'm hardly an expert in psychology," he said, "but people's attitudes toward members of the opposite sex are usually colored by prior marriages, prior relationships."

"What does my personality tell you about my relationship with Alex?" she asked, genuinely curious.

"Your self-reliance and independence tell me you probably were the strong one, or at least that you shared the burdens equally."

"Alex was a dreamer, and being married to him prevented me from having the luxury of dreaming myself, that's true. I suppose I did assume a lot of the responsibility."

"And now it's hard for you to let go, to rely on others."

"Like you, for example?"

"Like me, for example."

"Chase, the paper we share is a ten-page contract, not a marriage certificate. I can't afford to get soft."

He glanced at the fire, which had caught well and was beginning to crackle. "I know that. I wish for your sake, though, that you could relax a little."

Jessica contemplated him. He looked back at her, curious.

"You know what?" she said. "You're a dreamer, too. A more successful one than Alex, but a dreamer none-theless."

"I've always thought of myself as eminently practi-cal."

"No, you're a dreamer. You just don't realize it."

Chase smiled, his broad mouth and chiseled features handsome in the firelight. "And what if I am?"

"It means I have to be on my guard, because in their innocence dreamers have a way of hurting themselves, and sometimes other people."

CHASE GLANCED INTO THE KITCHEN and decided to leave the mess for Maggie. He had rinsed everything, so cleaning up wouldn't be too bad a job. And he knew she wouldn't mind, because he'd given her the extra day off. He switched off the light and went to the front door, checking to make sure it was locked.

Before mounting the stairs he looked into the sitting room to ensure the fire had died down sufficiently to leave for the night. After Jessica had gone to bed he had sat watching the flames for a long time, thinking about their conversation and about her.

What a strange and remarkable woman she was. Every time he thought he had her tamed in his mind, she'd sur-prise him with some previously unseen quality. Every time he thought he had mastered his desire for her, she found some new way to intrigue and beguile him, though he knew it was the farthest thing from her mind. Per-haps it was the lack of intention that made it so effec-tive.

Weary from his long day, Chase slowly climbed the stairs. In the hallway above a dim night-light burned, casting a mellow glow through the upper part of the house. At the top of the stairs he turned toward his wing, when he heard someone in the hall behind him.

He spun around as Jessica spoke his name. "Chase..."

"What are you doing up? I thought you'd be asleep by now."

"I couldn't sleep."

He saw that she had slipped on her robe, though it hung open, revealing the swell of her breasts under her nightgown. "Want some hot milk or something?"

"No, I'm fine. Actually, I just wanted to talk to you."

They stood facing each other in the dim light.

"I wanted to thank you for your support today, for coming back to be with me when Jamie was hurt."

"There's no need to thank—"

"Yes, there is. Not everyone would have done it."

"I don't know about that, but I couldn't ignore either your plight or Jamie's."

"I realize that, and I want to thank you for it, for being there when I needed you."

Chase could see that the gratitude she expressed was heartfelt. It touched him and a sheen of moisture glazed his eyes. He smiled. "Thanks for saying so." Then, unable to resist, he stepped over and put his arms around her, gathering her close. Jessica let her head rest against him, almost childlike in his embrace. He stroked her hair.

"You've given me so much, Jessica. There's no way I could truly compensate you."

"Considering the future you've given Jamie and me, I could say the same."

He took her by the shoulders and held her. A grin crept across his face. "Then maybe this hasn't been such a bad deal, after all."

She smiled. Taking her chin with his fingers, Chase leaned over and lightly kissed her lips before sending her back down the hall and to her room.

CHAPTER THIRTEEN

JESSICA AND CHASE were at the hospital at eight the next morning. When they entered Jamie's room Jessica could tell by the expression on the nurse's face that all was not well.

"I'm afraid Jamie ran a temperature most of the night, Mrs. Brandon. It's back to normal now, but doctor wants to observe him for a while and run a few more tests before we send him home."

Jessica looked at Chase, then at Jamie with the panda propped up beside him. She went to the boy, kissing him. "How are you feeling, honey?"

"Fine."

She looked at his eyes. He seemed subdued, but otherwise normal. "Does your head feel better?"

"It hurts."

"Does it?" She lightly stroked the side of his head. "This will make it better."

"I want to go home."

"I know you do. But the doctor has to check you over first to make sure everything's fine. Then we'll go home and you can see your toys."

"My pony, too, Mommy?"

Jessica glanced back at Chase. "I think you'll have to rest awhile, Jamie, before we go on pony rides."

The boy's face crumpled and Chase stepped up to the bed. "Hey, partner, if the pony was sick you wouldn't want to make him go out in the cold, would you?"

Jamie shook his head, looking up at the man through tear-brimmed eyes.

"Well, the pony doesn't want you to go out, either, until you're feeling better. As soon as the doctor says it's okay we'll go for a ride. I promise."

Jamie considered the words for a moment. "I'm better now."

Chase chuckled. "Let's see what the doctor says. I bet it won't be long."

"Tomorrow?"

"Chase has to go away, Jamie. He won't be able to tomorrow."

"Is he going away like Daddy?"

Jessica and Chase exchanged glances.

"No, darling. Nothing like that. On an airplane. He'll be back in a few days. Then you can ride the pony cart."

"Excuse me, Mrs. Brandon," the nurse interjected, "but we have to get Jamie ready for more lab work. Would you mind waiting for us downstairs? Someone will let you know when he's done."

They left, making their way to the waiting room.

"When's your flight, Chase?" Jessica asked, sitting on the couch.

"I don't have to be at the airport for a couple of hours, but I'm thinking I ought to cancel."

"You can't do that. The races are tomorrow."

"The horses can run without me."

"No, I don't want you to miss the races. It's bad enough that you flew back here yesterday. Meade's coming. Jamie and I can ride back with her."

"No, I think—"

"Chase, I insist. The minute Meade arrives I want you to get to the airport."

Just then Meade Phillips came breezing in the door. Chase and Jessica looked at each other, then laughed.

"You two are certainly in good spirits this morning. I take it Jamie's feeling better."

"Yes, but he ran a fever most of the night," Jessica replied, "and the doctor wants to do more tests."

Meade looked at them quizzically. "Then why the mirth?"

Chase got to his feet. "Because just before you walked in Jessica announced she was banishing me the minute you arrived."

"Good heavens, why couldn't I make you disappear so easily when we were kids?"

"Because *you* were always the one tagging around after *me*, remember?"

Meade sat next to Jessica. "I suppose you do have a point."

Chase looked at his watch. "Well, I'd better be off."

"Where to, big brother?"

"Lexington."

"That's right, Keeneland. When is it?"

"Tomorrow."

"Good luck."

Chase grinned. "I need more than luck. I need new breeding stock. I'm not looking forward to tomorrow."

"Well, hurry back, then. Life in Westchester is infinitely more interesting."

"Yes, I'm beginning to realize that." He leaned over and pinched Jessica's cheek. "Take care of that son of yours." He winked at his sister. "See you soon."

Jessica watched him go, feeling the fire in her cheeks at his touch. She hadn't been the same since he had kissed her the night before.

"Well," Meade said, "has my big brother been taking care of you?"

"Yes, he's been very kind."

"Chase can be overprotective—it's his nature. His intentions are always good, though. You can rely on that." Meade examined Jessica's face. "But it still bothers you, doesn't it?"

"His kindness?"

"No, Chase generally. Your relationship."

"You're very perceptive, Meade."

"I sensed the attraction."

"And it's a problem.... I don't want that kind of a relationship. It's too hard to deal with, considering the baby and all." Jessica's hand grazed her abdomen, then she caught herself and moved it away.

"Want some advice?"

Jessica turned to her.

"Don't fight his attempt to help. What he wants to do benefits you both. Accept his generosity and make it as easy on yourself as you can."

But how do I protect my feelings? Jessica wanted to say. *How can I protect myself from being hurt?* She shook her head. "It's not easy."

Meade watched her in silence for a minute. Then she said, "Funny how ironic things can be. You and Chase get pregnant and it's a problem between you. Roger and I can't have a baby and it's putting a strain on our marriage."

"You're talking as though Chase and I *have* a relationship, Meade."

The woman smiled. "You do Jessica, whether you want one or not."

She avoided Meade's eyes. She thought about her words and wondered if she didn't have a point. Maybe it was time to start facing up to her feelings and decide what to do about them.

BY MIDMORNING the doctor had given Jamie a clean bill of health and Jessica and Meade took him home. It turned out to be nothing more than a "good rap on the noggin," as the doctor put it, but Jessica watched the boy carefully and worried anyway.

Chase called from Kentucky that afternoon and seemed greatly relieved at the news. "I'll be getting back Friday evening. Let's have a special dinner or something."

"Don't forget there's the party Saturday evening, the gallery opening."

"That's right, I'd forgotten. Do you have a dress?"

"I was planning on getting one this week."

"Why don't you wait until I get back? We can go shopping together."

Jessica felt uncertain about the proposal, but agreed. She hadn't been shopping with a man since Alex died.

JAMIE SLEPT most of that day, but by the next morning he was virtually his old self. Jessica and Anne Bascom spent the morning with him, but he was so anxious to get out of bed that the nurse took him downstairs after lunch to let him play for a while. Jessica used the opportunity to go out to the studio and get in a little work.

In the few hours she spent painting she managed to accomplish quite a bit. Off and on she thought about Chase, wondering how the races were going. That night he called with the disappointing results. Two of his horses had run that afternoon: one finished fourth, just out of the money, the other, in the major race of the day, had finished seventh. Chase was not pleased.

"So how's your social life?" he asked, sounding a little maudlin.

"Oh, a virtual whirlwind of activity! How's yours?"

"Passed up most of the parties."

"You poor boy."

But he didn't laugh. He wasn't in a joking mood. Silence hung on the line. "Jessica," he finally said, "I miss you."

The words were unexpected, but the gravity of the sentiment didn't go unnoticed. She fumbled for a response. "We miss you, too."

"Do *you*?"

She hesitated. "Yes."

He managed a lighter tone. "Then I'll definitely come back. After today I was considering staying and cleaning out my stables—horses, trainers, the lot."

"What does that mean? That you consider this breeding experiment to be your only success?"

"As a matter of fact, I do. I've told you I value you like a prize filly."

She knew it was intended as a compliment. "Well, I suppose if my foal doesn't turn out to your liking you can always try another woman."

"Do you think I would?"

She heard the answer in the question, but couldn't resist teasing him. "I guess the only limitation is the extent of your bank account."

He laughed. "And I thought you understood me."

CHASE'S FLIGHT in from Lexington was late. He didn't get to the farm until after everyone was in bed. Breakfast the next morning was the big reunion.

"There's the patient!" Chase exclaimed when Jessica carried Jamie into the breakfast room. He went to them and took the boy. "How are you feeling, partner?"

Jamie was pleased to see him. "Fine."

"If you're really fine this afternoon, when your mom and I get back from shopping, you and I will go for a pony cart ride. How does that sound?"

"Let's go now!"

"No, ladies first. Your mom wants a new dress so she'll be real pretty for the party."

Jamie let out a wail of protest.

Chase looked at the boy with dismay. "Those are pretty strong feelings. I wonder if there's a compromise."

Jamie didn't understand the words, but he sensed a softening of Chase's position. He stopped crying when Chase put him on his shoulders. After a slow gallop into the sitting room and back the child was giggling. They came to a halt in front of Jessica, who looked longingly into Chase's handsome face. He leaned over and kissed her sweetly on the lips.

"Sort of like kissing a totem pole, isn't it?" he asked with a grin.

Jessica smiled. "Now that you mention it . . ."

"Well, better kiss the top totem, then. After all, he's the wounded party." The man leaned way over so that Jamie could touch his mother's face. She kissed the giggling child.

Chase looked into her sandy beige eyes and at the rosy clearness of her skin. She had a fresh, healthy glow that excited him by its very vibrancy. Gone was the spare, lanky beauty of the fashion model. Jessica was beginning to look the expectant mother she had been in his mind the past months.

"You look wonderful," he said, barely above a whisper.

"I'm getting fat."

"More beautiful by the day."

"You just want your baby to show."

"Horsey!" Jamie cried, and began bouncing on Chase's shoulders.

Glancing up at the boy Chase chuckled and began galloping around the room.

"Haven't you had enough horse racing?" Jessica asked, laughing.

"Quite the opposite, my dear. After this disastrous week, not enough." He came to a halt in front of her again. "Get any painting done?"

"A little."

"That's good." Chase swung Jamie off his shoulders and sat him on the floor at their feet. They stared at each other for a long tentative moment, then he took her into his arms and held her close. The soft perfume of her tawny hair touched him and he remembered the magical evening when they had nearly made love.

He felt her arms loosely around his waist and the warmth of her breath on his neck. She wasn't exactly rigid in his embrace, but Chase could tell she was hesitant. He knew he'd have to be careful.

"Pony, Mommy. Let's ride the pony," Jamie protested from below.

"This afternoon will be soon enough, darling."

Chase laughed. "Easily said."

"You haven't been the one who's had to hear about the pony the past few days."

He reached over and lightly touched her face. "How've *you* been?"

She gave him a gamine smile. "To be honest, as anxious to go shopping as Jamie has been over the pony."

"Anything to do with me?"

"Not a thing."

THEY DIDN'T GO into New York as Chase suggested, but settled instead on a shopping mall in White Plains. The notion of going with him to buy a dress had a curiously erotic effect on Jessica. Until they were in the store, she hadn't realized how intimate the occasion really was.

He seemed to examine *her* even more than the dresses she modeled, which Jessica found particularly exciting. She let herself enjoy the sensation. Chase seemed to be having fun, too. There was electricity in the air, just as there had been at fashion shows during her modeling days.

"Have you ever done this with a woman before?" she asked. As he watched, she turned in front of the mirror in an aubergine silk theater suit with a sleeveless shell that she had on for the second time.

"I'll take the fifth on that."

She looked at his smiling face in the mirror. "When have you... Oh, never mind!" she snapped when his smile broadened into a grin.

"Believe me, the model wasn't nearly so lovely."

"Oh, shut up! I never should have opened my mouth."

Chase laughed.

"I was going to pay for this dress myself," Jessica announced, "but now I have half a mind to make you pay."

"I paid for it last time I did this."

She spun around to face him.

"Well, it'd be a shame to break your string, wouldn't it?" They were both teasing, but Jessica could hear a touch of jealousy in her own words. "On second thought, I won't let you pay for it."

"Why the sudden change of heart?"

"This way I won't have to feel guilty when I wear it out with other men."

Chase rubbed his chin in mock seriousness. "You aren't planning on something while I'm in Europe, are you?"

"Chase, you know I'd never violate the *letter* of our contract."

He laughed. "That makes me feel much better."

She looked at herself in the mirror and turned around slowly, then glanced at the approaching sales clerk. "I've decided on this one," she said, feeling very pleased with what had transpired.

THEY ARRIVED AT THE GALLERY early that evening and Chase introduced Jessica to the owner, a slender little Spanish gentleman with a wizened face by the name of Cordena.

"*Señora*, if you paint you must show me some of your work," the man said with exaggerated courtesy.

"I'm afraid Geisel has gotten to her first," Chase explained.

"Ah, Helmut," Cordena said, shaking his head. "The man has an eye for art, that I must give him. You must be very talented."

Jessica beamed at the attention.

"I regret, *señora*, that I am not familiar with your work, but should you ever have the need do not hesitate to come and see me."

"Thank you, Señor Cordena."

"Please, to you and Señor Hamilton, I am Carlos." He smiled at each of them. "Now please, make yourselves at home. There is champagne waiting."

They wandered farther into the small gallery to a table where a man in a tuxedo was pouring champagne. Chase asked if he had mineral water that he could pour into a flute for Jessica. When he handed her the glass, she let her annoyance show.

"I don't see what harm one little glass of champagne would do," she protested under her breath.

"Doctor's orders."

"No," she said dryly, "Chase's orders." She didn't really want the wine, but he was almost too insistent, too controlling, and at times she felt resentful.

Chase looked wounded by her comment, and Jessica felt badly. "I'm sorry. I didn't mean to snap."

He took a glass of champagne and they stood sipping their drinks for several minutes. There were only a dozen or so people there, but a large group was coming in the door and it seemed the place would be crowded before long.

Jessica was happy that he had brought her to the party, but she had a feeling that he was going to try to spend the evening promoting her work. The notion was gratifying in one sense, but there was also a proprietary aspect to it that bothered her. She wanted to succeed at her work, but *she* wanted to feel responsible for her success.

"Chase," she said hesitantly, "would you be terribly offended if I circulated for a while on my own?"

He looked at her blankly for a moment. "No, if you'd like to, that's fine."

"I promise I won't drink any champagne," she said, giving him a coy little smile before slowly walking off.

He watched her move through the gallery, eventually bumping into a young woman of about her own age with whom she exchanged excited greetings. Chase thought it must be a friend from Jessica's days in New York, or perhaps someone from art school. He observed her and the happy, animated expression on her face for a time, then turned and picked up another glass of champagne.

JESSICA'S CHEEKS WERE WARM from the crowded room and the glow of excitement. Though she hadn't had any wine, she felt as light-headed as everyone around her. She was enjoying the heady feeling of almost belonging. One couple she met had even heard her name via the grapevine and asked when she would be exhibiting her work.

Apart from the wife of one of her instructors at art school, the only person Jessica had met previously was Arthur Netley, Chase's attorney, who came up to her and chatted briefly. She hadn't realized that he, too, was a collector of contemporary art. After a few moments they each drifted into other conversations.

Jessica had been busy rubbing shoulders for the better part of an hour, when she realized she hadn't seen Chase the entire time. Since the gallery was small it didn't take her long to search the crowd, but she couldn't find him. She was about to seek out Carlos Cordena to ask if he had seen him, when she saw Chase coming in the front door in the company of a willowy auburn-haired woman.

After watching them for a moment, Jessica was able to detect an easy familiarity between them. The woman, in her mid-thirties, wore a dark green designer suit and seemed very relaxed. She turned to Chase and, laughing, patted him on the cheek. He didn't seem to mind the gesture, and Jessica could tell they were old friends.

She watched them until they began moving in her general direction, then quickly turned to look at a painting on the wall next to her, not wanting to be forced into an embarrassing encounter. Staring at the contemporary watercolor, in the theme of Madonna and child, she prayed they wouldn't see her.

"Jessica!" She heard his voice behind her but didn't react, trying to appear in deep concentration.

"Jessica!" Chase touched her arm and she slowly turned. "I'd like you to meet a friend," he said brightly. "This is Carolyn Waitley. Carolyn, Jessica Brandon, the artist I told you about."

"How do you do?" the woman said, extending a gloved hand.

Judging by her lightly accented speech, Jessica decided she was British. "Nice to meet you."

Carolyn Waitley began removing her gloves and glanced around the gallery. "Carlos managed to scare up a large crowd, didn't he? Are you enjoying the party, Miss Brandon?"

"*Mrs.* Brandon."

"Pardon me. *Mrs.* Brandon." She gave Chase a sly, amused little look and scanned Jessica's theater suit. "I understand Chase discovered you."

"He bought my first painting, if that's what you mean."

Carolyn playfully tapped Chase on the arm with her gloves. "Collectors are prone to hyperbole, I suppose."

He looked a little annoyed. "I believe 'discovered' was your term, Carolyn. I was telling you about Jessica's growing success."

Carolyn Waitley looked across at Jessica and spoke to her in an overly familiar tone. "Don't you just love the man?'' She paused, eyeing Jessica with curiosity. "I once did.''

Jessica looked at Chase.

"Carolyn and I were engaged a few years ago.''

She suddenly realized who the sophisticated woman was, remembering the story about the decorator who didn't care for horses and children.

"Oh, you're the decorator..."

"You've seen Chase's place, then,'' Carolyn said with a questioning glance at him.

"Yes....'' Jessica regretted having stumbled into a situation involving Chase and another woman. She wished she could quickly and gracefully slip away.

"Jessica is staying at the farm,'' he explained.

"I see,'' Carolyn said with a touch of ice, though she tried to maintain her equanimity. "Then perhaps it was accurate to say you discovered Mrs. Brandon, after all.''

Jessica felt her stomach tighten as the drift of the conversation became clear. She was desperate for escape, a change of subject, anything to avoid unpleasant feelings. A quick look at Carolyn's face told her of the woman's jealousy.

Carolyn was looking around again, letting her eyes rest on the painting Jessica had been studying when they'd come up. "I don't know why painters insist on doing this sentimental drivel,'' she intoned, "and why dealers hang it.''

They all looked at the watercolor.

"I rather like it,'' Jessica said, not seeing what was so offensive.

"It's an appealing theme,'' Chase added. When he smiled at her, Jessica caught his drift and blushed.

Carolyn didn't appear to understand the subtle communication, but clearly detected the intimacy between them. Her eyes flashed, and she was obviously struggling to remain calm. "Well, Chase, it seems you haven't been entirely candid with me."

He looked at her quizzically, but Jessica understood immediately what the woman was referring to. She felt dreadful, hoping the situation wouldn't turn nasty.

"I assume, Mrs. Brandon, that you're divorced or soon will be?"

"No, I'm widowed. My husband died in an automobile accident a few years ago."

"I'm sorry to hear that." The look she gave Chase said a lot more than Jessica understood.

She wondered if it meant something along the lines of "Can't resist taking in a stray, can you, Chase?" Jessica colored, not liking Carolyn Waitley very much just then.

The woman glanced back at the painting. "If you both find the theme appealing," she said a bit caustically, "maybe you're better suited for each other than you think." She gave Chase a tight, bitter smile. Then she looked past Jessica into the crowd. "I should say hello to Carlos. Would you two mind if I go look for him?"

Neither of them spoke.

Carolyn's eyes passed over Jessica. "Nice to have met you, Mrs. Brandon."

"And you, as well."

"Goodbye, Carolyn," Chase said.

"Ciao. Oh, and thanks for coming to walk me over." She tapped him a final time with her gloves and disappeared into the crowded room.

Jessica sighed and he put an arm around her shoulders.

"I'm sorry about that. I didn't know Carolyn would be a spoiled brat."

"She wasn't spoiled, Chase."

"What do you call it, then?"

"She still loves you."

He looked at her with surprise. "Loves me? That's ridiculous. It's been over between us for years."

"That's what you think."

He looked after the woman, into the crowd. "No, Carolyn is just a little bitter that it didn't work out, that's all." But his voice lacked conviction.

"Do you still love *her*?"

He stroked her cheek with the back of his fingers. "No, of course not."

"Why 'of course not'? Maybe you should have married her."

"I didn't want to, not in my heart of hearts. That's why I didn't."

"*You* broke it off with her?"

"It was mutual. That's why we're still friends."

Jessica couldn't help a little scoff at his words. "You don't understand women, Chase."

He lifted her chin with his finger. "Don't I understand you?"

"Not really. But, then, I wouldn't expect it."

"Why? Because I'm just a man?"

Jessica smiled.

He looked around. "Had enough networking for one night?"

She nodded. "I'm getting tired."

"Come on, then," he said, taking her arm. "Let's go home."

CHAPTER FOURTEEN

DURING THE RIDE to Westchester County Jessica couldn't decide how she felt about Chase Hamilton. He wasn't her lover, but he was clearly more than a date. They were having a child, but they weren't mates, though in ways he seemed like a husband. The baby had receded into the background, though it controlled their lives completely.

Jessica looked at him behind the wheel of the Bentley as they sped along the Saw Mill River Parkway, and wondered what thoughts were going on behind his serene visage. "Are you thinking about Carolyn?"

He grinned in the darkness. "Yes, as a matter of fact. I was thinking how fortunate I was our relationship ended when it did."

She contemplated him. "Is that really what you were thinking?"

"Yes, exactly." He glanced over. "Why? Don't you believe me?"

She shrugged. "If you say so. I thought she was lovely myself. Very sophisticated."

"She is."

"But you don't love her?"

Chase hesitated. "Let me put it this way. Seeing the two of you this evening, I realized it would have been a disaster if Carolyn and I had married. We'd have been miserable, probably divorced by now."

"What do I have to do with it?"

"Let's say you're the symbol of my present state of contentment."

Jessica gave a little laugh. "I've never been described as a symbol before. What are you referring to? My condition of servitude?"

"No, your wonderful maternal aura."

"Chase, you're going from bad to worse. Women like to be appreciated for themselves, not for their childbearing ability."

"I appreciate you for yourself, of course. You happen also to be the mother of my child. It's something we share. That sets you apart from someone like Carolyn, with whom this wouldn't have been possible."

"Did you try offering her a hundred thousand?"

He gave her a disapproving look. "I wish you wouldn't insist on degrading it so."

"I think you're just trying to romanticize something that's very cut-and-dried."

"Your motives?"

"Yes, my motives. I'm like one of your horses, the only difference being I had to be bribed instead of coerced."

"No, the only difference being my horses don't talk back."

Jessica fell silent. They drove for several minutes.

"Why so quiet?"

"I'm trying not to talk back."

Chase laughed, then reached over and took her hand. "I never said I didn't like it that you talk back. Actually, it's one of your most endearing qualities."

Jessica couldn't help a little smile, liking the feel of Chase's thumb as he stroked the back of her hand.

WHEN HE TURNED OFF the engine of the car and the quiet of the night enveloped them, Jessica could feel Chase's eyes on her. Ever since his return from Kentucky—since Jamie's accident, actually—she had sensed a growing affection. It was a pleasant thing, something she couldn't easily spurn. Now, sitting alone with him in the darkness, she was acutely aware of it.

"You're really a very lovely woman, Jessica," he whispered, breaking the silence.

She turned to him, touched by the overture.

"We've teased a lot about horses," he said softly, "and my feelings for the baby are obvious enough, but I don't regard you as a brood mare. You're a very special person, and I'm very fond of you."

She blushed at the sentiment. "Thank you."

They left the car and walked in the crisp night air to the house, hand in hand. Chase sensed that she had let down her guard somewhat, though he didn't know why.

No one in the house was up, though it was not terribly late. He suggested that they build a fire and have a cup of tea or hot chocolate. Jessica agreed but said she wanted to look in on Jamie. By the time she came back downstairs, he had a fire going.

"Doesn't that look inviting!" she enthused, and Chase turned around to see the glow of the fire on her smiling face. She sat down on one of the couches and he stared at her, watching the light play on her skin, the pretty curve of her mouth, the stark whiteness of her teeth.

Resting her elbow on the arm of the couch, Jessica leaned toward him, her long beige-tipped fingers against her cheek, the gilt wisps of her hair a spumy crown. Her delicate, fragile beauty touched him.

"Have I mentioned how nice you look tonight?"

Her lips curved happily at the corners. "Yes, I believe you have."

Chase tossed another log on the fire, then rose to sit next to her. Taking her hand, he held it on his knee.

She was watching the fire, but she sensed his admiration again.

"'Nice' isn't the right word, really," he said. "'Beautiful' is better."

She turned toward him and was greeted by penetrating eyes, dark in the firelight. There was a slight smile on his lips and it struck her again how very handsome he was, the shadowed planes of his face angular, masculine. But there was a look in those eyes—an unfathomable look. It was one she had seen before.

"What are you thinking?" he asked.

"About how much you look like you did that first day we met at Harriet's."

"But that wasn't a very friendly meeting."

"No, that's not what I'm referring to. It's the look in your eyes. It seemed as though you were searching for something and expected to find it."

"Perhaps I was. Both then and now."

It wasn't clear exactly what he meant, but Jessica sensed it was weighty. Her eyes dropped.

Chase lifted her chin and kissed her softly, but deeply, on the lips. When he released her, the sensation hung. Jessica felt weak. She took his hand and pressed it against her cheek.

Chase inhaled her fragrance, intoxicated by its heady effect.

"Jessica," he whispered.

She looked at him as he shifted closer, his mouth moving toward hers. Her lips opened as he covered them, his hand sliding over the supple flesh of her stomach, resting over her womb, large, warm and protective.

His infinite tenderness flooded Jessica with emotion. Their lips parted and she looked at him through misty eyes, her fingers caressing his cheek, her heart filled equally with awe and desire.

"Oh, Chase..." Her mind was a swirl of confusion, but she was helpless to do anything but accept his affection. She wanted it too badly, too fiercely, to do anything else. No warning, no threat, no admonition could dissuade her. Where it would end she wasn't sure, but there was no way she could stop it—not now.

Chase ran his fingers along the side of her neck and up into the wispy fringes of her hair, sending shivers along her spine, tremors through her body. Jessica pressed her face against his neck, drinking in his manly aroma, feeling the need for his intimate embrace.

He traced her skin at the edge of her neckline, his hands slipping under the fabric to stroke her. Under his touch her breasts began to throb and she wanted him to take them more fully. She remembered the feel of his lips and tongue the last time, and her nipples hardened.

She rolled against him, wanting the pressure to penetrate their clothing. He embraced her eagerly, spreading kisses over her face.

"Jessica... I want you."

She answered with a kiss, clutching him to her, telling him of her desire with her tongue.

Gently he broke free and pulled her to her feet, holding her as the shadows of the fire danced around them. Jessica clung to him, savoring his scent and the taste of him on her tongue.

"Jessica," he whispered into her hair, "I want you. Now."

Her eyes sought his questioningly, but he didn't wait for a response. He reached down and lifted her into his arms, kissing the swell of her lower lip before carrying her to the stairs.

What she had been wanting for so long now seemed imminent, and with each step he took she asked herself whether she ought to stop him before it was too late. Her mind was still debating the question when they had reached the top of the stairs. Chase paused, his breathing deep and heavy, his heart beating forcefully against her breast.

"Chase, I don't think we should." But there was no conviction in her voice, and she could tell he knew it, too.

Without a word he proceeded down the hall toward his rooms, and Jessica pressed her face against his neck, fearing her own submission as much as she feared his will.

Inside the dimly lit chamber she saw a large bed and soft leather chairs—the mood, the scent of the place, distinctly masculine. She sensed the danger, but it excited her, too.

Chase carried her to the bed and put her down gently. He stood over her for a moment, studying the lovely face, aware of the heavy pounding of his heart and the insistent voice of desire within him.

Jessica didn't move, she just looked up at him, feeling trepidation. She knew she was within his power, beyond retreat, incapable of escape. He loosened his tie, pulled it off and tossed it behind him, his eyes riveted still to her face. He began unbuttoning his shirt.

When he was stripped to the waist he sat on the bed beside her, touching her breast at the opening of her shell. She looked at his naked skin in the half-light and laid her

hand against it, intrigued by the soft mat of hair beneath her fingers.

His flesh tingled under the feathery caress of her hand
as it slid lightly over his arm and shoulder. He gazed into
the wide innocence of her eyes, feeling wonder, desire. He
hardened, aching for her.

When she touched his lip with the end of her finger he
captured it, teasing the sensitive tip with his tongue. In
Jessica the sensation was electric, causing her body to
tremble and her womb to pulse.

"Oh..." she murmured, aching with desire.

Chase unfastened her dress and slipped it off her
shoulders so that he could kiss the naked hollows of her
chest, running his tongue lightly across her skin. She
gasped at the sensation.

He unclasped her bra and let it drop away, exposing
her swollen breasts. Leaning down, he lightly touched the
tip of one bud with his tongue, then painted a patch of
moisture around it, making it harden more and throb.

Jessica closed her eyes and the evening on the hilltop
returned, her breasts tingling and the place between her
legs moistening.

"Oh, God, how you excite me," she moaned, sitting
up a little and crushing his face into her breast. He took
it into his mouth, sucking her greedily. Then, when she
released his head, she fell back against the pillow.

He looked down at her half-naked body, her eyes
closed, waiting for him to take her. Seeing her that way,
he could wait no longer. It took only a few seconds for
him to finish undressing her.

He stood up then and Jessica looked at him through
hooded eyes. There was desire on her face, and touches
of fear, but he knew he would have her.

As he undressed, Jessica pulled down the bed covers and slithered under them. He stood motionless beside the bed, completely naked.

There were a million things at the back of her mind just then, a million things to think of and consider, but none of them touched her consciousness. Nothing was more important or immediate than the man beside the bed. She let her eyes follow the shadowed contours of his torso to the triangle of his loins, the distended essence of his manhood.

He was large and swollen with desire. Her own body was alive in expectation, her feminine hollows fully moistened, ready. And yet, despite her boundless hunger for him, she was afraid. To permit him to enter her, to know her, was as wrong as it was inevitable. She knew she must have him, and equally that she couldn't.

Chase didn't wait for an invitation. Carefully, slowly, he lifted the covers from her, revealing her naked body. Her legs were together, her arms at her sides, the tawny fringe of her feminine down exposed. The flesh of her stomach was slightly swollen with the child, her breasts ripe, her nipples enlarged. She didn't exactly look pregnant, but he knew the baby was in her womb—his child, the product of their bodies.

As he crawled onto the bed beside her Jessica watched his eyes, seeking their message, searching for signs of love amid the desire. The skin that touched hers was fire; the leg that wedged between hers was rock; the low rumble of his voice was distant thunder moving nearer.

"I've waited and dreamed about this moment for months," he said huskily. "You'll never know how much I've wanted you."

Desire opened her legs to him; need lifted her pelvis to take him; love beckoned him to take her, to have her, to merge their bodies into one.

She felt the rigid enormity of him slipping into her opening and she gasped with pleasure and pain. Her body had not known a man intimately since Alex, and the feeling was alien, yet natural and beloved.

Chase stopped the downward pressure until he felt her muscles relax again and her hips rise once more to take him in fully. The gradual penetration, the feel of her body around him, was a sensation like no other on earth. He yearned to thrust deep inside her but held back, wanting it to be pleasurable for her, wanting her to love his love.

"Oh, take me, please take me," she whispered into his ear as her fingers sank deeply into his back and her legs lifted and wrapped around him.

With a slow, smooth thrust he sank to the bottom of her core and she gasped.

"Oh, God!"

And he froze, afraid to move, hoping with all his heart that he hadn't hurt her. Then the tiny cries of pleasure coming from deep within told him of her joy. He withdrew slightly, then slowly, incrementally, moved into her again. Jessica opened herself wider and lifted her hips eagerly to him. He clutched her against him, more forcefully than he had dared before.

Feeling his excitement double and redouble, Chase began the rhythmic dance of lovemaking, the hard length of him sliding outward then deep inside her. At first he kept the pace slow and controlled, but as he became more excited he gradually lost himself to the act and to the woman. Jessica felt the mounting excitement inside her, the rush of passion, the need to be one. Soon their bodies were heaving against each other intractably. They entered the storm together, moving at a fever pitch.

"Oh . . . oh . . ." she cried.

The ultimate heave of his body sent Jessica beyond herself and she cried out in climax. Answering her, he exploded, and she felt his life force fill her.

They clung together then while the pulsing throb of their fulfillment slowly dwindled. Yet even as the minutes passed, they remained one.

A LONG TIME LATER he was still inside her. Though his body was large and heavy upon her, Jessica was content. Chase had drifted into half sleep, enabling her to savor the continuing sensation of their intimacy.

It had been long, so long since she had been fulfilled, and it had never been lovelier, sweeter, not even with Alex. Chase had given her yet another gift, one greater in a sense than all the rest.

Feeling his warmth against her, she wondered what would happen next, what she wanted to happen. Would there be other times? Would she permit it? Should she?

This protracted connection of their bodies was profoundly intimate, and Jessica sensed it was more than sex. More than just the two of them. Their child had been there, too. This lovemaking was its procreation, after the fact.

What was Chase thinking? About the baby, or about her? He had expressed the most profound and sacred sort of affection, but did he love her?

She felt him stirring, and she squeezed him between her legs a final time, knowing he would soon leave her feeling void, empty. He lifted his weight onto his elbows and Jessica felt the air flow freely into her lungs.

"Am I hurting you?" he asked in a low whisper.

She shook her head and he kissed her on the temple. Slowly he began withdrawing and Jessica wanted to protest, but she couldn't. Time was pulling them apart.

"I wish it were tonight that you had gotten pregnant," he said softly, settling beside her.

He *had* been thinking of the child. "Why?"

"Because then you couldn't pretend it wasn't ours. If it had been conceived this way it would have been our love child, not something that happened at a clinic."

Jessica lay quietly, listening to his words as she played them over again in her mind. There wasn't bitterness, but there was sadness, a touch of regret. But what was he really saying?

He turned toward her and kissed her hair. "I'm glad we had this, Jessica."

Why? she asked herself. *Why is it important? Because of us or because of the baby?* A sinking feeling settled over her as she began to see what had happened in a different light. Had Chase made love to her, or was he just consummating the pregnancy? Clearly he wanted her, clearly he needed to make love with her, but for what reason?

"It was important to you that we made love, wasn't it?" she asked.

"I've wanted to for a long time."

"Why?"

He gave a little laugh. "Isn't it obvious?"

"No."

He looked at her with concern now, realizing she was upset about something. "Didn't you want to make love with me?"

"Yes."

"Why did you?"

"Because I care for you."

"Well, it's the same with me, Jessica. I care for you, too."

"Do you?"

He lifted his face over hers. "What is it? What's the matter?"

She bit her lip, suddenly feeling weepy. "Nothing."

"Did I say something, do something that upset you?"

"No."

He turned her face, making her look at him. "Jessica, what is it? What's wrong?"

Tears welled and she tried to stop them. It was absurd to cry, but the frustration was terrible. There was no way to tell him, no way he could understand what was wrong.

"Is it the baby? Are you upset because of the baby?"

A tear overflowed and ran down her cheek. She nodded, fighting back her sobs. "Yes."

He sighed anxiously. "But isn't it better now?"

"No, it makes it harder."

"That we made love? Why?"

She couldn't control herself any longer. "Because you weren't making love with me," she sobbed. "You were making love with the baby's mother."

"That's nonsense. I was making love with you."

"I know you weren't," she said through her tears. "I could tell."

"What are you saying?"

"Don't you see? It was wrong to do this! How can I make love with you and be the surrogate mother to your child? It's not right!" Her voice had risen to an almost hysterical pitch.

"Jessica!" he said, taking her firmly by the shoulder. "Whatever I said that upset you, please forget it."

"It's not you, Chase," she lamented as the tears streamed down her cheeks, "it's the situation. Everything about it makes what we did wrong. I was just too weak. I wanted your love too much."

"But you have my love," he protested.

"No. You're so blind you don't even see it yourself."

"Jessica . . ."

But she had rolled away from him to the edge of the bed. Crying softly, she picked up her clothes and stepped into them. Quickly gathering the rest of her things, she ran toward the door.

"Jessica!" His voice was more insistent, but she didn't stop.

Fearing he might follow her, she ran as fast as she could toward her rooms at the far end of the house and locked the door behind her. Miserably she turned to a bed that wasn't even hers.

CHAPTER FIFTEEN

THE NEXT MORNING Jessica stayed in her room until Maggie informed her that Chase had left for the city. She didn't want to see him until she had decided what to do, what to tell him. She knew that after the previous night something would have to be done.

She considered going to the studio to paint, but she was in too much turmoil to concentrate on her work. Instead she put on a jacket for protection against the brisk autumn air and went for a walk. Her meandering eventually took her to the hilltop where she had gone with Chase that summer evening only two months before.

Looking down on the house, the crisp breeze blowing through her hair, Jessica realized that the wondrous night in his bed had thrust her life to the point of crisis. She decided she couldn't live with him as a lover—that was impossible. The baby made it so.

To have a broken love affair would not be just another failed relationship, it would be disaster. How could she love him without loving the baby? To love is to risk a part of oneself, she knew, but with Chase she would be risking two loves, not one. It was more than any woman should bear.

Jessica knew that Chase Hamilton was a very hard man to resist. The previous night had very nearly been her undoing. With half a mind she wanted to believe that he truly cared for her, but the rest of her questioned and feared.

Jessica knew her doubts were partly a product of her own insecurities, but she didn't have the luxury of letting time clear up any uncertainty. The child inside her, the tiny creature she had so resolutely locked from her heart, was like a time bomb ticking away.

And what if he resisted—fought her decision? She would simply stand firm. She had no other choice.

Chase had said when they first met that he would never marry just to have a child. Except for the fact that he had made love with her nothing had changed. She had no reason to believe he felt any differently now. And even if he did, Jessica knew that she would never marry just to play the role of mother, whatever promises, threats or offers he made.

What she wanted seemed hopelessly impossible: to be loved for herself alone, without thought of the child growing in her womb. She realized all too poignantly that she didn't really want to be a surrogate mother at all.

AFTER MR. VALTICOS HAD FINISHED the physical therapy and Jamie had lunch, Jessica took the boy out to the fence surrounding the paddock to see his pony. The farmhand, Mack, saw them staring wistfully across the field and brought the pony to them at the fence. Jamie petted the animal for a while and Mack gave the boy an apple to feed to him.

Jessica watched her son in his joy, and thought of all the advantages living at the farm afforded, including the therapy, which seemed to be progressing remarkably, but she knew in her heart she'd have to end it. There was no way she could go on.

Mack wandered back to where they were after a while, watching Jamie. "Would you like for me to hitch up the cart for you, Mrs. Brandon, so you can take the boy for a ride?"

"No. I'm afraid I wouldn't know how to drive it."

"There ain't nothin' to it. I'll show you how. If you're worried, I'll keep an eye on you."

Jamie looked up at her longingly, but Jessica realized that if she was to wean him from the life at the farm she might as well start now. "No, but thank you for offering."

Jamie let out a whoop of protest, but Jessica picked him up and began marching back toward the house, leaving Mack and the pony behind. Before they made it to the back door the Bentley came around the house. On seeing them, Chase tooted the horn.

Jessica stopped, then watched him get out of the car and walk to them.

"Coming in from a walk?"

"No, I took Jamie to see the pony."

Jamie saw Chase's arrival as a reprieve and began protesting again. "Ride the pony, Mommy. Please. Please."

Chase grinned. "Half a loaf is no loaf at all."

"Jamie just has to learn that we can't always have what we want in life." She heard the irritation in her own voice.

"I somehow get the feeling your point has implications beyond the issue at hand."

Jessica stared up at him, reflecting. "You're very perceptive, Chase."

"Can we talk?"

"Yes, I think we should."

They went inside, where Jessica turned Jamie over to Anne to be taken upstairs for his nap. Then Chase led the way into the sun-room, where they sat at the table, Jessica carefully taking the chair opposite him.

His expression was foreboding. He maintained his silence, waiting for her to speak.

"What happened last night was a dreadful mistake," she said simply. "I can't go on living here. Jamie and I will have to leave."

"Was it that cataclysmic?"

"Yes. For me it was."

"Do you feel I took advantage of you?"

"No, that's not the point."

"What is the point?"

"Maybe what it boils down to is that I can't trust myself. I don't trust you, either."

"Was it that bad that we made love? I mean really that bad?"

"Chase, if you don't see it, there's no way I can explain it to you. I don't want this kind of relationship. It's not good for me and I'm not about to be miserable for the duration of this pregnancy. The physical discomfort will be bad enough."

"Doesn't it matter how I feel?"

"Frankly, no."

"Then you're the only one you'll consider. Never mind me, the baby, your own son for that matter."

"Be pious if you must. The fact is that despite your generosity you've managed to look out for yourself very well during this entire ordeal."

"Ordeal? It's gone from a mistake to an ordeal?"

"I'm sorry, you know that's not what I meant."

"No, I don't know what you meant. In fact, I don't understand you at all. Someone listening to this conversation would think I raped you, for God's sake."

"I take my share of the responsibility."

"Yeah, you said that the last time." Chase's eyes flashed. "Maybe taking responsibility means more than just not saddling me with all the blame."

"What do you mean by that?"

"I mean this damned habit of yours of running hot and cold." His voice rose. "I've got feelings, too, you know. I don't enjoy your teeter-totter any more than you like the way I make love."

Jessica gave a wary look toward the open door. She lowered her voice. "Look, this has nothing to do with the way you make love. It has everything to do with the fact that I'm carrying your baby as a bought-and-paid-for surrogate mother, and we slept together!"

"It's not your normal situation, I'll grant you, but—"

"Chase, there's no point in arguing. It's apparent we don't see eye to eye. The fact of the matter is I'm leaving and I'd like your cooperation."

"You're threatening to invoke your clause—the one you had Arthur Netley add to the contract."

"I'm not threatening anything, but I'll do what I have to. You know as well as I that there's no way you can keep me here against my will."

Chase stared at her, his blue eyes hard, his wide mouth taut. They had become adversaries. Jessica realized she had pushed things to a point of certain rift. She could only pray he'd let go gracefully.

He slowly shook his head. "Last night meant that little to you."

"Don't try to shame or manipulate me, Chase."

He nodded. "Maybe you're right. You might have seen something all along that I didn't. Perhaps it's just as well."

She waited, hating the circumstances, but she was unable to hate him. There was no real target for her anger.

He rose to his feet. "Give me a while to figure out the best way to handle it."

"You agree, then?"

"I don't have much choice." He looked at her for a long time, doubt and hurt in his eyes. Then he glanced at his watch. "I've got some horse people coming this afternoon and I'll be tied up with them until after dinner. We'll be going out, but if I'm not home too late let's discuss it then. All right?"

"Yes, that would be fine." Jessica watched him walk from the room, his jaw set, his stride purposeful. She realized that for the first time since meeting Chase Hamilton, she had won. But she didn't feel triumphant. The victory left her empty. It seemed the memory of those luscious moments in his bed would be the only prize she'd carry with her from the battle.

JESSICA WAITED DOWNSTAIRS all evening, but Chase didn't come home. She finally went up to her room and got ready for bed, worrying that he was off plotting, that he would find some way to thwart her. Why did he need time? What remained to be settled? She had made it plain enough what she wanted to do.

She resolved to go out the next morning and find a place to live, regardless of what Chase said or did. It was the sort of situation that called for action. She was deep in a melancholy review of events, when there was a knock on her door. She climbed from her bed, slipped on her robe and went to see who was there. It was Chase.

"I saw your light was still on and thought you might be anxious to get this business settled," he said matter-of-factly.

She opened the door to admit him.

He walked in and went to an armchair. Jessica sat on the corner of the bed nearest him.

"I've decided it would be better and simpler for everyone if I left instead of you."

"You? That's ridiculous. This is your home, not mine."

"I realize that. Believe me, I'm not being noble, just practical."

"I can't force you out of your own home."

"You're not forcing me, I'm choosing it."

"No."

"Yes. And here's why." He lifted his hand and began ticking off the reasons. "First, I'll feel better about my baby being here. Forgive my bluntness, but Maggie and Miss Bascom can look out for my interests in my absence."

"You mean supervise me?"

He ignored her sarcasm. "Second, Jamie can complete the physical therapy program I've set up for him."

"He can have therapy elsewhere."

"Not like this and you know it." He grasped his third finger. "Finally, it's easier for me to move than for you."

"But where would you go?"

"I checked this afternoon. I can get the apartment in New York now that had been reserved for you for the first of March. When it's time for you to move to be near the hospital, we can switch places. Very clean, very simple."

"But it's only the middle of October, that's a long time away. What about your business, your friends?"

"I'll be in Europe for much of that time anyway. I had planned on keeping it to a month, but now there's no reason to hurry back."

Jessica suddenly felt heartless. She knew she really was depriving him. His hurt was genuine. "The last thing I wanted to do was punish you, Chase."

"I have my conditions. You needn't worry about me."

"What conditions?"

"I still want to go with you to the clinic for your visits to the doctor, at least when I'm in town. And I'd like to come out once a week to take care of routine matters here and to visit Jamie. We can arrange it at a time when you're normally in your studio, so that you aren't inconvenienced."

"You're making me feel like a heel."

"That's not my intent. I'm trying to show good faith."

"Your conditions certainly aren't onerous. And if you're *sure* you really want to leave your home, I'll agree to your proposal. I think I ought to pay rent or something, though."

"Just to keep things businesslike I'd accept, but the money doesn't mean anything to me, so you may as well keep it."

Jessica sighed, contemplating Chase's stony countenance. "I'm really sorry it worked out like this."

"There were bound to be problems of one sort or another. Deep down I guess I didn't have any illusions."

"I hope I haven't cheapened it for you—spoiled it in any way."

Chase stood. "No, the payoff for me is in March. And that's what this is all about, isn't it?"

She bowed her head. From the corner of her eye she saw him moving toward the door.

"Good night, Jessica."

DURING THE DAYS after Chase moved out Jessica spent many fruitless hours in the studio, struggling with her work. She managed to apply a good deal of paint, but the results were uninspired. She preferred to think it had nothing to do with Chase, but she knew it did. He was always on her mind. She was tormented with doubt about what she had done, but common sense told her she had had no other choice.

What distressed her most was not that she had given up Chase, but that her work was not going well. She, in effect, had the arrangement she wanted from the beginning, but was unable to do anything with the opportunity.

One morning she stood at her easel, staring irritably at a still life that had all the originality of a can of soup, when her frustration spilled over and she angrily smashed her palette against the canvas. The easel tumbled over and Jessica stomped out, kicking a rag on the floor as she went.

Outside a blustery wind was blowing, the cool air chilling Jessica's fiery cheeks. She hadn't bothered taking her jacket, and she didn't care. Nothing seemed to matter just then. She didn't give a damn if she came down with pneumonia. Aimlessly she strode past the house and down the driveway toward the road.

Just as she reached the highway, a station wagon pulled into the driveway and stopped beside her. The electric window slid down. Meade Phillips, in a fur jacket, smiled at her.

"Jessica, what are you doing out here without a coat on? You'll catch cold."

"It was warm inside. I'm just out for a walk."

"Well, for heaven's sake jump in. I don't do a very good Florence Nightingale."

Jessica started to protest, but she was feeling chilled and she had burned off most of her anger and frustration. Compliantly she went around to the passenger side of the car and climbed in.

"You may as well ride back with me, because I'd just have to wait. I drove over to see you, you know."

"Oh?"

"I know I didn't call, but I'm bearing gifts. I thought you'd forgive me." She gestured with her thumb toward the rear of the car.

Jessica looked back and saw stacks of boxes. "What's all that?"

"Maternity clothes."

She looked at Meade in surprise.

"Chase's orders. He said you're starting to show and don't have the wardrobe for it. It's his obligation under the contract, so here I am, Santa's helper."

"Meade, you didn't have to do that."

She laughed. "Are you kidding? I wouldn't have missed it for the world. The vicarious pleasure I got was worth every minute." She laughed again as they pulled up in front of the house.

Once inside Meade requested tea from Maggie and the parcels were brought in. The two women went straight upstairs to the guest suite. Jessica sat down, feeling like an errant schoolgirl as she watched Meade supervising the delivery of the packages. When everything had been brought up, Meade had Jessica take off her painting smock.

"What makes Chase think you're starting to show? Except for a little fullness in the face you look the same to me."

Jessica thought of him caressing her nude body, knowing how he'd come to that conclusion. But she could hardly explain it to Meade. "I've gained."

"Not since I've met you. You must have been a rail, Jessica."

They looked at each other, Jessica wondering just what Chase had said to Meade, what she knew. So far she had given no indication that anything was amiss, but Jessica decided that was intended to spare her feelings. There was no point in ignoring the facts.

"What did Chase tell you, Meade?"

"About his leaving? Oh, he gave me some cock-and-bull story about business obligations and the fact that it would be easier for you with him gone. I didn't believe it for a minute."

"I didn't ask him to leave."

"You wanted him to stay?"

"No, I planned to move out myself."

"The reasons are none of my business, so don't feel you have to justify or explain."

"I just didn't want you to feel badly toward me."

"Of course I wouldn't. I'm sure if anyone's to blame it's my brother. He's not the most diplomatic man on earth."

"No, it's not Chase's fault. It's the circumstances."

"Is there anything I can do?"

"Just understand that I did what I had to do."

"If you say so, Jessica. I'm not here to judge. I hope we can be friends."

They smiled at each other.

"Well, shall we look at the goodies?" Meade went to the bed and picked up a box. "I hope I didn't miss your taste by much, but don't worry, we can take back anything you hate."

Jessica watched Meade open a box and hold up a pale blue corduroy jumper. "They had it in forest green, too, but I thought with your coloring the blue was better. What do you think?"

She didn't have the heart for it, but she could see that Meade was enthralled. "It's very nice. I like the blue."

"You know," Meade said, hardly having heard Jessica's response, "I dreamed about the green jumper last night—it's the color I would have gotten for myself. In the dream I put it on and my stomach started growing." She chuckled. "Can you imagine? Roger said it was a hell of a lot easier than what we've been through, but not nearly as much fun."

"It wasn't much fun the way I did it, either."

Meade looked at her thoughtfully. "No, I suppose not. But I wouldn't hesitate to trade places with you." She picked up another box.

Jessica quietly sighed, thinking this was the last thing she needed. But she realized that Meade didn't know she preferred keeping the pregnancy completely from her mind.

"Oh!" Meade exclaimed, peering into the box. "This is one of my excesses, but I just couldn't resist." She held up a tiny pair of baby pajamas in blue, complete with dangling feet. "Isn't it adorable? And just to hedge my bets I got this." She pulled out an identical pair in pink.

Jessica stared blankly at the little items of clothing, suddenly feeling dreadful.

"What do women do, buy everything in yellow? I don't imagine everyone's as extravagant as I." She folded the baby things and put them back in the box. "Maybe women just know whether to get blue or pink." She looked up at Jessica. "Did you know with Jamie? Were you just sure he was going to be a boy?"

"No, Alex and I were both expecting a girl." Jessica felt her stomach clinch, not liking the conversation at all.

"Then I guess you won't be any help with this one, given your track record," Meade said good-naturedly. "Or do you have a clear premonition this time?"

"No, Meade, I haven't thought about it."

Hearing something in Jessica's voice, Meade looked over at her sober face. "You aren't enjoying this, are you?"

"No, it's all right. I guess I just have trouble getting excited about maternity clothes."

"I shouldn't have shopped for you, should I? I'm interfering."

"No, no, it's not that at all. I suppose somebody had to do it. It's just as well that you did."

"Would you prefer to look at the things alone? I don't need to see them on or anything."

"I'm grateful that you went to the trouble, Meade. I really am."

Maggie came in with the tea service and placed it on the table beside Jessica. Meade came over and joined her. "You don't need to pour, Maggie. I'll do it."

The housekeeper withdrew and Meade took a cup and saucer from the tray and placed it next to Jessica. She took one for herself, lifted the lid to the teapot and peered inside.

"I think I'll let it steep awhile."

Jessica sank back in her chair and looked tentatively at the woman, who was placing napkins and spoons on the table. She didn't know what to expect.

"You know," Meade said, "the clothes don't worry me nearly as much as the baby's room. How are we going to decorate it? We can't wait until he or she is born, and

I do hate yellow. It's so...indecisive. What do you think?''

"That's entirely up to you and Chase. It's no affair of mine."

Meade looked up in surprise. "Lord, you are upset. It's the baby, isn't it. You don't want me talking about it."

Jessica felt the sting of tears and got to her feet. She went to the window.

Meade followed her. Jessica didn't turn around.

"I'm sorry if I upset you. I wasn't thinking."

A tear brimmed Jessica's eye and trickled down her cheek. She felt Meade's hand on her arm.

"Can you forgive me?"

Jessica sniffled and wiped her cheek with the sleeve of her blouse. "I'm sorry. I'm just feeling emotional. Let's talk about you." She walked over to the dresser and took a tissue. "When's your operation?"

"Heavens, I had it two weeks ago."

"You did?" She wiped her eyes. "What happened? What did the doctor say?"

"My tubes are scarred. That's the bad news—no baby the traditional way. But the good news is my ovaries are fine and they think I'm a good candidate for in vitro."

"A test tube baby?"

Meade smiled happily. "Roger and I have to go in and talk with the doctor, and there are tests, but it's a possibility."

"Meade, that's wonderful! I'm so happy for you."

"Well, I'm trying not to get too excited. I'm preparing for the worst and keep telling myself the child you're carrying is the only baby I'll ever have."

"I wish I could give it to you now."

They looked into each other's eyes and quietly embraced.

WEARING THE BLUE MATERNITY JUMPER, Jessica took the train into Manhattan the following week for her checkup at the clinic. She was terribly nervous and dreaded seeing Chase. But as she rode up in the elevator, the thought struck her that he might not be there. The little clutch of regret she felt told her that she really wanted to see him, after all.

He was in the waiting room when she arrived. "Hello, Jessica."

She looked at the familiar face that, though sober, was still dear, like that of an old friend. "Hello, Chase." She moved past him, sitting a few seats away.

"How's Jamie?" His voice was calm, resonant, but it betrayed a discomfort, not unlike her own.

"Fine."

"How's the therapy coming?"

"Very well. The other day Mr. Valticos told me Jamie's legs are much stronger. He thinks he may be ready for lighter braces."

"That's great."

Jessica searched his face for messages that weren't in the conversation. She couldn't decide if what she saw in his eyes was coldness or hurt. He somehow looked a little sad and older, though it had to be the mood. It had only been a few weeks.

"You look good," he said.

She smiled politely. "I've gained two more pounds, if that's what you mean."

Chase chuckled. "I guess it's all a matter of perspective as to what's good."

She nodded. "Yes."

"I wanted to tell you that I'm leaving for Europe day after tomorrow. I'll be returning just before Christmas."

"That long?"

"Yes. And unfortunately I'll be missing the next appointment or two here at the clinic." He smiled. "But I'm sure you can handle it on your own."

"I guess I can." She looked down.

"Incidentally, I didn't think about holidays when I set up our new arrangement. The past few years we've established a tradition of sorts. Meade and Roger always come for Christmas. Would it be a problem if we all join you for the day?"

"No, of course not! How could I keep you away from your own home on Christmas?"

"Perhaps Meade and Maggie can coordinate things in my absence."

"Since it's a family occasion, Jamie and I can certainly go away for a few days, if that would make it easier."

"No, I wouldn't consider letting you do that. Christmas is for children. The farm's Jamie's home now."

They sat quietly for a time. Neither spoke.

"I see you got the maternity clothes."

"Yes, Meade did a wonderful job. And thank you for buying them for me."

"It was my obligation."

Jessica hated the formality, the stiffness, though she didn't know what else she could reasonably expect. "Listen, Chase," she said, after another silence. "I've felt badly about running you out of your home. I know you've got to resent me terribly for it." She looked at him imploringly. "Do you?"

Just then the nurse opened the door. "Mrs. Brandon, you can come in now."

She sighed, feeling the futility of the moment. She got to her feet.

"Jessica," Chase said, stopping her just before she went through the door, "the answer to your question is no. Don't worry about that, or anything else."

"Thank you," she whispered in a barely audible tone. "Thank you."

IN THE DAYS THAT FOLLOWED, Jessica slowly began to find her stride in the studio. Her evenings were lonely, though. Once Jamie was in bed she was left to her own devices. If her mind wasn't on Chase it was on the baby and her stomach, which seemed to be growing by the hour.

She thought often of their brief conversation in the waiting room and the few minutes together with the doctor after her examination. She was glad he wasn't bitter, but the situation, their separation, still weighed on her.

One evening Maggie wandered into the sitting room to find Jessica by herself, a magazine on her lap but staring off into space.

"You look all forlorn sitting there alone, Mrs. Brandon, if I might say so."

Jessica smiled up at the woman. "I enjoy my time alone, Maggie."

She was aware Chase had talked to the staff before he had left, but he hadn't revealed the true reasons for his departure. In deference to Jessica, he attributed the necessity to business obligations.

"It's a shame Mr. Hamilton has gone and left you by yourself, ma'am. Mind, I know you're not married and

such, but the baby is the both of yours, and you oughtn't
to have to live like a widow lady."

"But I am a widow lady, Maggie."

"Pardon me, ma'am, but I mean to say your life now
should be different."

"I appreciate your concern, but I'm fine. I'm like any
other woman who's pregnant. I'm just waiting for the
time to come."

"There's ways to wait and there's ways to wait. A lady
expectin' should work with her hands, do needlework.
Now I know you're a painter, but in the evenin', especially on a winter night when there's a fire burnin', you
should have a piece to work on, somethin' for the baby."

"I'm afraid I don't know how to do any needlework,
Maggie."

"You don't know how? Your mum didn't teach you?"

"My mother died when I was a little girl. I missed a lot
of that sort of thing."

"Oh, Jesus and Mary, I'm sorry, ma'am. I didn't
know."

"There's no way you could. Don't worry."

Maggie hesitated. "Would I offend you if I offered to
teach you, ma'am?"

"Teach me needlework? No, of course you wouldn't
offend me. But I don't know that I would make a very
good student. I have trouble sewing on buttons."

"It's simple as pie, ma'am. It truly is. There's different kinds, of course. Some women prefer knittin', but
I've always been partial to needlepoint. You bein' artistic, you might like it, as well. I'm sure I have a simple little piece of some sort in me rooms if you'd like a little
lesson now. Then, if you like it, you can buy somethin'
more challengin', somethin' suitable for the baby."

Jessica smiled at the woman's earnest manner. "Well, if you don't mind...but I hate to take your time, you put in such long days."

"Don't think a thing of it, Mrs. Brandon. There's nothin' on the telly tonight, and it would please me to teach you."

Jessica proved to be a better student then she expected, catching on very quickly. At a needlework shop in Mount Kisco she bought a large needlepoint bunny that would be sewn and stuffed when she was through. Jessica decided to make it a gift to the baby, something the child could remember her by. Maggie estimated the five remaining months of her pregnancy would be just about how long the project would take if she worked diligently.

A COUPLE OF WEEKS after Chase flew off to Europe a cold northern wind moved down the Hudson Valley, sending autumn leaves tumbling along the roads, covering lawns with a fine coat of frost and turning children's cheeks rosy pink. Mittens and parkas, scarves and overcoats were retrieved from the backs of closets as winter threatened to arrive before Thanksgiving.

Jessica's life regained its solitary character with all the world but Jamie, Maggie and Anne Bascom on the other side of the fence. She painted earnestly by day, sat with Jamie and worked on her needlepoint bunny by night. She watched her stomach grow and waited impatiently for her time to come.

Meade came by for tea several times and took Jessica and Jamie shopping once. She invited the two of them for Thanksgiving, but Jessica didn't want to impose. Instead she invited Harriet, who like herself had no family. Maggie and Anne were off. Jessica cooked the three of them a small turkey.

"So you've decided not to become Lady Hamilton after all," Harriet said when they had gotten Jamie to bed and were having their coffee by the fire.

"I never considered it."

Harriet gave her a skeptical look. "Lord, I'd have already checked the title on this place, made sure there was room for another name on the deed."

Jessica shook her head. "It's all over, Harriet."

"Says who?"

"Says me!" she snapped. "Who do you think?"

Harriet sank back into the couch. Jessica realized immediately that her outburst was out of line.

"Oh, Harriet, I'm so sorry. I'm in a foul temper. I didn't mean to snap."

"Poor thing. You're having a rough time, aren't you?"

Her eyes closed. "Why couldn't I have listened to you?"

"You love him?"

"It doesn't matter now. All I care about is that Jamie and I get through this in one piece."

"That's really all?"

"My sanity depends on it." It sounded facile, she knew, but the course of her survival was clearer to her now than it had ever been in her life. There were long months ahead, but even harder would be the few hours she'd have to spend with Chase Hamilton.

CHAPTER SIXTEEN

BY MIDMORNING ON CHRISTMAS EVE it had begun to snow. At first they were just lazy flakes, but the weather report indicated the snowfall would turn heavy by nightfall. Jessica stood at the window, watching the snow and thinking about Chase.

He was flying in from London early that evening, and because of the storm Meade and Roger decided they would come to the farm Christmas Eve instead of Christmas Day. The Phillipses would drive over from their place in Connecticut after lunch, Chase would drive up from the airport when he got in, and they would all be snug in the house for the blizzard.

With Meade there to help, Maggie and Anne had been given a couple of days off. So the evening before Christmas Meade and Jessica worked in the kitchen, making a lobster bisque, fettuccine Alfredo and salad for dinner. Having learned that Chase's flight was delayed in London, they listened to the radio for weather and traffic bulletins, worried that he might not make it in before the airports were closed.

Roger called the airline and was told that some incoming flights were being diverted from New York. The status of Chase's flight was uncertain, and Jessica realized that the bittersweet encounter she had been anticipating might not happen after all. Roger, Meade, Jessica and Jamie ended up eating dinner alone.

After the boy had been treated to Auntie Meade's reading of "The Night Before Christmas" in front of the fireplace, he was put to bed and the Phillipses volunteered to help Jessica play Santa Claus and set everything up around the tree. They got all the gifts arranged—Meade bemoaning the fact Chase wasn't there to enjoy it, too—except for the miniature electric train that was to be Jamie's principal surprise.

For a while Roger fiddled with it, but it soon became apparent that his skills ran in other directions. He threw up his hands in exasperation.

"No man is perfect," Meade lamented, "but when we moved into our first house and he called a carpenter to install ceiling hooks for my plants, I should have realized I married a mechanically deficient specimen."

"Be thankful I can pay for professionals to do things properly," Roger retorted.

"Yes, dear, but a plumber to repair a running toilet?"

"How was I to know shaking the handle would fix it?"

Meade turned to Jessica. "Maybe *my* plumbing isn't the reason we haven't gotten pregnant yet."

"*That* I know how to do," Roger interjected.

His wife smiled. "That's true. I didn't marry you for your advertising jingles alone, dear."

Jessica picked up the instruction sheet for the train set. "This is my fault. I didn't realize it was so difficult to put together."

"It'd be a shame to give it to Jamie like this," Roger said. "I remember my first model plane. I opened the box expecting to find an airplane and instead there were a million little pieces of balsa wood."

"What did you do?"

"I cut out the picture on the box and hung it on my wall."

"Well, that won't do for this train," Meade said. "Maybe I'll have a go at it." She looked at her husband. "You're still weak from that bout of flu. Why don't you go on to bed so you'll feel well for tomorrow? I'll stay up and help Jessica."

THE GRANDFATHER CLOCK SOUNDED the half hour and Jessica realized it would soon be midnight. Meade was still on her knees on the floor, pieces of the train set scattered around her, partly assembled.

"Oh, Meade, this is no way for you to spend Christmas Eve. Let's just leave it for tomorrow."

"No, you just lie back and rest or, better yet, go on to bed. I'll finish this if it kills me."

Jessica was tired, but she couldn't abandon Meade. She stretched out on the couch, watching the shimmer of flames among the burning logs, picturing Chase's face and worrying about him.

Resting her hand on her swollen stomach, Jessica thought about their child. She didn't normally, but the baby was the only tie—or link—to Chase. The thought of his child in her womb was comforting in a strange sort of way. Despite their separation, it was a tentative bond that kept them together.

As she lay back, her eyelids heavy, her cheeks warm from the fire, Jessica felt an unexpected stirring in her womb. It was just a feathery sweep of a tiny arm or leg— not the robust motions she remembered from the latter stages of her first pregnancy—just the fragile caress of Chase's child. The sensation brought a smile to her lips and she let herself hold the little bulge in her abdomen.

CHASE TRIED ROCKING THE CAR back and forth from low to reverse, but the tires just spun ineffectually, digging deeper and deeper into the snow. Finally the rear end began slipping sideways into the ditch and he stopped the car, set the hand brake and turned off the engine. Almost immediately the snowflakes began accumulating on the windshield. In just a few moments he could hardly see out.

He cursed his luck and began going over the options in his mind. He estimated he was still three or four miles from the farm. Even if he could get to a phone there probably wasn't much hope of getting a tow truck on Christmas Eve. And it would take at least an hour to walk home. Eventually a snowplow or emergency vehicle would come along, but would it be within an hour?

Chase got out of the car, wishing he were dressed for the expedition. Dress shoes and a top coat were not going to do well when snowshoes and a parka were appropriate. He pulled his lapels tightly across his chest and wished he had waited out the lines at the airport phone booths and called the farm.

He started walking through the snow, distinguishing the road from the adjacent fields by the fences and trees. There was one house within sight, but it was dark and well off the road. He was trying to remember what other homes lay ahead, when he heard the muffled sound of a vehicle in the snow-filled air.

Turning around, he saw the faint gleam of headlights in the darkness. A smile crossed his face and he thought it might not be long before he was home, after all.

THE SHERIFF'S CAR STOPPED at the porte cochère, Chase climbed out, thanked the officer and bounded up the front steps of the house. Inside he brushed the snow from his coat and was hanging it in the closet, when Meade came rushing into the entry hall.

"Chase, you made it!" She bussed him on the cheek. "We were worried your plane would be diverted."

"It nearly was. I think it was the last one to land before they closed the airport. Where is everybody?"

"Roger's getting over the flu. He went to bed. I'm helping Jessica put together Jamie's train, but without much success."

They stepped to the doorway leading to the sitting room and Meade pointed to Jessica curled up and asleep on the couch. Chase stared at her, the firelight casting a mellow glow over the room and the woman.

"Are you too tired to help with the train so we can all go to bed?"

"No, it's morning where I came from. I'm ready to start my day." He had slipped off his suit coat and tossed it on a nearby chair. "There's no need for you to stay up, Meade. I'll put the train together."

"Shall I wake Jessica?"

"No, I will. Go on to bed."

As he walked toward the sleeping woman, he could see the little round bulge under her mauve panne velvet caftan. Her hand was resting on her stomach, the light from the fire turning her tawny hair strawberry blond. For a moment he froze there, awestruck. He wanted to go to her, but couldn't. He wanted to awaken her, but he wasn't willing to disturb the lovely vision.

He sat on the couch opposite her, moved by what he saw. The face was exquisite—fuller than before, but even more beautiful than he had remembered. Her lips were slightly parted, the soft feminine wisps of her hair a perfect crown to her delicate features. Jessica's long slender neck was so lovely and inviting in the muted light that he wanted to kiss it.

He couldn't though. She was as untouchable as a fine portrait, arousing his emotions, yet removed and inhabiting another world.

After savoring her beauty a bit longer and thinking of the child she carried, Chase got down on the floor and began examining the scattered pieces of the toy train.

CHRISTMAS MORNING Jessica awoke from a deep sleep, feeling disoriented and vaguely alarmed. She remembered being awakened the night before by the sound of Jamie's train and seeing Chase on the floor beside the tree in his shirt sleeves. They had exchanged only a few words, mostly about the train and how she was feeling, then he had taken her upstairs and she'd gotten in bed, falling asleep almost immediately.

Jessica rubbed her eyes as impressions of Chase slowly drifted back into her mind. She hadn't even asked him about his trip, or the reason he was so late. The only impression that stuck with her was his gentleness and the polite deference he showed.

In the next room Jamie was stirring and Jessica hurried out of bed. She knew he wouldn't be patient while she prepared herself for her first real encounter with Chase. She would have to be quick.

When she carried Jamie down the stairs, Meade, Roger and Chase were in the sitting room, having a cup of coffee while they waited to witness the child's excitement. The men were dressed, but Meade, like Jessica, was in a dressing gown.

"There they are! Merry Christmas," Meade exclaimed, and rose to go over and greet them. "Jamie, come and see. I think Santa's been here," she enthused, taking the boy.

Glancing at Chase and Roger, Jessica went to an empty chair near the tree to watch. Jamie was on the floor, squealing with joy at the sight of the train. Everyone was sharing in the child's excitement, but when Jessica looked up Chase was staring at her, a little smile on his face. He calmly sipped his coffee, but said nothing.

She turned her attention back to her son, watching him tear into the package Meade had placed before him. She tried to get into the spirit of the event, but Jessica knew it would be a long, hard day with Chase Hamilton so near.

WHEN CHASE HAD FINISHED operating the train for Jamie and renewing their friendship, he set him near Jessica's feet to play with a game Meade and Roger had given him. It was time, Roger said, for the adults to get their toys, so Meade began handing out the gifts.

Chase's presents for everyone were especially nice—not just expensive, but carefully considered. He had given Jessica a tigereye bead necklace he'd found in Paris. It wasn't terribly expensive, but it was simple and pure. Meade agreed that it suited her perfectly.

Jessica's own gift for him was less imaginative—a tie— but it was a Polo and quite expensive. Feeling it was a little inadequate under the circumstances, she excused herself and went upstairs to get something else.

She returned a few minutes later with an unwrapped carton about the size of a shirt box. "I was going to give this to you in March when I left," she said, "but it seems more appropriate that you have it now."

He took it from her, surprise on his face. "The tie is lovely. You don't have to give me anything else."

"It's not a shirt," she said shyly as he lifted the lid.

Chase removed an object wrapped in tissue paper and uncovered it to find a framed miniature landscape on wood. Jessica's initials were in the corner.

"It's gorgeous!" He held it up for Meade and Roger to see. "It's the farm. I recognize the hills."

He stood up and kissed her on the cheek.

"Something to remember me by," she explained, but her voice broke and emotion suddenly welled up. She quickly retreated to her chair, her eyes glossing over with tears.

Chase sat down again and silence settled over the room, save Jamie's chatter as he played happily by himself.

"Well," Meade said cheerily, "who would like some breakfast?"

JESSICA WAS PLEASED that Chase made it easy for her the rest of the day, keeping a polite distance, minimizing the tension as much as possible. He spent a great deal of time with Jamie, and she was in the kitchen a lot, even when it wasn't necessary.

Christmas dinner was pleasant, and Meade got it started well with a surprise announcement. "This is a family occasion," she said with prideful tone. "So Roger and I want for you to be the first to know that we've been approved for the in vitro program."

"Well, congratulations!" Chase exclaimed.

"How wonderful!" Jessica added. "I'm so pleased for you."

Chase picked up his wineglass. "To our growing family."

"It's a little early to begin counting chickens," Meade cautioned. "I'm one setting hen who still needs help."

"I'm sure it'll work out fine," her brother assured her.

"We thought we'd concentrate our emotions on your baby," Roger said, "to avoid painful disappointment." He grinned. "Of course, with half a dozen name books on our coffee table, that's easier said than done."

They all laughed.

"By the way, what's this celebrated kid going to be called? Picked a name yet?"

Chase glanced at Jessica. "We haven't . . . I mean, I haven't picked one yet."

In the uncomfortable silence that followed Roger seemed to see that he had ventured into dangerous waters. "Hey," he said, trying to carry the jest off, "why don't I take it to the agency? I'll put up a poster in the coffee room and we'll have a name-a-kid contest."

"Roger..." Meade said out of the corner of her mouth.

"It's a good idea," he insisted. "It'd cost a client ten or twenty thousand for us to name a product, maybe more. Look at all the free brainpower you'd have at your disposal. Of course, if you offered lunch to the winner you'd probably have more enthusiastic participation."

"I think we'll pass on that, Roger, but thanks," Chase said.

His brother-in-law shrugged. "It's the price. People always turn their nose up at free service. If we named children for three hundred dollars a pop there'd probably be a line at the door."

"I'm sure there would be, dear," Meade said, showing a little irritation. She turned to her brother. "So how was Europe, Chase? We haven't heard a word about it and you were gone so long."

BY EVENING the storm had blown itself out, but because of the holiday they had doubts many of the secondary roads would be plowed. Meade planned on staying until

Maggie returned, but Roger had an important meeting the next morning and decided to drive home. He'd had the foresight to bring a four-wheel-drive vehicle and offered to take Chase down the highway so he could pick up his car.

While Meade helped Roger pack his things, Chase sat with Jessica in the sitting room.

"Sorry about that business with the baby's name," he said sympathetically. "I hope you weren't embarrassed by it."

"Not at all. Actually, it struck me as strange that the subject hasn't come up before. Have you decided what you want to call the baby?"

"I've thought about it, but haven't made a firm decision."

"Mind if I ask what names you're considering?"

"No, not at all. I was thinking Andrew if it's a boy and Emily if it's a girl."

"Hmm."

"What do you think?"

"I like Andrew."

"But not Emily?"

"Not a lot."

"What would you pick?"

"The girl's name I wanted for Jamie was Catherine. I'd have called her Kate."

"Kate. Yes, Catherine's nice." He reflected. "Let's see. How would it sound?" He cleared his throat. "And now ladies and gentleman, playing Chopin's Etude in E Major, Miss Catherine Hamilton."

Jessica chuckled. "No, Chase. It goes like this—and now I'd like to present to the executive committee the new vice president of marketing, Catherine Hamilton."

They laughed.

"I suppose you'd prefer that Andrew play the piano," he teased.

"Well . . ." The comment was completely unexpected. "I guess I don't prefer anything. It'll be your son or daughter, not mine."

"I'm sorry, Jessica. I wasn't thinking."

She knew it was her own fault for chiding him. "Don't be silly. No harm done."

But Chase could see it upset her.

They heard the Phillipses coming down the stairs. He got up and stepped over to her. "Look," he said, "I know this was a difficult day. I just want you to know how much I appreciate it."

"Don't mention it."

"And thanks for the painting. It means a lot to me. It'll hang in the baby's room. Always."

Jessica swallowed hard but couldn't stop a tear from brimming her eye.

"You ready, Chase?" Roger called from the hall.

The farewell was quickly done. Roger was affable. Chase gave his sister a hug and gently pinched Jessica's cheek. "Take care."

The men went out the door into the crystalline air.

Both Jessica and Meade turned away with misty eyes.

THE DAYS from January to early March moved at a glacial pace. Jessica didn't see Chase again. He came to the house three or four times, but when he did she was either in the studio or at the clinic. Each time he stayed just long enough to spend a few minutes with Jamie and take care of the business that brought him home. Jessica was sorry he didn't ask to see her, but knew she had no basis for complaint.

The visits to the clinic were more frequent, but Chase didn't bother to go with her—or didn't want to. She wasn't sure if he was sparing her or himself. In any case she was glad. She missed him, but it was easier not seeing him.

Meanwhile, everything seemed to be growing: her stomach, the snowdrifts against the buildings and along the roads, the numbers of paintings lining the studio walls, Jamie's impatience, and even the needlepoint bunny, which she finished by the end of February. Although the baby seemed constantly active in her womb, Jessica managed to keep it at an emotional distance. During those months her mind, her heart and her body were not one.

Jessica gave Maggie the bunny to give to Chase. It didn't seem it ought to come from her directly.

"The little tyke will cherish it his whole life, I'm sure, Mrs. Brandon," Maggie said, running her fingers over the stitches. The housekeeper was unable to say more. She wiped her eye with her sleeve and Jessica had to turn away.

Meade came by occasionally, mostly to make arrangements for the baby on Chase's behalf, but she asked Jessica to join her for tea several times. Their conversations were like always, but they both sensed the baby's birth would be the end of their friendship.

DURING THE FIRST WEEK of March a storm blew down out of Canada, blanketing the Eastern Seaboard with a foot of new snow in the first two days. Everything came to a halt. At the farm the power was out for a number of hours. Mack wasn't able to get to the farm to feed the horses and Maggie, Anne, Jessica and Jamie were stranded.

Chase called and talked to the housekeeper, telling her he would have the man who normally plowed the drive get out as soon as possible. Like everyone else, he was powerless to help. They had no alternative but to wait out the storm.

The evening of the second day Jessica didn't feel well. She didn't go down for dinner, so Maggie brought her soup on a tray. But she wasn't hungry. She felt strange, not at all her normal self.

Lying on her side in bed, Jessica pulled the covers close around her neck, wrapped her arms around her stomach and waited. The baby was very active, pushing first one way, then another. She wondered if it wanted to be born as badly as she wanted it.

Within an hour the contractions began. With Jamie there had been false labor pains during the final month, but they had never come to anything. These seemed different. She couldn't be going into labor, though—the baby wasn't due for nearly three weeks.

Maggie came up to look in on her just as Jessica was experiencing another bout of pain.

"You all right, Mrs. Brandon? You're looking very pale."

"I'm having false labor pains, but I don't ever remember them being so bad or so frequent."

"Perhaps it's best I call the doctor, ma'am. Mr. Hamilton said to me, 'Call first, ask later.' Better safe than sorry."

"Let's wait and see if they pass."

"But with the storm and all, we'd best not take a chance."

Jessica saw the concern on Maggie's face, but tried not to let it worry her. This baby had behaved normally for more than eight months. There was no reason to think it would decide to come early now.

"You wouldn't get angry if I called Mr. Hamilton, now would you, ma'am?"

"No, if it would make you feel better, call him."

"Then I shall. If you'll excuse me."

Jessica watched Maggie leave as the contractions continued rippling through her abdomen. She listened to the wind blowing outside and thought of the snow.

CHASE HAMILTON LOOKED OUT the window at the snowy obscurity of the Manhattan skyline. The gray-white atmosphere was slowly turning black as night approached. He turned and looked impatiently at the telephone, hating his impotence.

He tried not to worry, telling himself he was fortunate that Anne Bascom was there—at least she had had some elementary training. Still, he wouldn't be able to relax until he knew how serious it was.

Finally the phone rang and Chase went to it instantly.

"Mr. Hamilton, Dr. Duckett."

"Yes, doctor. Were you able to reach them?"

"I just got off the phone a few minutes ago."

"And?"

"I spoke with both the young lady there and with Mrs. Brandon. Frankly, it's difficult to tell how serious it is without examining her, but as a precaution I've suggested they go into the local hospital. I believe Mount Kisco's closest."

"Yes. Transportation will be a problem, though. I wonder if I can get an ambulance to them."

"I would think some sort of emergency vehicle could get through, though as I understand it your place is pretty remote."

"It'll depend on how much plowing they've done. I'll get on the phone. How about you, doctor? I suppose even getting up to Mount Kisco will be difficult."

"I'll investigate that, Mr. Hamilton. But even if I'm unable to get through, I can consult with the attending physician by phone. Fortunately Mrs. Brandon's pregnancy is without complication. There should be no cause for concern once we get her to the hospital."

Chase hung up, his palms moist with perspiration. As he dialed information for Westchester County a surge of fear went through him. What if this was it? He might be about to have his child and he wasn't prepared. Things were not working out as he had planned.

He pictured Jessica, and wished to God he could be with her.

CHASE LOOKED OUT the tow truck's window at the snow-filled streets of Mount Kisco. Cars were buried everywhere and very few vehicles were moving. The driver, wearing an old mackinaw and a leather cap with woolen earflaps, gripped the wheel and glanced at Chase.

"We'll be at the hospital soon, mister. It's just up the street."

"I hope I'm in time. It's taken me four hours to get here from New York."

"Must be your first."

Chase nodded. "Yeah."

"The wife and I have five. It gets pretty routine after a while. With the last one we was in the middle of a TV show when the labor started. Neither of us wanted to miss the ending—" the man laughed "—so we waited till it was over."

They slowly inched around a stalled car.

"They brung your wife in by ambulance, then?"

"Some sort of four-wheel-drive emergency vehicle."

"Poor little thing, and her first, too."

"No, it's Jessica's second. My first."

"Oh. Well, better you than her, huh?"

"Yeah, better me than her."

They pulled into the emergency entrance of the hospital. Chase handed the man two twenty-dollar bills and climbed out of the truck. "Thanks."

"Thank you, mister, and good luck to you and the wife."

Chase waved and hurried inside.

He was directed to reception, then to the maternity ward, where he found a nurse sitting behind the counter. She looked up as he approached.

"How's Jessica Brandon? She was brought in during the night."

"Are you Mr. Brandon?"

"No, my name's Hamilton. I'm the father."

"Oh. Well, then, congratulations, Mr. Hamilton!" she said, beaming. "Two hours ago Mrs. Brandon delivered a baby girl."

Chase suddenly felt weak. He blinked, trying to make his mind accept the words.

"Both the mother and child are fine. The baby was a few weeks early, so she's on the small side, but she seems to be healthy and normal."

"Thank God."

"Mrs. Brandon is sleeping now, but you can look in on her if you wish."

Chase was in a daze. *A child. A daughter!* He looked at the nurse, feeling so lighthearted he could almost fly. "A little girl."

"Yes, sir." She smiled. "Did you want to see your...uh...Mrs. Brandon?"

"No, I don't want to wake her now. But thank you."

"The baby's in the nursery."

"Yes. Where do I go to see my daughter?"

JESSICA STOOD BESIDE the hospital bed, looked through her small suitcase to see that everything was inside and closed the lid. Harriet Thomas turned from the window and smiled at her.

"Well, at least the snow has stopped and they've got most of the roads open."

"Thank goodness for small favors."

"Better this than the way it was when you arrived, Jessica."

"Yeah. My life doesn't seem to lack excitement." She looked at her friend. "When did Anne leave with Jamie?"

"They left Chase's place this morning. They'll be at the apartment when we get there."

"It's creepy to be moving from his house to his apartment."

"Well, it's just until you find a place. And it's free."

Jessica nodded and started to pick up her case.

"No, leave that. I'll take it."

"I'm not an invalid, Harriet."

"You're going to have to ride out of here in a wheelchair, so you might as well get used to it."

"Do I really have to hold the baby?"

"I'm afraid so. There's no way out of it. The hospital won't give her to anyone but you."

Jessica's stomach was in a knot. She felt nauseous. "Will you tell the nurse to have her covered with a blanket? I don't want to see her, Harriet. I really couldn't handle that."

"Sure. Don't worry, everybody understands."

Jessica took a shaky breath and exhaled slowly.

"I have to give her to Chase?"

"Yes, he'll be out front in his car. I've got a cab waiting for us."

Jessica gingerly sat on the edge of the bed. "When can we go? I want to get this over with."

"Let me check with the nurse." Harriet started to the door.

"Harriet."

The other stopped and turned.

"Tell her to hold the baby as long as possible—until the last minute."

"Okay." She left the room.

A few minutes later an orderly arrived with a wheelchair. Harriet helped Jessica on with her coat, then the young man assisted her into the chair. They went out into the hallway, where the nurse stood waiting with a pink bundle in her arms.

Jessica looked at the woman's face, then at Harriet. "Let's go," she whispered.

They went down the corridor to the bank of elevators. No one spoke. When the doors opened they all went in, the nurse with the baby on one side, Harriet on the other. Jessica prayed the baby wouldn't cry or coo.

The doors opened, they exited and went down the hall to the main entrance, where they stopped. Jessica didn't look up, but she sensed the nurse shuffling uncomfortably beside her.

"Here, Mrs. Brandon. I'm afraid you'll have to take her now."

Jessica bit her lip and accepted the pink bundle, staring straight ahead, her body quivering almost imperceptibly.

They went through a double set of doors and into the icy air. Instinctively Jessica pulled the baby against her, but she didn't look down. After a moment she realized that the Bentley was at the foot of the walk. Through the window she saw Meade's face, watching as they approached.

At the same time the door on the driver's side opened and Chase got out. Jessica could see that he wore an overcoat and gloves. His head was bare and vapors billowed from his mouth as he breathed. The expression on his face was somber. He was looking at her, but she didn't see his eyes. The silence and solemnity reminded Jessica of a funeral and for an instant recollections of Alex's burial flashed through her mind.

When they arrived at the car she saw that Chase had a long white envelope in his hand, which he immediately gave to Harriet. The cold air stung Jessica's eyes and she blinked several times, looking away, feeling empty and confused. She knew what was expected of her, but nothing seemed to happen. No one moved, no one spoke.

Jessica glanced at Harriet and realized that it was up to her. Looking up at Chase, she lifted the baby and extended her toward him. "Here's your daughter," she said, her voice cracking.

He leaned over and took the bundle, the vapors of his breath mixing with hers. Jessica looked at him. Then he straightened, the baby clutched awkwardly to his chest. He didn't move; he just met her gaze.

Jessica saw light glistening on his cheek and she realized it was a tear. She looked at him for a moment, then closed her eyes, unable to bear it any longer. "Please go, Chase. Please go."

She dropped her face into her hands and waited until she heard the car door open, then close. Still unable to look, she listened to the sound of his footsteps as he went around to the driver's side. She heard the engine start, the gears engage and the crunch of the tires on the icy pavement as they pulled away.

When she was sure they had gone she opened her eyes. Harriet touched her shoulder and signaled for the cab to pull up. Jessica rose from the chair and the orderly helped her into the back seat.

As the taxi pulled away Harriet put her arm around Jessica's shoulders, then pressed the envelope into her hand. Jessica didn't look at it. She just stared out at the drifts of dirty snow and naked trees that lined the streets.

CHAPTER SEVENTEEN

THE SNOW MELTED almost as quickly as it had come. A week after Chase had taken the baby to the farm, there were only patches left in the fields. He was able to walk along most of the lane without being thwarted by melting drifts or mud.

He climbed to the top of the hill—Jessica's hill, as he had come to think of it—and looked out over the bleak landscape. A curl of smoke emanated from the chimney of the house and he thought of the cozy familial feeling that it suggested. His daughter was there, safely in the care of Anne Bascom. Maggie was there, too, and frequently Meade. They all doted on the baby, loving her in their way, though none more fiercely than Chase himself.

He had never known such joy as when she was in his arms, such pride. And yet, it was not right. Something was missing. Jessica.

Chase had known for a long time that he loved her, though how much had only become apparent when she and the baby were no longer one. He hadn't really seen her as just Jessica Brandon for a long time—not since the previous May. But in his mind now that was exactly who she was. He felt her absence from his life, acutely.

Chase had debated for several days when it would be best to go to her. There were reasons for going now and reasons for waiting. But his own anxious desire was the most persuasive argument of all. Though he had no idea how she would react, he decided to contact her.

JESSICA WAS LYING on the bed, doing exercises, working avidly just as she had for the past few days, when the phone rang. She slowly got up, pressing the flabby tissue that still hung around her middle. The doctor had cautioned her against doing too much too quickly, but she couldn't wait.

She picked up the phone. "Hello."

"Jessica, I want to see you."

She recognized the voice immediately, but still was shocked to hear it. For a moment she didn't respond. "Chase, why are you calling? Is anything wrong?" She had visions of something having happened to the baby, and her heart stopped.

"No, I'd like to see you. Can we meet in town for lunch or dinner?"

"Oh, my God," she said, letting out the breath that had been wedged in her lungs. "I thought something had happened to the baby."

"No, no. Nothing like that. She's fine. Couldn't be better. I'm calling for myself, not about her."

"Lord, you scared me to death. I couldn't imagine why you'd phone unless there was an emergency."

"Is that the only reason you thought I would call you?"

"I hadn't thought about it, actually. But listen, do me a favor and don't ever call me like this. I don't mean to sound hard-hearted, but I don't want to hear about her. Whether good or bad, I don't want to hear about her."

"Jessica . . ."

"That baby's out of my life now and I want to keep it that way. I've *got* to."

"What about me?"

"It's the same. I'm sorry, but it is. You're her father and I can't see you either." Anger and sorrow boiled up spontaneously. "Chase, can't you understand that? Do you know how hard this has been for me?"

He heard her sob and his gut wrenched. "Look, Jessica, you belong here with us. You and Jamie both. I want you to come back. I want—"

"No!" she screamed. "This is killing me. It's just tearing me up. I can't take it. It's all I can do to pull myself together. Please, Chase, please let me be, let me get over this," she implored.

Then she began weeping and tears filled his eyes. "Okay," he said softly.

"I'm sorry. I'm so sorry, Chase," she managed between sobs, "but I can't."

The telephone clicked and the dial tone in his ear was the most mournful sound Chase Hamilton had ever heard.

IT WAS MID-APRIL in New York. Jessica stood on the balcony of her new apartment; Jamie and the baby-sitter were inside reading a book of fairy tales. Harriet would be coming by soon and they would be leaving for Helmut Geisel's gallery and the first-ever Jessica Brandon exhibit.

After a rocky start back in town, her first good day had been the afternoon she and Geisel looked over her paintings. He was pleased. Sparing with his praise, he had nevertheless selected twenty-two of her canvases and scheduled the show. Invitations had been sent out, preparations made, and Jessica had returned to her own life, except for the fact that Chase Hamilton and his daughter were always lingering in the back of her mind.

For almost nine months she had denied her feelings, but she couldn't deceive herself any longer. She thought about her daughter frequently, and even now cried herself to sleep at night.

Jessica knew that becoming obsessed was the last thing she ought to do, but her instincts told her to get her feelings out in the open and to grieve, so that they wouldn't eat at her insides like a cancer. In a way, Chase was a more difficult loss to deal with, because he had offered his love and she had rejected it.

As she drank in the brisk spring air, Jessica tried to convince herself that life was wonderful: she and Jamie had everything they needed, including security. There was nothing missing—except for a man who had touched her like no other had and a baby girl whom she had never seen.

WEARING AN ELEGANT peach, off-the-shoulder gown that hugged her already-trim figure, Jessica arrived at the gallery with Harriet Thomas well ahead of any of the guests. Geisel walked up to greet them. He took Jessica's hand.

"Is it really happening, Helmut?"

"Of course it is," he said, kissing her on the cheek.

Jessica introduced her friend and the art dealer took them back to where a champagne bar had been set up.

"You are looking wonderful," he said, handing Jessica a glass. "No one would know that you only last month had a child." He ran his tongue slowly across his lips.

Feeling uncomfortable, Jessica glanced around at the walls of the gallery and the canvases she had lived with for the past months. "I want to show Harriet my paintings before the crowds come, if it's all right. Do you mind if we spend a few minutes wandering around?''

"No, of course not. Tonight my place is yours.''

JESSICA STOOD IN THE MIDDLE of the gallery, watching the milling crowds in formal attire looking at her paintings. She held a glass of champagne, which she had hardly touched.

Harriet walked slowly over, beaming at her. ''Nothing but praise. I've been eavesdropping like crazy and everybody seems to love your work.''

"People have been complimentary, but that doesn't mean much.''

"Stop worrying. You're a success, love. You can feel it in the air.''

Helmut Geisel approached, a big smile on his face. ''Well, my dear, I think you and I are going to be making a lot of money together.''

"I certainly hope so.''

They glanced around the crowded gallery in silence.

"How many invitations did you send out?'' Jessica asked after a while.

"Hundreds.''

"To all of your clients?''

"Clients and everybody who's anybody.''

More silence.

"Did you invite Chase Hamilton?''

Both Geisel and Harriet looked at her at the same time.

"Yes, he is a valued customer. But he sent his regrets. Not many do, but he sent a note wishing us well, but pleading another commitment.''

Jessica felt suddenly deflated. She looked down at her glass. ''Oh, that's too bad. He never did see all my canvases.''

"Well, he owns a Jessica Brandon and that, at the moment, puts him in a rather exclusive group."

"Yes, I suppose it does." Jessica looked up to see Arthur Netley moving through the crowd toward them.

"Good evening, Arthur," Geisel said. "Have you had the pleasure of meeting the artist?"

"Yes, I met her through Chase Hamilton. How are you, Jessica?"

"Thank you, I'm fine." She turned to Harriet and introduced the lawyer. They shook hands.

"Jessica," Arthur said effusively, "it's a wonderful show. Some really lovely pieces. One in particular has caught my eye."

"Oh? which?"

"My favorite is the monochromatic treatment of the horses in the fields. Perhaps part of it is knowing where you got your inspiration, but it's a fine painting." He glanced at Geisel. "And you keep that under your hat, Helmut."

"Arthur, of course."

Netley turned back to Jessica. "Is Chase going to be here this evening?" he asked.

Jessica looked at Helmut Geisel. "Helmut was just saying he'd sent his regrets."

"Oh, what a shame."

During the ensuing silence Harriet touched her arm. Jessica turned to her friend and saw that she was staring at the door. Looking up, she was amazed to see Chase Hamilton standing in the doorway. Her heart stopped.

In his arms was a bundle, a blanket. *My God, would he? How could he bring the baby here?*

Jessica stared at him in disbelief. Chase was looking around the crowded room. A diaper bag was slung over the shoulder of his suede jacket.

Just then he spotted her and immediately headed in her direction. Jessica was frozen, speechless. The others turned and watched. The unexpected sight of a man casually dressed with a baby in his arms brought much of the crowd to a surprised silence.

When Chase got to them he glanced at the others, nodded a mute greeting and looked directly at Jessica. "I'm sorry to interrupt the party, but I'd like a word with you."

She blanched, looking down at the tiny pink face amid the folds of blanket. "What are you doing, Chase?"

"I've brought you the baby. Her name is Kate, by the way."

She gasped. "Brought me the baby?"

"I've changed my mind. I don't want her."

She stared at him in disbelief. "What are you saying?"

"I don't want her, Jessica. You're her mother. She's yours." He deposited the baby in her arms like a loaf of bread. Then he reached into his pocket and pulled out a slip of paper. "Here's her feeding schedule. She's due to eat shortly." He tucked the slip into the blanket.

Jessica looked down at the tiny sleeping face, then at Chase. He swung the bag off his shoulder and dropped it at her feet. "There are plenty of supplies until tomorrow. You'll find a check in the bag to cover expenses. I'll be sending one each month."

Jessica's mouth was open. "What about our agreement?"

"I'm changing it. If you don't like it, sue me." With that he turned on his heel and walked out.

MOMENTS LATER Jessica was standing at the curb, looking up the street, the brisk breeze fluttering the tendrils of her hair. In her arms was the baby. Harriet was standing beside her.

"I could kill the man," she said through her teeth. "I could just kill him! Tonight, of all nights!"

"What are you going to do?"

"I'm going to his place and get this settled right now. I'll be damned if he's going to push me around like this."

Jessica waved futilely at the passing taxis, but they were all either occupied or on call. She felt bitter tears of anger.

After a minute or two of anxious waving, a cab cut across three lanes of traffic and stopped at the curb. The driver leaned down and looked at her through a half-open window. "Where you goin', lady?"

"Westchester. Near Cross River."

"That'll cost a bundle."

"It doesn't matter, I'll pay it." She got in the cab, carefully clutching the baby to her breast. She looked up at Harriet. "Tell Helmut I'm sorry, would you? And check with the sitter on Jamie?"

"Sure." Harriet managed a smile. "Good luck, kid."

The taxi pulled back into the flow of traffic and disappeared up the boulevard.

For a while Jessica just stared out the window at the city, trying to ignore the baby. Finally she pulled back the blanket and peered down at the tiny face. Kate was sleeping, but her lovely little features were plain to see. She was beautiful.

Jessica looked at her for a long time in the sweeping light of lampposts as they passed. A tiny hand was clutched to her cheek, fine wisps of blond hair swirled downlike around her head. Jessica searched the sleeping face for traces of herself and found them, mingled there with hints of Chase Hamilton. It was a devastating dis-

covery, because her heart opened and she felt love for the
baby as she never had. It was her daughter in her arms,
and Jessica kissed her.

DURING THE REST of the drive to the farm Jessica was
emotionally wrought and utterly confused. She still
seethed with anger toward Chase, but with each passing
mile she clung more fervently to the baby in her arms.
With one dramatic, cruel gesture, he had turned a faceless entity into her child.

She rubbed Kate's cheek with her finger and cooed,
trying in some way to tell her who she was. *Can you ever
forgive me? Will you ever understand?*

Finally the baby gave a little cry—the discomfort of
hunger—and Jessica pulled out the slip of paper with her
feeding schedule from the diaper bag. Looking at her
watch, she realized a bottle was past due. But they were
nearing the farm and Jessica decided to wait. She'd let
Chase deal with the problem, though her aroused maternal instinct fought the notion.

Now that Kate was awake Jessica propped her more
upright, pulling back the blanket a little to see what she
was wearing and if she approved. The pink pajamas with
soft lace collar betrayed the hand of Meade Phillips and
Jessica wondered who Kate regarded as her mother. Was
it Meade? Maggie? Anne?

Jessica indicated the turnoff to the cabbie and readied
herself as they went up the familiar drive. Though the
adrenaline started flowing through her veins, she realized she hadn't the vaguest idea of what she was going to
say. All she knew was that she felt outrage.

She asked the driver to wait, and he reluctantly agreed.
"Make it fast, though, lady. I won't sit out here all night
in the boonies, waiting time or no."

Jessica climbed the steps to the front door and rang the bell, wondering if Chase would be there. She rang again. Finally Maggie answered, wearing her bathrobe.

"Mrs. Brandon!"

"Hi, Maggie. Is Mr. Hamilton home?"

"I believe I heard him come in a while ago, ma'am, but I can't be sure." She glanced at the bundle in Jessica's arms. "Is that tiny Kate?"

"Yes."

"Lord a'mercy, come in out of the air."

Jessica stepped into the hall. "Could you tell Chase I want to see him, please?"

"Yes, ma'am. I surely will."

The housekeeper mounted the stairs and Jessica sat on a straight chair in the entry hall. Kate let out a little cry, and Jessica looked at her anxiously.

A few minutes later Chase came down the staircase, wearing pajamas and a bathrobe. Maggie was behind him.

"Jessica, what a surprise."

She rose to her feet, glaring at him.

"What brings you to Cross River this time of night?"

"You know damned well," she seethed under her breath.

Chase glanced back at the housekeeper, who hovered in the background. "That'll be all, Maggie. Thanks."

"Yes, sir." The woman nodded at Jessica. "It was awfully nice seein' you, Mrs. Brandon."

"Thank you, Maggie. Nice to see you, too." She turned back to Chase as the housekeeper left the room, her eyes narrowing. "You bastard," she hissed.

Chase glanced down at the baby in Jessica's arms and shrugged. "Sorry. I changed my mind."

"Oh, just like that!"

There was a honk outside.

"Who's that?"

"My cab."

"Didn't you pay him?"

"No. He's waiting to take me back to New York. I'll have to borrow some money. I don't have enough cash."

"I'll just pay him now. What did you agree to?"

"I didn't. Whatever's on the meter."

Chase gave a half smile. "Take Kate into the living room. I'll go upstairs and get my wallet."

"Tell him I'll just be five or ten minutes more."

He was already heading up the stairs. Jessica wandered into the sitting room, where a single lamp burned in the corner. Kate cried and she began bouncing the baby, trying to calm her.

A minute later Chase came downstairs and went directly outside to the cab. The baby was getting quite adamant about eating, so Jessica rummaged through the diaper bag and pulled out a bottle of formula. As she turned the nipple she heard the taxi's engine start and the crunch of gravel. Chase came in an instant later.

"Did you send my cab away?"

"Yes. The man wasn't being reasonable, so I paid him and sent him on his way."

"Then you can call me another."

Chase sat down next to her. "All right. But I imagine this is not a social call, so why don't you say what you have to, first?"

Jessica just looked at him, unable to believe his cavalier attitude. "Isn't it obvious?"

"You aren't pleased to have your daughter back."

"*Your* daughter."

"Let's compromise. *Our* daughter."

Jessica stared at him in disbelief. "You aren't taking this a bit seriously, are you? Chase, this is a human being I'm holding."

"I'm well aware of that. I've been aware of that longer than you, I believe."

"Why are you doing this to me?"

He let a long emotional moment pass, his eyes filming with moisture. "Because I love you."

She searched his eyes, not fully comprehending, afraid to believe.

"I love you *and* Kate," he said simply. "But I won't keep her without you."

"But she's the most important thing in your life."

"Not more important than you. And if I can't have you, if you won't stay with me, it's better she be with you."

Jessica heard the weighty conviction in his voice. He was willing to sacrifice the child that meant so much to him to prove his love.

Kate let out a loud cry of protest. She had lost her patience entirely.

Chase smiled. "I think she's hungry."

Jessica took the bottle and finished fixing the nipple. "Yes, I'd almost forgotten how the world stops when it's time to eat." She got the nipple into Kate's mouth and the baby began sucking eagerly. Jessica watched her for a second, feeling all her maternal instincts boiling up from within. She looked at Chase, almost in tears. "How am I going to give her up now?"

"You aren't. Ever."

"But how can you?"

He studied her face thoughtfully. "You know, in a way you were right about me, Jessica. In the beginning, when we met, I was just breeding a child. But when I got to know you, I began looking at it through different eyes. You were already pregnant by the time I realized that you were very special to me, and it was too late when I finally figured out that I wanted the baby to be the product of our love.''

''I don't think I would have believed you no matter what you said.''

''I guess I knew that. Besides, I didn't know exactly what my feelings for you meant until a few weeks ago. But I know now that I want you to be with me always.'' His mouth twisted at the corners.

''Oh, Chase, I love you so much. I have for a long time.''

Kate gurgled as she eagerly sucked on the bottle. Jessica took a cloth from the bag and wiped her chin. When she looked up at him there were tears in his eyes.

''You can't imagine how wonderful it is to see you with her.''

''Oh, Chase.''

He moved to her side, gathering both mother and child into his arms. He kissed Jessica's wet cheeks, taking her face between his hands. ''I need you, Jessica. I love you.''

EPILOGUE

THE MARCH WIND BLEW across the paddock and Chase looked over the fence at the brown grass and scattered patches of dirty snow. It wasn't exactly springlike, but it was a far cry from the blizzard that Kate had arrived with the year before. He was staring thoughtfully at the barren landscape, when he heard a car horn toot back at the house.

He turned and saw Meade and Roger climbing out of their station wagon. As she stepped around the car, Meade waved. Chase waved back, noticing that his sister had gotten much bigger in the month since he's seen her. He walked over to meet them.

"Well," he said, embracing Meade and kissing her on the cheek, "you can't be accused of letting pregnancy get in the way of high fashion."

Meade stepped back, turning around and beaming. "Do you like it?"

Chase looked admiringly at the tailored black wool coat. He turned to his brother-in-law and extended his hand. "Roger."

"Meade asked if I thought a maternity coat was too ostentatious," Roger began.

"And you said?"

"Not if we have at least three children and all of them are spring babies."

Chase laughed and gestured toward the horses in the field. "I've got two mares in foal myself. Of course the important one is down in Kentucky."

"The one you bought in England?"

"Yes, Victoria Cross. The sire carried the best bloodlines I could find in Kentucky. He's a grandson of John Henry."

"I'm pleased for you, Chase," Meade said, smiling. "An expectant father again."

"No. After the real thing, I'm content thinking of the horses as my business, not family."

"Speaking of which..." Meade glanced toward the house.

"Yes, we'd better go in, or they'll have the party without us."

"Are you excited?" she asked, as they walked. "I am."

"Jessica said the first birthday is always the one the parents remember best." He grinned. "This is my first, first birthday."

"How's Jamie taking it?"

"Oh, he's proud of his little sister. He did a picture of her at nursery school the other day. It was a relatively flattering representation," he added, chuckling.

"How sweet."

They were nearing the house. "Jessica says the three of them have planned a surprise for us."

"A surprise?"

"Yes, I think something to do with Jamie's getting his braces off. You did know he got them off this past week, didn't you?"

"I knew it was supposed to happen sometime soon."

"Jessica's been ecstatic. She flew back from the opening of that exhibit in Washington to take him in herself."

"What exhibit?"

"She was one of ten contemporary American women painters selected for a special exhibit they did at the Corcoran Gallery. She was far and away the least known, but there were two or three selected as representatives of the new, young set. She was absolutely thrilled to have a piece in the same room with Georgia O'Keeffe."

"How wonderful!"

They went up the front steps. "Well," Chase said, "my instructions were to take you into the living room. Act surprised, whatever happens."

They went inside and Chase hung their coats in the hall closet. Meade led the way into the sitting room. "Doesn't the fire look wonderful?" She walked over to the fireplace, rubbing her hands together to warm them.

"Chase, is that you?" Jessica called from the other room.

"Yes, we're all here."

"I'll be right there."

A moment later she appeared in the doorway, wearing a pale lavender cashmere sweater over a pearl gray wool skirt. Her face was bright with excitement. She came in and kissed Meade and Roger.

"You look wonderful, Meade. How's it going?"

"Perfect." She smiled broadly. "That is, perfect if I can get Roger to drop the dreadful name he's come up with."

Jessica looked at Roger questioningly.

"The contest at the office I organized . . ."

"Can you imagine?" Meade interjected. "He picked a winner without consulting me!"

"Which was?"

"Barclay," she intoned.

Looking at them both, Jessica shrugged. "I won't get in the middle of that one. Just be glad you don't have to worry about girl's names."

"I've already invested a lunch in Barclay," Roger protested mildly.

"Well, I'm investing nine months, and it's going to be Spencer."

"Mommy," Jamie called from the next room, "now?"

"Just a minute darling!" she replied. "Come on, everybody, it's time for the surprise. Sit here, facing the door."

Meade, Roger and Chase sat on the couch. Jessica sat on the arm, next to her husband. She rested her hand on his shoulder. "Okay, darling," she called out, "now."

An instant later Jamie appeared in the doorway, standing behind a little toddler in a pink dress and white lacy pants, holding her hands.

"There's the birthday girl!" Meade exclaimed.

Kate giggled and took a couple of awkward steps toward them, Jamie behind her, holding her hands.

"And look at you, Jamie. No braces!"

The boy beamed and nodded shyly. "Katie can walk all by herself," he said proudly.

"She can?"

The children were about halfway to the couch, both smiling happily. Chase slipped his arm around Jessica's waist and pulled her against him.

"Watch," Jamie said. Then he knelt down, his hands under Kate's arms. He whispered in her ear and pointed to Chase.

The toddler took several halting steps toward her father, then made a staggering run toward him. He caught her just as she was about to fall at his feet.

"Whoa there, young lady! Don't want any falls on your birthday." He picked her up and plopped her onto his lap.

Meade touched the pink bow in Kate's thin little wisps of hair. "Don't you look precious."

Jamie came over and leaned against Chase's knee. "I did a picture of Katie," he said proudly.

"You did? I'd like to see it," Meade said, stroking his head.

"Okay!" He ran from the room, a bit awkwardly but with enthusiasm.

Kate looked around at the fawning adults, obviously in her glory. Meade glanced up at Jessica.

"Sitting in Chase's car a year ago at the hospital, I never would have thought . . ."

Chase scoffed. "Meade, you have no faith in me. I had it planned all along."

Jessica poked him playfully with her elbow. "I wish you'd told me, and saved me all that trouble."

"Nonsense," he said, kissing her. "I know Thoroughbreds, and a spirited filly has to be brought along carefully. Very carefully, indeed."

Take 4 best-selling love stories FREE
Plus get a FREE surprise gift!

Harlequin Superromance

COMING NEXT MONTH

#246 LOVE SONGS • Georgia Bockoven
Jo Williams's relationship with some of the senior
citizens who frequent her yogurt shop brings Brad Tyler
to her door one night, and once there, he never wants to
leave. But Jo soon realizes she'll have to help Brad over
the pain of a lost love for them to have their chance at
happiness. She'll have to risk losing him to gain his
heart forever.

#247 MASKS • Irma Walker
Despite appearances, Tracy Morrison is not a lonely
heiress. She's a reporter for the *Cincinnati Herald*,
working undercover to trap a couple of con artists—and
write the hottest story of the year. When Chris Collins
falls into her trap, she knows she's struck pay dirt. He is
manipulative, dangerous . . . and absolutely irresistible.
But, as Tracy will discover, he's not what he seems. . . .

#248 CHERISHED HARBOR • Kelly Walsh
U.S. Marshal Daniel Elliott and his latest assignment,
Marcy Keaton, are like night and day. Yet, as they fight
for their lives, they find themselves sharing passion-
filled nights and dreaming of a future they can't
possibly share. . . .

#249 BELONGING • Sandra James
Mayor Angie Hall believes the small city of Westridge
is hardly the place for a tough ex-cop from Chicago like
Matt Richardson. But her new chief of police proves
her wrong. He fits in perfectly. . . *too* perfectly for
Angie's liking.

HARLEQUIN HISTORICAL

Explore love with Harlequin in the Middle
Ages, the Renaissance, in the Regency, the
Victorian and other eras.

Relive within these books the endless ages of
romance, set against authentic historical
backgrounds. Two new historical love stories
published each month.

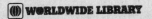

ATTRACTIVE, SPACE SAVING BOOK RACK

Display your most prized novels on this handsome and sturdy book rack. The hand-rubbed walnut finish will blend into your library decor with quiet elegance, providing a practical organizer for your favorite hard-or soft-covered books.

Only $9.95

Approximately 16" x 8" when assembled

Assembles in seconds!

To order, rush your name, address and zip code, along with a check or money order for $10.70* ($9.95 plus 75¢ postage and handling) payable to *Harlequin Reader Service*:

> Harlequin Reader Service
> Book Rack Offer
> 901 Fuhrmann Blvd.
> P.O. Box 1325
> Buffalo, NY 14269-1325
>
> *Offer not available in Canada.*

*New York residents add appropriate sales tax.

BKR-1R